THE DIVINE SAGE

JOHN PAUL CUNNINGHAM

The Divine Sage is a work of fiction. The story is based on the voyage of Captain
Basil Hall as detailed in his published book, *Extracts from a Journal, Written on
the Coasts of Chili, Peru, and Mexico, in the Years 1820, 1821, 1822* (first edition,
1824), together with further information that appears in the surviving log of the
HMS *Conway* and letters written by Basil Hall and George Birnie. Though
many of the characters that appear in *The Divine Sage* are real, their portrayal
within the novel, together with the plot itself, is the product of the author's
imagination.

ISBN: 9780648846901

Printed by IngramSpark and Amazon.

Cover design by Predrag Markovic, with kind permission to use a photograph
taken by Bruno Zehr.

www.thedivinesage.net

It matters not how strait the gate,
How charged with punishments the scroll,
I am the master of my fate:
I am the captain of my soul.

—WILLIAM ERNEST HENLEY, *Invictus*

THE LETTER

25th September 1844
Royal Naval Hospital at Haslar
Plymouth

Dear Mr Birnie,

As you may be aware from recent reports in the newspapers, Captain Basil Hall passed away on the 15th of this month having suffered for nearly two years from a degenerative disease of the mind characterised by violent fits and progressive dementia. Basil and I had been close friends for many years before his incarceration at Haslar, and I can assure you that during his time with us, he was afforded the best treatments we have available and resided in a private room with a view of the hospital garden. It might also give you comfort to know that he never once was taken downstairs to the lower corridors of the asylum, where the less fortunate patients must live out their days in such torment.

I have enclosed with this letter a notebook belonging to Basil, the contents of which were written in the last few weeks of *his life, at a time when the fits he was experiencing were daily occurrences and his body and mind were steadily weakening from these cruel and relentless blows. As you will soon discover, the narrative within bears no small resemblance to Basil's book, published to considerable acclaim some years ago, 'Extracts from a Journal Written on the Coasts of Chili, Peru, and Mexico'—inasmuch as the dates and stopping points along the way appear to be, for the most part, the same. But for the rest, I cannot say; except that, having read the notebook from start to finish, I am concerned for the captain's reputation and for the wellbeing of his surviving family, should this material fall into the wrong hands.*

Although it is my personal belief that the notebook might better be destroyed, Basil's last wish was that I give it to you. On the evening he passed away, I entered his room to find him standing by the window with his fingers pressed against the pane, his face lit by the light of the setting sun. It is a moment I shall never forget as long as I live. He turned to me, and I saw in his eyes the old friend I have loved and admired for many years. "I am returned, John," he said. "I have passed through the invisible, and now I am returned." It was then that he insisted I find you, Mr Birnie, wherever you were in the world—and then, just like that, the light in his eyes went out, and he fell into the grip of a severe fit. It was one from which he did not return.

Under normal circumstances, the transfer of material belonging to a patient at Haslar would be strictly prohibited, but in this instance, I find myself able to do so, as this can be considered a matter of medical interest passing from the hands of one physician to another. As such, if you choose to read the enclosed notebook, I trust that you will do so as a physician who has sworn an oath to never divulge secrets of a patient's life that ought not to be spoken. For my own part, I have no intention to discuss the contents of the notebook further, either with my colleagues or with Basil's surviving family—nor will I speak of its existence beyond this letter.

The Divine Sage belongs to you now, Mr Birnie.

Respectfully,
Dr John Richardson, FRCS.
Head Physician

The Divine Sage

PART ONE
CHARLES

ONE

HMS *Conway*, Cape Horn, 26th November 1820

IN ALL MY DAYS, I have never seen anything quite so beautiful as the aurora australis, which I had good fortune to witness on the night we navigated Cape Horn. The mysterious celestial light appeared shortly after nightfall, first as a shimmering arc of green fire over the southern horizon, then growing by degrees until its luminous tendrils stretched high into the starlit heavens, wavering and dancing above the *Conway*'s creaking masts and flapping sails.

Our passage up until that point had been one of little excitement. "Rounding the Cape" is widely regarded as the foremost test of seamanship, and I had spent the weeks before our departure from England poring over maps and seeking advice on how best to survive the unpredictable tides and strong winds that dominate these latitudes—but upon entering the chilly waters of the Southern Atlantic, we experienced only clear skies and favourable breezes. Indeed, when earlier that same evening we finally spotted the jagged coastline of the

Tierra del Fuego on the western horizon, I could not help but feel a little disappointed. There it was, the infamous promontory that has gained such celebrity in nautical history, silhouetted against the dying rays of the sun: yet, as ship's captain, what had I done besides pace back and forth on the icy deck, puffing on my pipe and listening to the wind whistling through the ropes?

At any rate, the aurora was to change all that. It was every bit as breathtaking and otherworldly as the salty accounts one hears from old mariners in the taverns of Plymouth Docks. Down on the main deck, the men stood in an eerie silence, open-mouthed, with clouds of breath collecting over their heads. Some of the more nimble sailors had climbed high into the rigging, as if drawn up in a rapture towards the bewitching luminosity that snaked between the constellations, shining with such brilliance that the *Conway*'s sails were dyed a ghostly green.

Alone on the quarterdeck with the collars of my coat pulled in tight about my neck, I took in the heavenly show. I found myself in a deep contemplation as to what forces lay behind its manifestation—the vagaries of weather and accumulations of atmospheric particles that must coincide to bring such a magnificent display into existence. What purpose did the aurora serve, in the grander scheme of things? Did it exist solely to strike awe into the hearts of lonely sailors? To remind us that the majesty of the universe will forever outdo the majesty of men, its secrets remaining forever beyond our grasp?

I was snapped out of my train of thought by the appearance of a swinging lantern, which wove its way across the main deck. A shadowy figure climbed the ladderway and walked towards me, his shoulders hunched against the cold.

It was George Birnie, the *Conway*'s surgeon.

"Have you ever seen the like?" I said, still gazing up at the shimmering light.

Birnie gave the aurora only a momentary glance. "I'm afraid I have some troubling news, Captain. We have lost Mr Gillies."

John Gillies was our only paying passenger, and suffered from incipient consumption—a chronic form of the disease that does not kill its victims outright, but leaves them lingering in ill health for many years. Eight weeks previously, I had watched two of my midshipmen escort Gillies onto the *Conway* at Plymouth Docks. His sallow complexion, bent posture, and unsteady gait made him look twice his twenty-eight years. If the truth be known, I did not expect the man to survive a fort-night, let alone the three-month voyage to the coasts of the New World.

I placed a consoling hand on the doctor's shoulder. "We shall have a burial at first light. And I will write a letter to his next of kin."

Birnie raised the lantern, the flickering flame reflecting in his spectacles. "Mr Gillies is not dead, sir. He appears to have *vanished*."

"What?"

"I cannot find him anywhere, sir."

"I thought you said the man was confined to his cot?"

"He was," the doctor insisted. "This afternoon, when I paid him a visit, he could barely lift a glass of water to his lips."

"Men do not simply vanish," I told him. "Mr Gillies must have awoken in a delirium and stumbled out of his cabin. Is he being administered laudanum?"

Birnie shook his head. "He refuses to take anything but those herbal concoctions of his. I have searched every cabin, cupboard and storeroom—all the way down to the hold."

I gazed into the darkness beyond the railings. The constellation of the Southern Cross, that much-loved celestial anchor for mariners, was rising above the horizon.

Taking out my tinderbox, I relit my pipe while I considered the situation.

"Well then, the only explanation remaining is that the poor fellow has found his way up here and fallen overboard."

The doctor rubbed his forehead with his gloved hand. "I don't believe John was capable of—"

"Then what *are* you suggesting?" I said, grabbing hold of one of the lines to steady myself as the *Conway* leapt over a succession of waves. A sprinkling of snowflakes fell from the rigging above. "That our Mr Gillies has been...spirited away?"

"No, sir, of course not."

Our conversation was interrupted by the arrival of Lieutenant Wollaton on the quarterdeck. Wollaton was the lowest in rank of the *Conway*'s three lieutenants, despite being the oldest—a situation that he had not ceased complaining about since our departure from England. The lieutenant's dour and cynical disposition was evident at his interview, throughout which I listened to a diatribe of criticism against his previous commander, and summarily pegged the gloomy Yorkshireman sitting across my desk as the kind who was quick to find faults in others whilst being quite oblivious to his own shortcomings. But alas, it transpired that I had little choice in selecting him for the voyage: having served for more than two decades as midshipman without receiving a promotion, the Admiralty had already decided that Wollaton should be given a chance to prove himself.

"Still no sight nor sound of Mr Gillies?" the lieutenant asked, dragging his vowels as Yorkshire folk tend to do. "Mind you, I always knew he were trouble. One of them clever types who thinks himself above the rest of us, an' tekkin' a voyage halfway around the world in such a state of poor health... Makes you wonder."

My fingers tensed irritably around the stem of my pipe as I sought to relight it. "From what I gather, Mr Gillies was braving this passage to benefit from the mild climate Chile has to offer."

"Aye, well, there were always something queer about that man if you ask me," the lieutenant went on, taking little heed of what I said. "I heard he were dismissed from another ship owing to a matter of misconduct involving a young officer. The lad died of a fever, so they say, but there were rumours he were poisoned by one of Mr Gillies's medications."

"That is absolute rubbish!" Birnie interjected sharply. "Mr Gillies retired from the navy owing to his declining health, and for that reason alone." He threw me an exasperated glance before turning back to Wollaton. "And for your information, the young officer was dying of yellow fever. I can assure you Mr Gillies would have done all he could to save his life."

"Aye, an' you doctors stick together." Wollaton tapped his nose conspiratorially. "That 'ippocritic oath you swear by."

Birnie rolled his eyes. "*Hippocratic* oath. And it has nothing to do with doctors sticking together."

The lieutenant shrugged dismissively. "At any rate, I were going to say that we found him." He pointed across the deck towards the bow. "Mind you, I think he might be frozen stiff."

"Why didn't you say something before?" Birnie snapped.

"I were getting to it," Wollaton replied, clearly enjoying his petty triumph over the doctor. "Mr Legge is seeing to him. Sounds to me as if this might have been his fault...but I shall leave it to him to explain."

The doctor and I hurried across the deck and climbed the

stairway to the bow, finding Lieutenant Legge crouching beside a pile of frozen ropes under the foremast.

"I am dreadfully sorry, sir," he gabbled, and then stood up and saluted, all pale-faced and ruddy-cheeked in the lamplight. "This is all my fault. I was called to Mr Gillies's cabin earlier. He said it was the doctor's orders that he should get some air."

Birnie held his lantern aloft, revealing a pair of skinny legs sticking out from a bundle of snow-covered blankets. "I said no such thing. When was this?"

"Shortly after sunset, sir."

"Did he say *which* doctor gave these orders?" I asked, clambering over the bowlines to take a closer look at the body swaddled in blankets.

Legge looked confused. "No, sir."

"Mr Gillies is a former surgeon for His Majesty's Royal Navy," I explained. "He may have been referring to himself."

It was Gillies all right, frost clinging to his mutton-chop whiskers and eyebrows, his spectacles sitting crookedly across his nose. He looked dead enough to me, sunken-cheeked and blue-lipped as he was.

Reaching down, I placed the back of my hand on his cheek. It was cold, but the skin was still soft—he might yet be alive. Clutching his jaw, I moved his head about. "Birnie, come take a look."

The doctor stepped between the lines. Pressing his fingers against the man's neck, he felt for a pulse. "We must get him below deck."

As we positioned ourselves to lift Gillies, there was movement beneath his eyelids, as if his eyeballs were rolling about. All at once, he awoke and glanced around wildly before looking me straight in the eye.

"I saw you," he gasped, his voice strained and hoarse. "Down there in the darkness. It was *you*."

"Yes, well, I am up here too," I said, assuming him to be in a delirium. "You must try and stay with us, Mr Gillies." I removed his spectacles for safekeeping. "We are going to carry you to my cabin and get you warmed up."

His eyes darted towards the sky, widening further still as he took in the aurora, a luminous green ribbon billowing directly over our heads.

"The light," he whispered. "He is watching us, Captain!"

Gillies remained with his eyes locked on the aurora for a few moments more before slipping under. He did not speak again, nor show any signs of returning to consciousness while we lumbered him across the deck and down the companionway steps to the Great Cabin. Stretching him out on the seating beneath the long window, I covered him with a thick woollen blanket.

"If he pulls through, there must be no more incidents like this," I said, taking three glasses from the cabinet and pouring each of us a whiskey. "Aside from all the kerfuffle, I do not want the crew thinking our only passenger has lost his marbles. You know what it's like." I handed the two men their drinks. "If they see Gillies staggering around in a delirium, they will start gossiping, and the next thing you know, there will be all manner of stories flying about. Sailors have active imaginations, as you well know."

I took another look at Gillies. He was out cold and wore an oddly contented look on his face. I suppose I could hardly blame the fellow for hoodwinking Legge like that in order to catch a glimpse of the aurora—especially given the man could have precious few nights left on this earth to enjoy.

Only then did another thought occur to me.

"Of course, it might be possible," I began, holding my whiskey up to the light to admire its deep golden sheen, "that Gillies was not expecting to return tonight at all."

Birnie frowned at me. "You think he deliberately went up on deck knowing he would perish out there in the cold?"

"He muttered something about seeing the light," I replied with a casual shrug. "Is that not what dying men talk of?"

Leaving the two men to keep watch over our frozen passenger, I climbed back up the ladderway into the chilly night. I was on deck just in time to see the last traces of the aurora fade away before my eyes.

Leaning against the mast, I gazed up at the star-encrusted heavens. Venus was out tonight, and Jupiter too. I mused a little over Gillies's words—*He is watching us, Captain*—trying to imagine what the world must look like from up there in the icy firmament: the contours of the many continents, separated by vast stretches of black ocean; and what the *Conway* must look like: a speck of white, inching its way through the narrow strip between the tail of South America and the polar ice caps of Antarctica.

TWO

HMS *Conway*, Valparaiso, Chile, 19th December 1820

A LOUD CHEER rang out across the deck as we rounded the headland and the whitewashed houses and church spires of Valparaiso slipped into view. The Chilean port had gained quite a reputation for its well-stocked taverns and lively dance halls, and after four months at sea there was considerable excitement on board the *Conway*.

Standing on the quarterdeck, I drew the eye of my telescope along the crescent bay. A crowd was gathering on the beach to welcome us, men and women dressed in colourful ponchos and children running about excitedly on the sand. I focussed the lens on the bell tower of an official-looking building in the centre of the port. It was in all likelihood the town hall—and, no doubt, where I would be spending much of my time over the coming months, engrossed in matters of trade.

A curious notion then struck me. I felt as though I recognised the place—not just the town hall, but the entire port. The way it was hemmed in by steep cliffs, the houses crowded into a narrow strip along the bay and forming strag-gling lines up the ravines. Even the old fort seemed familiar, situated as it was on a rocky outcrop at the southern end of the bay.

Cannon fire cracked through the air to mark our arrival, and the *Conway* fired her cannons in a return salute. I followed the tendrils of smoke as they rose up from the battlements of the fort, moving the glass eye along the line of the cliffs and then surveying the uncultivated hills beyond. I came across an isolated house, perhaps a farmhouse. Morning sunlight glinted back from the upper windows. I could make out a winding track curling around the hillside towards the house, and a garden scattered with trees.

There it was again: that odd sense of familiarity.

Just then, a strong gust of wind blew across the deck, sending the sails flapping against their masts. It felt gritty against my cheek.

"Where the devil did that come from?" Lieutenant Darby said from beside me on the quarterdeck.

"A squall from the mainland," I suggested, rubbing my eyes. "A dusty one, at that."

Walking across to the barometer, I checked the needle. It was steady, no sign of bad weather.

Turning my gaze in the direction of the port, I noticed the inhabitants were making a quick retreat from the beach. The hills in the distance were disappearing from view, concealed by a rust-coloured haze.

The wind suddenly veered and strengthened.

"All hands on deck!" I cried out.

Without warning, the ocean beneath us rose up into a swell and the *Conway* began rolling and pitching on her hull. The crew braced themselves, holding onto the railings and shrouds with their eyes turned towards the quarterdeck in eager anticipation.

"Send orders to shorten sail," I ordered Darby. "And free the head sheets!"

Darby turned on his heel and hurried down to the main deck echoing my commands, his black hair whipping about his face. Before the crew had time to seize the clewlines and hoist the topsails, the ship sliced through a breaking wave with a heavy jolt. Water surged over the bulwarks, sweeping Darby into a line of men who were heaving on a chain, all of whom then lost their footing and landed in a tangled heap. Above me, a man was left clinging like a cat to one of the yardarms. Another dangled from the rigging, kicking his feet in an attempt to regain his foothold.

The *Conway* lurched helplessly to windward, then crashed over another wave, drenching us all. As she rose out of the swell, the bowsprit swung towards the southern cliffs, where white surf churned over the exposed rocks.

"Put down the helm!" I yelled from the railing.

The men slipped and slid about the deck, bellowing out to one another to hold tight as they fought to regain control of the ship. Enshrouded now in a cloud of orange dust, the *Conway* began shuddering violently from stem to stern. Slowly but surely she began to turn, the bowsprit sweeping in a counterclockwise direction until it pointed once more towards the shore.

"Come hang, come haul together,
Hooray, hooray!
Come hang for finer weather,
Hang, boys, hang!"

The crew were in their element, bawling out sea shanties as they steadied the sails and we cut determinedly towards the bay. As if realising it was defeated, the dusty squall died away as quickly as it had come. Within minutes the sea was calm again, the sky returning to its former dazzling blue. Indeed, were it not for the little mounds of dirt in the corners of the deck, I might easily have been convinced that I had imagined the entire thing.

We dropped anchor a couple of hundred yards from the beach and began making the necessary preparations to take the boats ashore. While speaking with the bosun, I saw Mr Gillies appear on deck, walking unsteadily with a cane. Gillies was not a tall man, and his height was further diminished by his stooped posture. He was dressed in a tired-looking brown jacket, but wore a colourful green neckcloth with gold spots. Tucked beneath his arm, he carried a sketchbook.

I called out his name, beckoning him to the quarterdeck.

"She is a lively port by all accounts," I said, helping Gillies up the stairs. I had not laid eyes on the man since the night we found him on the bow, half frozen to death. In the daylight, he was a funny-looking fellow. His face was small and round, and his hair was a mass of tightly knotted curls. His skin, tinged yellow by his illness, looked delicately thin, and was peppered with freckles beneath his eyes.

"I doubt I will be here for long," he said, squinting through his spectacles in the direction of the beach.

I presumed that Gillies was lamenting his failing health, until he added, quite to my surprise, "I am heading northwards, to Mexico."

"Mexico?"

He fixed me with his sharp, grey-green eyes. "As is the *Conway*, I hear."

"Perhaps," I said. "But I cannot say when." Seeing the puzzled frown on his face, I then went on to explain. "I receive orders only days before our departure—the Admiralty refrain from disclosing the destination earlier in order to protect British interests. It could be several months, or more than a year."

"I know how it works," Gillies said, dismissing my words with a flick of his hand. He pointed to a patch of shade near the bulwarks. "Might I sit down over there? I find all this sunlight rather intense."

"Mexico is several months' voyage by sea," I went on, watching him lower himself slowly down onto the deck. "Once you cross the equator, the heat will become oppressive. And you will not find refuge in the comfort of your cabin, either— you will be driven up onto the baking deck with the rest of the men."

"Then I suppose I will have to bake," he said with a sigh. Fumbling in his pocket, he withdrew a pencil.

"I am just saying that if I were you, I would stay right here. Given your illness, a voyage—"

"I appreciate your concern, Captain," he interjected, opening his sketchbook with a lukewarm smile in my direction. "But I am afraid I am not very good at listening to advice."

I was still staring at the man in resignation when Wollaton approached the quarterdeck. He threw Gillies a disparaging look. I very much doubted the lieutenant was as pleased as I was to see he was still alive.

"We were hoping you might give permission for a swimming race to the shore," he said, tipping his hat. "The conditions couldn't be better, an' they all fancy a bit of a flutter."

I glanced down at the main deck to see a hundred grubby faces looking expectantly back at me.

Why not? I thought. *The men have worked hard. They deserve a little fun.*

I walked over to the railing and called out, "Ten shillings goes to the first man on the beach!"

Coins and tobacco exchanged hands as the competitors stripped down to their slops and began jumping and stretching on the wooden boards. Contrary to what one might think, sailors are often poor swimmers, but on any ship there are a few who excel in the water and relish the opportunity to show off their talent.

"If I might offer you a tip, Captain," Wollaton muttered through his beard. "Place a wager on Slick. Unbeaten in three such races on the *Alceste*." He nodded in the direction of the man in question, a sinewy deckhand elbowing his way through the rabble. "I have two shillings saying he'll take this lot."

Slick was listed in the ship's muster book as a Mr Jacob Allen. He was a dirty-nailed, mean sort, and I often wondered whether his nickname had arisen from the greasiness of his hair or the general oiliness of his character. Leaning back against the gunwale, he punched the air with his fist as if he had already won the race.

Gillies glanced up from his sketchbook. "Two shillings. Is that all?"

Wollaton shot him a look. "What's it to you?"

"I just thought it rather a measly sum," Gillies replied with a casual shrug. "Given your assuredness that Slick is our champion."

"And what great sum are you willing to wager?" the lieutenant said, his lip curling into a smirk.

Gillies reached into his pocket and brought out a small purse. He tossed it up and down in his hand, making as if to calculate its weight. "I should say there is at least fifteen shillings in here."

"Save your money for a tailor," Wollaton said. "Fix the holes in that moth-eaten jacket of yours."

"If I win, I shall buy myself a new jacket." Gillies began proudly plucking at his cuffs. "And trousers to match. I will wager fifteen shillings, sir, if you are game?"

Wollaton lifted his hands, implying he had tried his best to convince the man otherwise. "If you insist on being a fool, sir, then who am I to stop you? Choose your man."

Gillies got to his feet. Walking to the railing, he looked down at the competitors. Having already climbed over the gunwale, they were now shuffling in a line along the channel board, clinging to the shrouds for support.

"Must I select one of these ruffians?"

"Unless you wish to swim yo'self?" Wollaton mocked.

Gillies turned and looked at me. "What I meant was, may I chose *any* man—if he agrees to swim?"

"Choose whomsoever you like," I said in exasperation. "So long as you are quick about it."

He stood for a while, pursing his lips, then pointed in the direction of the mainmast. "Aha! There he is. Our champion."

I followed the line of his finger. "Mr Legge?"

He nodded. "A sure winner. Skinny legs and big feet."

The young lieutenant was leaning against the mast with his arms folded and his face turned towards the sun.

"Officers do not usually take part in such races," I said. "I am sure you are quite aware of that."

"I thought you said I could pick anyone I liked?" he replied. "And I like Mr Legge."

There were no rules to these swimming races, and in the past I had seen many a dirty tactic secure an unworthy winner —which is why I was not at all happy with the idea of one of my lieutenants taking part. But then, Charles Legge was a smart lad, one who would not risk compromising his standing amongst the crew.

It occurred to me then that Gillies might have chosen Legge as a way of getting out of the wager, and I decided to play along in the hope I could stop the silly thing from going ahead.

"Very well. You may ask Mr Legge," I said. "But if he declines your request, the wager is off."

"And if he accepts?" Gillies said.

"Then let it be on his head—and yours too."

Picking up his cane, he made his way gingerly to the stairs and climbed down to the main deck. I watched him weave through the men to the lieutenant.

"I said he were trouble," Wollaton remarked. "He'll be up to no good, mark my words."

Down on deck, the two men talked. Legge began rubbing the back of his neck and shaking his head. When he looked my way, I held up my hands to indicate that I had no part in this foolishness. Gillies, however, appeared to be quite persistent, and continued talking and gesticulating for a few minutes longer.

"He had better watch out," Wollaton said. "We all know what happened to the last lieutenant Mr Gillies took a liking to. He were dead before—"

"Might I suggest you take Mr Birnie's word on that matter?" I said, interrupting Wollaton before he annoyed me further. "And might I also suggest that you stop listening to idle gossip. There is nothing so low as wilfully damaging another man's reputation for the sole reason of having something to say."

The conversation between Gillies and Legge came to a close, leaving the young lieutenant scratching his brow. I was about to turn away, satisfied that the matter was done with, when I noticed that Gillies was now whispering in the ear of Mr Lange, the purser, as he collected the bets from the men. Lange beckoned to Legge with his hand.

"What on earth are they up to?" I said under my breath, as the two men disappeared down the companionway steps. Surely Legge was not about to take part in the race?

But alas, the lieutenant reappeared a few minutes later, bare-chested and wearing only a pair of cotton slops. He walked self-consciously through the cheering, stamping crowd, with his arms tightly folded. Clambering over the gunwale, he joined the nine other contestants on the channel board.

I had hoped Legge would be less impressionable. Having placed himself in a position where he no longer had seniority over the men, the lieutenant was in danger of compromising his authority in the future—if he did not handle himself correctly. Even now he looked vulnerable, his milk-white skin conspicuous in a line of tanned and brawny men.

I took a deep breath, maintaining my composure. I supposed that, if nothing else, this would serve as a lesson for the lad.

The rest of the contestants flapped their arms and shook their legs in readiness for the race, goading and nudging each other boisterously. With one hand clinging to the shrouds, Legge leant forwards and peered down at the water beneath him.

Gillies returned to the quarterdeck with a grin on his face.

"Was it entirely necessary to coerce him into this foolishness?" I said, as he settled back down in his spot in the shade.

"I prefer the term *gentle persuasion*," Gillies replied, picking up his sketchbook again.

"And what form might this *gentle persuasion* have taken?"

He shrugged his thin shoulders as if to make light of my question. "I merely informed him that his captain wished to see him win."

"I said nothing of the sort!" I snapped, glaring at him.

"And neither did I tell the young man that you *said* such a thing," Gillies replied coolly. "Simply what you *wished* to see. Am I not correct?"

For the second time that day, I found myself staring wide-eyed at Gillies. Before I had time to say anything more, however, we were interrupted by the arrival of one of the midshipmen, Mr Garvey, carrying the ship's horn.

"Let us get this over and done with," I said with a sigh. Taking the instrument, I turned back to the railing and shouted, "Swimmers, ready yourselves!"

The crew fell silent. The contestants stood poised with bent knees, gripping the edge of the channel board with their toes.

I blew a long, brassy note. The men leapt from the ship into the cobalt-blue water below. Reappearing a moment later, they began splashing frantically towards the shore.

"I have been reading your book," Gillies said, continuing with his sketching. He seemed quite disinterested in the race. "*Voyage to Loo-Choo*. A fascinating story."

"It is a factual account, not a story," I corrected him. "Taken from the entries in my journal while on board the *Lyra*. And there were no embellishments for the sake of storytelling, I can assure you."

A strict adherence to facts had been instilled in me at an early age. My father, Sir James Hall, had been an eminent geologist in his day: President of the Royal Society of Scotland, an exclusive club for the country's scientific elite. Indeed, I shall never forget the day of my very first voyage, when my father accompanied me to the docks. I was only fourteen years old and would be away at sea for an entire year. While the other parents hugged and kissed their boys, my father stood awkwardly on the quay, holding a package, which he thrust into my hands as I was called aboard.

"A journal for you to write in," he had said stiffly. "It is not a gift. It is a responsibility. Observe without bias and write accurately without embellishments. Your duty is not to please, it is to educate. So no silly flourishes."

I have never forgotten those words, nor the sentiment that followed. He clasped my hand in a formal handshake, as if we were two men having completed a business arrangement. Then, uttering the briefest of farewells, he turned and walked away.

With the glass to my eye, I followed the swimmers as they splashed towards the turquoise shallows. I was pleasantly surprised to see Legge out in front, though Slick was close on his tail.

"You should watch this," I said to Gillies. "Your man is winning."

"Is that so?" he replied, frowning as he scrutinised whatever it was he was sketching. "Mr Legge has quite the physique of a swimmer. Would you not agree, Mr Wollaton? Such well-defined latissimus dorsi."

Wollaton was standing next to the bulwarks with his telescope trained on the swimmers. "I am not one to spend my time looking at a man's lassamus dorsey," he said. "Nor any other part of his body."

There was shouting on the deck below. Several men were squabbling for possession of the few telescopes they shared amongst themselves. The rest crowded the railing, shielding their eyes from the sun as they stared in the direction of the beach.

"I think we just lost ourselves a lieutenant," Wollaton scoffed, turning to Gillies with a smirk on his face.

Through my own glass I could see neither Legge nor Slick. "What in God's name..."

A man broke the surface. It was Slick. To my relief, the young lieutenant appeared shortly afterwards, though seemed to be flailing. Slick began whipping something about his head—Legge's cotton slops. Tossing them well out of reach, he swam towards the shore.

"Your cleverness has cost you a pretty sum today, Mr Gillies," Wollaton said. He strode across the deck and snatched Gillies's purse, tipping the contents into his hand. "I count only twelve shillings here. Means you still owe me three."

Gillies seemed unbothered, slipping his pencil into his jacket pocket and stretching his arms in the air. "Is it over?" he said with a yawn. "Have we a winner?"

Down below, the crew began stamping on the boards and shouting Legge's name. Refocusing the lens, I was astonished to see the lieutenant running through the breakers and up onto the sandy beach, all blond hair and white buttocks in the morning sunshine. Slick hauled himself through the knee-deep water some distance behind.

A boy ran up to Legge and handed him a poncho, which he slipped over his head. Turning towards us, he raised his arms into the air victoriously.

A raucous cheer resounded across the deck.

"It looks as though your man has been well and truly beaten," I said to Wollaton, concealing my jubilation as best I could. "Give Mr Gillies his purse back and whatever you owe him. Twelve shillings? Or did you settle on fifteen?"

Wollaton took off his hat and wiped his brow with his sleeve, his thinning, iron-grey hair matted against his sweaty scalp. Scratching his beard, he began grumbling that he did not have sufficient money on his person and would settle the wager later.

"In the spirit of good sportsmanship, the debt must be settled immediately," I ordered, knowing full well that it would not be paid once we were ashore. "You will see to this right away, Mr Wollaton."

While we waited for Wollaton to return, Gillies showed me what he had been sketching: a half-finished portrait of a young man, whom I could already tell was Legge.

"Blessed with his great-grandfather's good looks," Gillies said. "But without a trace of the Proud Duke's legendary vanity."

"I see," I looked Gillies in the eye. "So you are aware of Mr Legge's heritage?"

He nodded.

"I trust you will keep this to yourself," I said. "I do not want the men thinking the lieutenant gained his position on my ship through family connections—because that was certainly *not* the case."

My own experience had taught me how difficult life could be for a young officer if the crew were led to believe he had attained his rank through privilege rather than ability. In Legge's case, the situation was especially sensitive, as he was the great-grandson of Charles Seymour, the sixth Duke of Somerset—a man nicknamed the "Proud Duke" after boasting of how his exceptionally good looks had won him favour within the Royal Household.

"Your secret is safe with me," Gillies said, touching his finger to his lips. "Charles Legge is a rare breed. Far more than just good looks and heritage." He climbed to his feet. "You will need to look after him."

"I am sure Mr Legge can look after himself."

Gillies shrugged his shoulders. "I am not so certain. He is a pure soul, a rose growing amongst a tangle of weeds."

"Then was it entirely necessary to coerce him into that swimming race?" I said. "And I have not forgotten how you placed Mr Legge in a difficult spot on the night of the aurora. Given you know about his heritage, I am inclined to wonder—"

"It will not do to be suspicious of my intentions," Gillies said, cutting me off. "We must trust each other, you and I. There is a lot at stake."

I found it a rather odd thing to say, but before I had the opportunity to ask him what he meant, Wollaton reappeared from below deck. Returning to the quarterdeck, he delved into his pocket and withdrew a handful of coins.

"Let us hope you live long enough to spend this," he said, thrusting the coins into Gillies's hand and avoiding his eye.

"I shall buy that new jacket," Gillies said, grinning at me. "And when I die, I hope the Captain will bury me in it."

"You think yo'self so clever," Wollaton spat back at him. "All them clever words. We'll see how far they get you once we're ashore an' there's nobody to watch your back."

"Is that a threat?" Gillies asked.

"Now, now. There is no need for this," I said. "Mr Gillies won the wager, fair and square. Shake hands like good sports, and let us get on with more important matters."

Wollaton's hands remained firmly by his side, his fists clenched. "'Scuse me, Captain, if I return to my duties."

"You must shake first. That is an order, Lieutenant."

He did so, albeit begrudgingly, then left the quarterdeck in a sulk.

I returned to my cabin. There would be countless meetings with town officials and dignitaries once I stepped ashore, and I needed to ensure my affairs were in order. The trouble-free passage had given me ample time to prepare the paperwork, which sat in a neat pile on my bureau. Yet, as I flicked mindlessly from page to page, I felt anxious—as if I had overlooked something of importance. Something was missing, or out of place.

I paced across the floorboards, trying to rid myself of the unnerving feeling that prickled my neck and caused butterflies in my stomach. My mother used to call this the 'sixth sense'—an awareness of something that lay unseen in the future. My father would have argued it was nature's instinct, and that my mind was simply misinterpreting what was little more than common anxiety.

I poured myself a whiskey, knocking it back in a single hit.

"First voyage as captain," I said to the bottom of the glass. "Bound to come with a little apprehension, here and there."

Walking to the gilded mirror on my wall, I studied my reflection. I had my father's strong, straight nose and my mother's deep brown eyes. My hair was thick and black, and rose into a widow's peak high upon my brow. The beard I had begun growing lay as a dark shadow on my chin.

Examining my countenance in this way was a habit that I often performed before official engagements. The purpose was not for vanity, but rather a sense of detachment, and I continued this inspection until I felt the familiar sense of separation between my inner and outer self. The man returning my gaze was a captain and a commander. He had gone to sea as a boy and laboured as all the young boys had, without complaint. As a midshipman, he had taken the midnight watch whilst the other midshipmen slept in their cots; and as a lieutenant, he had used every ounce of his influence and intelligence to gain favour with the Admiralty so that they might consider him for a captain's post. The man in the mirror had climbed the ladder of ambition without ever looking down—and though he knew my darkest secrets, they did not haunt him as they haunted me.

I watched my ally straighten his collars and adjust his cravat, his steady eyes never leaving mine. He dabbed a little cologne onto his neck and inhaled its jasmine-and-musk scent, then plucked a stray thread from one of his epaulettes.

I trusted this man with my life.

Turning on my heel, I left my cabin and returned on deck.

THREE

WE ANCHORED in Valparaiso when the Yuletide celebrations were at their height and multitudes of people had arrived from the countryside to enjoy the festivities.

The main attraction of the season was the bullfights, which were quite unlike the bloodthirsty performances I had witnessed in Spain. The bullfights began with a crowd gathering at noon in one of the plazas, and the lumbering beasts would then be paraded along the main street to a makeshift bullring by the harbour. It was a noisy procession, accompanied by the sounding of horns and ringing of bells, which grew in size and fervour as the crowd passed the taverns and swept up drunken townsfolk and sailors alike.

The bullfights themselves were an amusing, if frivolous, affair—the bulls were never injured in the performance, merely chastised with blunt spears until they stamped and snorted and inevitably charged at their gaily dressed provokers, who ran around waving at the audience before leaping out of the ring to safety, all to roars of laughter and thunderous applause.

When the daytime festivities were over, the women and children retired and the revelry took on a more primitive and boisterous nature. By nightfall, the men were dancing under flaming torches on the beach, throwing themselves at one another in drunken embraces and bawling out unfamiliar ballads in hoarse and discordant voices.

I had taken lodgings in a suburb called the Almendral, or Almond Grove, situated on an elevated plain on the eastern side of the town. The narrow, cobbled streets and whitewashed townhouses of the Almendral were built by wealthy colonials who wished to recreate the flavour and charm of a Spanish pueblo on Chilean soil. It was here that the officers from visiting ships preferred to stay.

The days following our arrival in the port saw me engrossed in diplomatic business, but even this was suspended over Yule, giving me time to relax and attend a few social functions. Christmas came and went with its usual overindulgence of eating and drinking, and having survived a grandiose banquet on Saint Stephen's, I decided to hide away in my lodgings and venture no further than the tranquil plazas of the Almendral until the new year was in.

On a sunny afternoon at the end of December, Mr Legge paid me an unexpected visit. The young lieutenant arrived on my doorstep shortly after midday, dressed in a linen shirt and wearing a silly straw hat adorned with white feathers.

"Many happy returns, Captain," he announced as I opened the door, greeting me with a beaming smile. Taking his hands from behind his back, he revealed a second hat, this one with a yellow ribbon around its brim and yellow feathers to match. "A birthday gift for you, sir."

"Thank you. It is quite...splendid," I said delicately, taking the hat from him. It was my thirty-second birthday that day, and to be quite honest, I had given the occasion little more than a passing thought.

"I was rather hoping you might like to join me for the last bullfight of the season," Legge said.

I glanced past him into the plaza. There were only one or two people about, but the tranquillity was disturbed by a cacophony of bells and horns and the sound of people cheering from somewhere not too far away.

"I am afraid I must decline. I have work to do."

"Could you not spare an hour or two?" Legge asked, his face already taking on traces of disappointment. "The whole town has turned out in the marketplace. There is all sorts going on."

I liked Legge. Indeed, I had liked him on the very first day we met, when he had sat nervously in my office with flushed cheeks and sweat dripping from his brow. He had arrived twenty minutes late for his interview, having been sent to the wrong ship by a senior officer, in what I had suspected to be a cruel joke. Despite my initial reservations at this poor start, Legge proceeded to win me over during his interview. His previous post was as midshipman on a Mediterranean voyage, and the reference I had received from his captain was filled with praise for the lad's good nature, honesty, and intelligence. Having settled into the interview, Legge demonstrated a commendable knowledge of sailing. Indeed, my only minor concern had been that he looked too young to be a lieutenant— which I told him, adding in jest that I would only give him the position if he managed to grow some facial hair before we set sail.

And here he stood, with his hair platted into a ponytail and a downy red beard on his chin, trying to hide his disappointment at my having turned down his kind invitation.

Yes, I liked Legge, and I suppose I also wanted him to like me. I was ten years older than he was, and his captain—but it did not seem so long ago that I was a lieutenant. Back then, my commanders had been aloof and distant men. Aspiring to be as they were, I used to imitate them, secretly practising the way they walked; the slow and sagacious way they nodded their heads when listening to their officers; the way they interrupted a conversation to issue an order, leaving the man who was talking with the words hanging in his mouth.

In those formative years, I had moulded myself to become what I believed a captain should be, and the clay had hardened —but with Legge, the clay was still pliable and wet. And that morning, as he stood there on my step, I wanted him to see that his captain was not always such a detached and impersonal fellow, but that it was a necessary role I had to play as my duty to our country, and for the safety of the ship.

I placed the straw hat on my head. "I suppose an old man *should* have a little fun on his birthday," I said, reaching out and taking him by the shoulder. "Come along then—let us see what mischief we can get ourselves into."

We walked into the town and soon became caught up in the clamouring procession that filled the cobbled street leading downhill to the marketplace. Legge and I had not spoken on a personal level before now, and I listened with interest as he talked with great affection about his family; in particular his mother, to whom he wrote frequently.

I was, however, somewhat distracted by the reactions of the townsfolk as they caught sight of the lieutenant. Fair-haired sailors were not uncommon in the port, and certainly drew the attention of the Chileans—but with Legge, it went beyond simply stopping and staring. On several occasions, I witnessed people, men and women alike, pushing purposely through the crowds so that they could shuffle alongside us. I watched how they stepped in front of Legge, quite unashamedly, tripping over their feet as they spun around to take in his piercing blue eyes, which carried in their depths an unusual translucence. And as if simply looking were not enough to satisfy their curiosity, I noticed their surreptitious attempts to touch him, reaching out to place a hand on his shoulder, or his back, as they jostled forwards; or sidling up next to him so that they might brush their fingers against the white flesh on his exposed forearm.

Legge seemed oblivious to this attention. Perhaps, after several weeks in the port, he had become used to it.

The marketplace was crowded with merrymakers; the festivities spilling out into the surrounding streets and along the promenade. We stopped to watch two wild-looking horsemen prance about on all quarters, wielding swords above their heads.

In the middle of this frantic display, a young girl ran out into the street, and were it not for Legge's swift response, she might have been trampled.

"Dónde está tu madre?" Legge said, crouching down and brushing the hair away from her eyes. She was perhaps six or seven years of age and dressed in the tattered clothes of a beggar.

"En el cielo!" she cried, pointing her tiny finger to the sky.

Legge looked up at me, then asked the child, "Y tu padre?"

"Papá se está muriendo. Ayúdame, por favor!" she said desperately.

Legge was unwilling to leave the child in such a distressed state and enquired as to where her sick father was. She slid her hand into his, tugging on it so that she might lead the way. We followed her through the streets and into the ravines below the cliffs, a suburb known as the Quebradas. It was here that the poorest members of the community lived: the brick makers, day-labourers and washerwomen. The ramshackle houses of the Quebradas were small, single-storey buildings, built with crumbling stones and thatched with broad palm leaves. There was no trace of the affluence of the Almendral here, but having taken several walks in the area, I found the people richer in conversation and humour than their wealthy neighbours—and in generosity too, despite their meagre earnings.

We continued threading our way through one street after another until, rounding a corner into a dirty alleyway, the girl ran ahead and disappeared through an open doorway. We soon found ourselves in a miserable dwelling that comprised a single, comfortless room with a mud floor and a broken ceiling. I covered my mouth and nose with my hand—the air was fouled by the smell of faeces. In the dim light thrown from a single tallow candle, I could make out a worktable cluttered with carpentry tools, and a makeshift stove with smouldering embers. Upon a narrow bed in the corner of the room, a half-naked man was laid out like a corpse, his course black hair hanging over the side. He was groaning heavily.

"Estoy asustada," the girl said, tears streaming down her cheeks.

Legge crouched beside her, placing his hands on her shoulders. "There is nothing to be afraid of." Reaching into his pocket, he took out a clean white handkerchief embroidered in one corner with his initials. He used it to dab the tears from the child's face. "We are here to help."

The girl flung her arms around the lieutenant's neck and began sobbing as if her little heart would burst.

Upon hearing his daughter's voice, the man's eyes opened. His head turned towards her. "Luisa... Luisa..." he mumbled, reaching out. "Sé valiente, mi niña, se valiente."

The man was a ghastly sight, soaked in his own vomit. His bulging eyes stared wildly in my direction.

"We must fetch Mr Birnie," Legge said, gently freeing himself from the child's embrace.

"Birnie is still on board the *Conway*," I told him. "He plans to sort out old Radcliffe's foot this morning. Perhaps a local doctor from the hospital?" The man heaved, and I watched aghast as a river of spittle ran from the corners of his mouth. "We may already be too late."

"What about Mr Gillies?" Legge suggested.

I had not spoken to Gillies since our arrival in the port, but thought I might know where he was staying. On several occasions, I had spied him hobbling across the Almendral plaza before disappearing down an alleyway into a house with a blue door.

"Stay with the child," I said. "It's worth a shot."

I hurried back through the streets, pushing my way through the crowded marketplace, then climbing the hill to the Almendral with the sun beating on my brow and sweat trickling down my neck.

Arriving at the plaza, I made my way down the alleyway to the tired-looking blue door. I banged on it with my fist until, after quite some time, a surly-looking woman in a black dress answered.

"I must speak with Mr Gillies," I said, removing my straw hat and wiping my brow with my shirtsleeve. "It is a matter of some urgency,"

The door was summarily closed in my face, and I was left waiting impatiently on the step for several minutes. Just as I was about to recommence my knocking, the door opened again. This time, I was greeted by the familiar whiskered face and sharp grey-green eyes of John Gillies.

"Captain Hall, how nice to see you," he said, then frowning as he looked me up and down. "But I can see this is not a social visit."

"A man in the Quebradas is in a ghastly state," I said. "Mr Legge and I found him bedridden, with a high fever and swollen eyes. We hoped you might take a look at him."

Gillies stuck his head out of the doorway and glanced down the alleyway. "I am afraid I cannot help. It is rather a long way...and I am feeling a little out of sorts today."

"It was Mr Legge's suggestion that I fetch you," I said, tossing my hat down on the step. "There is a young child, the man's daughter. Legge is quite taken with her, and by the looks of it, she will be left all alone if her father dies."

"Yes, well, that is a pity," Gillies said. "But I doubt there is much I can do."

"I should say you owe Mr Legge a favour," I said. "You might not have been able to afford these lodgings were it not for his swimming prowess."

Gillies contemplated this for a moment, then sighed and nodded his head. "All right. Wait here while I retrieve my bag."

It took well over an hour for us to make our way back to the Quebradas. The streets were becoming steadily busier, and as I pushed a path through the crowds, Gillies hobbled along behind me with his cane, stopping every few hundred yards to catch his breath or cough hoarsely into a handkerchief. We entered the dwelling to find the room silent. Our patient looked as though he had fallen unconscious, and the little girl sat huddled in a corner with her arms around her knees. Legge sat on the floor next to her and scrambled to his feet as we entered.

Gillies spent some time examining the ailing man: prising his eyelids open and inspecting his eyeballs, looking into his mouth, feeling his brow, pressing down on his ribs, then lifting his arm and feeling for his pulse.

The man remained motionless.

"Is he...dead?" Legge asked quietly.

"Not yet." Gillies placed his satchel on the floor, then rolled up his sleeves. "I believe he has the *chaoo longo*, a local fever that can be fatal if left unchecked. We will need to make a tourniquet." He pointed to the worktable. "That strip of leather will do. Boil some water on the stove."

Gillies bound the man's arm above the elbow. Opening his satchel, he removed a thin knife and a piece of cloth.

"Cover her eyes," he said, nodding at the girl.

Legge took the child into the corner of the room. Meanwhile, Gillies made a clean incision in the man's forearm. I watched the blood run in a thick rivulet down his arm and went to fetch a pot to place underneath his bleeding limb.

"That should help relieve the pressure," Gillies said, wiping his brow and leaving a smear of blood on his forehead. "Now we wait."

In the minutes that followed, we stood in silence, listening to the blood dripping from the man's fingers into the pot. I watched in astonishment as the veins on his forehead withdrew. The swelling beneath his eyes subsided, and his breathing calmed and steadied. Half an hour later, our patient woke woozily from his delirium and began calling out for water. His voice was weak, but without distress.

"If he is strong, his body should fight off the disease in a few days," Gillies said. Returning to his bag, he brought out a brown paper packet and sprinkled what looked like dried herbs into the pot on the stove.

"The tea will control the fever. It must be drunk three times a day." Gillies held up three fingers to his patient. "Tres veces al día. Mañana, mediodía y noche."

The man nodded weakly. He shifted his head so as to glance about the room, his eyes searching for his daughter. "Luisa?"

We all turned to the darkened corner where the girl was squatting with her hands wrapped around her knees.

"Papá?" She seemed uneasy about going to him.

Legge went to fetch her. Crouching on his haunches, he swept the tangle of black hair from her face and looked into her eyes. Only then did she manage a smile.

"Todo lo que él necesita es tu amor," the young lieutenant said.

All he needs is your love.

It was a relief to be back outside in the sunshine. Straightening my back, I took several deep breaths to clear the rancid air from my lungs. Gillies leant against the wall of the house and gazed blankly across the lane.

"You saved a man's life in there," I said.

He glanced at me and shrugged. "Let us hope so."

"I have never seen such a dramatic recovery," I went on, meaning it quite sincerely. "The man was at death's door. It was incredible to watch."

"We were lucky this time," he said, managing a smile, and I noticed a look of sadness in his eyes.

I then recalled the piece of unkind gossip Wollaton had related about Gillies: how a young officer had died while under his care, and how the incident had led to his dismissal. Birnie seemed to think the young man died of yellow fever. Perhaps the situation had been not unlike today—except that Gillies had been unable to save his patient back then.

"Death's door," Gillies said. "Have you ever thought what it might look like?"

"Not really," I confessed.

"Do you think it has a handle?" he mused. "I suppose it does, but we're mostly afraid to look at it, aren't we? Let alone reach out and grab it with our hand." He rapped his cane against the wall. "At any rate, all credit goes to Mr Birnie for our patient's return to life. We had several long discussions about tropical fevers on the passage from England. It was Birnie who told me about the *chaoo longo*—I was merely putting his theory of bloodletting into practice."

Legge emerged from the dwelling, having said his goodbyes to the little girl. Setting off back through the Quebradas, we walked at a leisurely pace through the poorer quarter of town, passing the saddlers, tailors, and blacksmiths who supplied the markets and the wealthy merchants in the port. Many were closed for the festival.

Nearing the marketplace, we became caught up in the steady flow of people pouring into the central plaza. The bull-fight was over, and the festivities continued with flamboyant matadors swooping and swaggering through the crowds, yelling out, "Toro! Toro!" as children charged through their scarlet capes.

As Legge was keen to buy a few provisions for our patient and his daughter, I said I would accompany Gillies on the walk back to the Almendral.

"We could meet here later?" the lieutenant suggested. "I imagine the festivities will carry on well into the night."

"Yes, well, perhaps." I smiled at him. "But you carry on. Enjoy yourself. Get drunk or something."

"Aye aye, Captain." Legge tipped his straw hat, retreating backwards into the crowd. "I will keep a lookout for you."

I took Gillies along the promenade so as to avoid the crowds in the centre of the town. It was high tide, and the sea had all but engulfed the beach. There were several ships in the harbour, their flags flapping in the afternoon breeze.

Gillies leant on his cane and stared out to sea.

"I am intrigued about those herbs you administered," I said. "What were they?"

Gillies shrugged. "A little of this, a little of that. Foxglove for the pulse, hyssop for the lungs, a touch of St John's wort to lift his spirits." He winked at me, then signalled with his cane that we should continue walking. "Eye of newt and toe of frog."

We climbed the cobbled streets to find the Almendral plaza busy with merrymakers. Arriving at Gillies's lodgings, I looked around for the straw hat I dropped earlier, but there was no sign of it.

"Damn this rusty old thing," Gillies said, rattling his key inside the lock. "There is a knack, you know... One has to..." He kicked the door several times. Finally, it swung open. Gillies wobbled on his cane, then reached for my arm in order to regain his balance.

"You must take some rest," I advised him. "It has been a strenuous day, and—"

"And it is time for some tea," he said, letting go of my arm and stepping across the threshold. He beckoned me with his hand. "Don't worry, I will not keep you captive for long. There is something I have been wanting to show you, and I suppose now is as good a time as any."

FOUR

Valparaiso, Chile, 28th December 1820

JOHN GILLIES LED the way down the dimly lit corridor into the parlour. Upon entering the room I heard the rhythmical scratching of a scrubbing brush on tiles, and saw a woman on her hands and knees vigorously cleaning the hearth.

"Might I introduce my landlady, Señora Valdés," Gillies announced, sweeping his hand in her direction. "Señora Valdés, this is Captain Basil Hall of the British Navy."

The woman glanced over her shoulder. I recognised her as the prickly individual who had closed the door in my face earlier. She tossed her scrubbing brush into a bucket of dirty water and stood up, her knees cracking unpleasantly as she did so. Wiping her hands on her apron, she gave me a lukewarm smile. "Buenas tardes, señor."

The two began conversing in Spanish, and meanwhile I looked around the sparsely furnished room, taking in the two rectangular patches on the carpet and the empty picture hook on the wall above the sideboard. I wondered if Señora Valdés had been forced to part with some of her furniture to help make ends meet: the residents of the Almendral had once belonged exclusively to the Spanish upper classes, but since the revolution many had experienced a reversal of fortune.

My Spanish was rather poor, but I understood enough of what they were saying to know that Gillies was enquiring about the lock on his bedroom door being faulty—and more specifically, he was offering to pay for a locksmith to come and take a look at it. Señora Valdés, with her hands on her hips and glaring at him in indignation, said it had been broken for years and if he suspected her of being a common thief then he should find somewhere else to stay. Gillies tried to convince the woman that this was not the case and that he simply preferred to sleep with the door locked, but she remained tight-lipped and scowling throughout. In the end, he changed the subject and ordered some tea.

We left the parlour after that and Gillies took me up the stairs to the top of the house. His living quarters were cramped and less salubrious than my own across the plaza. The bed had been pushed tightly against the far wall to provide enough space for a round tea-table, a small bookcase, a bureau by the window, and two worn armchairs that sat next to the hearth. A large, gold-framed mirror filled the wall above the fireplace, giving the illusion that the room was larger than it was. A black carriage clock ticked contentedly on the mantle between two low-burning candles.

"When do you think you will sail north?" Gillies asked, opening a window to let in some fresh air.

"Within the next month," I told him. "The revolution in Peru is imminent, and we must be standing by to ensure the gates for trade remain open for England—whichever side may win."

The room had two west-facing windows and boasted an enviable view, which looked out over the red-tiled rooftops in the direction of the harbour. An American ship had sailed into the port that morning and I could see men the size of ants scurrying back and forth along the wharfs. The *Conway* was visible too, moored in the deeper waters of the bay.

On the bureau beside me, Gillies's sketchbook lay open next to a wooden paint box and a jar of lilac-coloured water holding a selection of brushes. The page on display bore a rather fanciful watercolour of a ship at sea, over whose masts flew a mythical creature of some sort, with the head of a serpent and feathered, emerald-green wings.

"I am calling it *Voyage into Purgatory*," Gillies said, walking over to the bookcase to remove a metal tin from one of the shelves. "The ship is sailing into the afterlife, watched by the eyes of Quetzalcoatl, the Plumed Serpent."

"It looks rather like the *Conway*."

"Inspired by that wonderful night when we rounded the Cape," Gillies replied.

"Ah, yes, the aurora." I recalled the magnificence of the sky that night. It was quite otherworldly. "Very good. So who is this Ket-sal...?"

"Quetzalcoatl," Gillies said. "He is one of the supreme gods in the Aztec pantheon. In Aztec mythology, Quetzalcoatl and his brother Tezcatlipoca created the universe. Quetzalcoatl brought order and light, and was the god of peace and the founder of civilisation; Tezcatlipoca, by contrast, was the Lord of the Night Sky, and brought chaos, destruction and darkness."

"Ah, the age-old battle between good and evil."

He shook his head. "Not at all. That is a Christian dogma. These ancient people understood that the fabric of the universe is built from opposing forces. After all, what is a star without the night sky? What is joy without sadness? Progress without first destruction? Tezcatlipoca was not at all seen as an evil god, though he was certainly feared." He glanced across at me. "We all fear change in our lives. A destruction of the old ways."

"The Aztecs were from Mexico," I remarked. "This Quetzalcoatl of yours is a little too far south, is he not?"

"He has come to welcome them at the gate." Gillies smiled at me. "Quetzalcoatl was, amongst his many roles, the god of merchants."

There was a knock at the door. While Gillies went to answer it, I flipped the page of his sketchbook and found myself looking down at the handsome face of Charles Legge. I recalled Gillies having begun the portrait on the day we arrived in the port, the day of the swimming race. Legge's well-bred looks, his solid brow and high cheekbones, the chiselled line of his jaw, had all been brought out by delicate shading.

The likeness was uncanny. His hair was not bound in a plait as it had been on that day, but fell down about his shoulders. And then there were his eyes. Gillies had captured that unusual translucence, and despite the lack of colour, they seemed somehow to radiate that same striking blue, gazing out from the page with all the amiability and cheerfulness that Legge managed so easily.

Yes, the likeness really was quite uncanny.

Hearing the door close, I glanced across the room to see Gillies holding a tray of tea things.

"Señora Valdés was forced to let her maid go earlier this year," Gillies said, making his way across the room. "Hard times have fallen on the poor woman."

"She is a widow?"

"Married to an officer in the Spanish royalist army," Gillies said, with a nod. "He was killed three years ago in the Battle of Chacabuco—not seventy miles from here."

"That is rather tragic," I replied, absently turning the page of his sketchbook. "The Royalists were surrounded, were they not—by General San Martín's men? Something of a grave miscalculation, by all accounts." I found myself looking down at another pencil sketch. This time, it was of a darkened prison cell in which a desperate-looking man sat chained to the floor with his head bowed low. "These are quite excellent, you know. Who is this character?"

Gillies seemed about to say something but then stopped himself, pursing his lips for a moment before continuing. "A fellow I once met...in a dream, of sorts."

"Not a very pleasant dream, by the looks of it."

I watched Gillies place the tray down on the table with something of a clatter. He looked unsteady and leant on the chair for support.

"Are you all right?"

"Yes, yes. I am quite fine." He blinked heavily, as if fighting against dizziness. "Right-hand drawer of the bureau, if you would be so kind. Bring the contents over here."

I stood staring at him a moment longer, then looked inside the drawer. It contained a collection of tattered-looking papers laid out neatly alongside one another. Seven in total, each divided into two columns of handwritten text and bearing colour illustrations drawn in a simple gothic style. The left-hand column of text was written in Spanish. I did not recognise the language in the right-hand column.

"They look rather ancient."

"Two centuries old," Gillies said, lowering himself into the armchair. "Taken from a sixteenth-century manuscript called the Florentine Codex."

"And this peculiar language?" I asked, carefully collecting up the pages. "There must be more than a dozen letters making up some of these words."

"Nahuatl. The language of the Aztecs," he said. "They were an illiterate race. What you see there was painstakingly transcribed from word of mouth by the author of the manuscript. The Spanish text alongside is its translation. You will find an illustration of Quetzalcoatl there too."

"Ah yes, the Plumed Serpent." I leafed through the pages, finding the picture with Quetzalcoatl's name beneath it. The deity wore a headdress of green feathers and carried a curved sword and a shield. There was a snake coiled around one of his legs and a rainbow-coloured bird flying over his head. *Quetzalcoatl: Dios de la Estrella de la Mañana,* the title read—*Quetzalcoatl: God of the Morning Star.*

"Quetzalcoatl was the divine combination of air and earth," Gillies said. "The bird you see there is a quetzal, a magnificent creature native to Mexico and revered by the Aztecs as sacred. *Coatl* means snake—an ancient symbol of knowledge."

I turned over the page. The dark-skinned deity pictured on the other side was dressed in a loincloth and the spotted pelt of what I presumed must be a jaguar. His headdress was made of lilac feathers and he wore a black-and-yellow stripe across his nose. *Tezcatlipoca: Dios del Cielo Nocturno—Tezcatlipoca: God of the Night Sky*. There were stars in the background, presumably signifying the heavenly realm over which he presided.

"Tezcatlipoca ruled mankind's destiny," Gillies said. "He was a master of deception, creating illusions that tricked mortals to look deep into their lives. His other name was the

Smoking Mirror—after the object you will see strapped to his knee there, a mirror made of polished black obsidian. Those who gazed into its smoking depths were confronted with their fate."

I inspected one of the other pages. It bore an illustration of a sacrificial ritual: a man in a loincloth lay upon a stone slab while several robed figures gathered around him. A figure in a headdress, perhaps a chieftain or religious leader, wielded a snake above his head. The sun, drawn in one corner of the picture, threw jagged shards of light into the recumbent man's chest.

"The Aztecs were a barbaric lot," I remarked, looking up to see Gillies scooping several spoons of dried herbs from the tin into the steaming teapot.

"They were a highly civilized race," Gillies replied. "Their capital city, Tenochtitlan, was as advanced in its architecture as any European city of the day. A formidable sight to behold, according to the accounts of the Spanish conquistadors, rising up from the centre of a lake with towering battlements on all sides, and accessible only by its four causeways to the north, south, east and west. The population thrived on fresh water supplied through a system of aqueducts; and the streets were lined with palaces and temples, glittering with gold in the evening sunlight. It is all in the Florentine Codex." He pointed towards the pages in my hand. "Two thousand five hundred pages of text in twelve hefty volumes. A veritable cornucopia on Aztec life—their gods, religious beliefs, politics, economics, knowledge of the cosmos, ceremonies and rituals, the crops they cultivated, the diseases they succumbed to... And cures, of course, all sorts of remedies made from the local flora. The Aztecs believed your health was determined to a large extent by the day on which you were born." Gillies examined his fingernails. "I suppose my birth date must have been an unlucky one."

"So what is going on in this illustration?" I asked, showing him the page I was looking at. "Death by snakebite?"

"The ceremony of *Tonatiuhtiz*," he said. "The name translates to *He will become as the sun*. It was the greatest of honours to be selected for the ceremony, and the Chosen One would first have to prove his worth by embarking on a dangerous quest. If he survived the quest and returned to the world of mortals, the ceremony would take place at noon on the summer solstice."

"Whereupon he was duly sacrificed."

"Transformed into sunlight." Gillies's eyes widened as he turned his gaze to a dusty sunbeam, which poured into the room from the corner window. "By a bite from the golden serpent."

"The poor fellow probably believed it too," I said, noticing the peaceful look on the victim's face. "Ignorance is bliss, is it not?"

"These ancient people were not as tied to this world as we are," Gillies said, smoothing out his trouser leg with a sweep of his hand. "They believed the fabric of existence was made up of many layers, of which the realm we inhabit is but one. Giving up one's body willingly, and for a noble cause, opened the door to higher realms."

"All very macabre, if you ask me." I handed the pages to him. "Where is the remainder of this manuscript?"

"It resides in the Basilica of San Lorenzo in Florence," Gillies said. *"La Historia Universal de las Cosas de Nueva España* is its proper title—*A General History of the Things of New Spain*. The Florentine Codex is its more common name. Contrary to what is generally believed, it is not housed in the main library. The monks keep it under lock and key in their inner sanctum three floors beneath the basilica." He raised his eyebrows. "I can tell you, it took a good deal of planning to get to it—and no small amount of luck. Not to mention the bribes— you would be surprised how easily monks will take your money. At any rate, there I was at four in the morning, with only half an hour to rifle through two thousand five hundred pages before the sun rose."

"Just a minute..." I said, suddenly catching on to what he was saying. "Are you telling me you *stole* these pages?"

Gillies returned a look that implied my question was in itself quite ridiculous. "When one uncovers a treasure map, one does not leave it behind for others to stumble upon."

I walked over to the mantelpiece and began filling my pipe, giving myself time to contemplate this unexpected revelation. For one thing, John Gillies was a thief. For another, he had stolen from the *Church*—and in no small way! Sacred pages from an ancient text, hidden away in a basilica in Florence...

And what was all this about a treasure map?

Gillies sat contentedly in his armchair with the pages balanced on his lap, one skinny leg crossed over the other, idly tapping his foot in the air as if keeping time to a melody.

Lighting my pipe from one of the candles, I puffed a plume of tobacco smoke into the space between us. "I presume this is connected with your desire to journey on to Mexico."

Although Gillies said nothing, the feverish look on his face spoke volumes.

"Listen here, I shall tell you a thing or two about treasure maps," I said, clearing my throat as I rested an elbow on the mantelpiece. "In fifteen years at sea, I have seen several such things—from scribbled notes on scraps of paper to elaborate charts rolled up and sealed with wax. One was simply an eight-line poem." I shook the smouldering bowl of my pipe in his direction. "And yet never once have I met a man who has found so much as a handful of gold coins, let alone a buried chest filled with pearls and rubies and what have you."

"This is entirely different." Gillies placed his hand gently on top of the pile of pages. It was a gesture not unlike that of a witness in court swearing an oath upon the Bible. "A great secret is no longer safe, Captain."

I shook my head in dismay. "Breaking into a basilica, Mr Gillies. Desecrating an ancient manuscript. Theft of a sacred text! You are lucky not to have been caught by the authorities and strung up by your neck already."

"What I did was out of necessity," he said. "It was only a matter of time before the pages were discovered. Should the golden serpent fall into the wrong hands, the consequences would be disastrous."

"The golden serpent—so that is your prize, is it?"

"That must remain between you and I." Gillies's face turned suddenly serious. "You must not tell a soul."

"Yes, yes, you have my word," I told him, somewhat flippantly.

Gillies reached into his pocket and pulled out his handkerchief, then fell into a bout of heavy coughing. When he took his hand away from his mouth there were spots of blood on the cloth.

"You are not a well man, sir." It was as good a time as any to speak plainly. "If the voyage to Mexico doesn't kill you, whatever lies waiting for you on this...this quest of yours most certainly will. Mexico is a dangerous country for even a well-seasoned explorer—which you are not! The terrain is harsh, the heat merciless, and the people...well, I very much doubt you will get a warm welcome from the natives when they find out you are there to steal their gold."

"Quests would not be quests if they were so easily achieved." He stuffed the handkerchief back into his pocket. "I did not come here to enjoy a comfortable retirement, Captain. What little time I have left, I intend to put to good use."

"Then why not help the poor in this town?" I asked, still hoping I might be able to reason with him. "You are a skilled physician. Look what you did this morning—you could save lives."

A silence fell between us. Gillies sat with his arms folded, collecting his thoughts from the ceiling. Meanwhile, I listened to the ticking clock on the mantelpiece, wondering what it was he was about to say—because I was quite certain there was more to come.

"Let me tell you a little more about the man who compiled the Florentine Codex," he said at length, his sharp eyes scrutinizing me from behind his spectacles. "His name was Fray Bernardino de Sahagún, a Spanish monk of the Franciscan order, and he arrived in Mexico in 1529, not long after the Spanish conquest of the Aztec Empire."

"A missionary?"

Gillies settled back into his chair. "On a divine summons. An apparition of the Virgin Mary appeared at the end of the young friar's bed one night, declaring, in all her resplendent glory, that a holy destiny awaited him across the ocean in New Spain."

While I stood sucking on my pipe, Gillies went on to explain that as the monk had very little money, he could afford only the cheapest of passages to Mexico: on an old sloop whose captain was a drunkard and crew were an unwashed bunch of petty criminals. As chance would have it, there were a number of native folk on board the ship whom he befriended—the Nahua people, from the interior of Mexico. They were being returned to their homeland after what Gillies described to be "a rather ludicrous affair involving the King of Spain"—though he refrained from going into further details.

"Nevertheless," Gillies went on, "it gave Fray de Sahagún the opportunity to pass the time on that dreadful voyage learning the language of the natives. He believed that if he were to understand and speak Nahuatl, he might build a deeper connection with these ancient people, which would ultimately help him deliver the message of God. But when the ship dropped anchor on the shores of Mexico, the friar discovered his ability to communicate directly with the natives was to lead him on a very different path."

Gillies continued then in a more solemn tone. "While the other monks spent their days listening to the tales of the Spanish soldiers, about how they brought peace and harmony to the squabbling tribes, ridding the country of its *barbaric* ways, the accounts Fray de Sahagún was privy to were dark and horrifying. The natives told the young friar of how the conquistadors stormed the Aztec capital of Tenochtitlan, slaughtering innocent men and women without so much as a hint of remorse in their eyes. How they ransacked the ancient temples, stealing what they coveted and destroying what they did not care for. How these fine and virtuous Spanish soldiers marched through the interior, wielding the sword and the cross triumphantly as they burnt down the villages, butchering and defiling and murdering as they went." His eyes fell to the stolen pages. "Appalled by the atrocities committed by his own countrymen, Fray de Sahagún swore he would devote the rest of his life to preserving what he could of this dying civilisation. And true to his word, he spent the next fifty years travelling from village to village, listening to the tribal elders and transcribing their knowledge into words and illustrations. And so his *histoire*, the Florentine Codex, was born." With a sigh, Gillies reached over and lifted the lid of the teapot. He peered into its steamy depths. "I think this is about ready."

The distinct aroma of liquorice wafted in my direction. I tried not to pull a face, as I cannot abide the stuff. "Would you mind awfully if I got on my way?" I said, followed by a theatrical glance at my watch. "Mr Legge will be waiting for me in the marketplace."

"Mr Legge. Yes, of course." Gillies gathered up the pages and held them out to me. "Take them."

Naturally, I was quite baffled by this gesture.

"They are to be delivered to our mutual friend, Sir Walter Scott," he then explained. "When you return to England."

I felt my jaw drop in surprise. How on Earth did Gillies know of my acquaintance with Sir Walter? I first met the famed literary genius at a Royal Society dinner hosted by my father some years ago, and we had since become good friends. It was Sir Walter who helped me edit and publish the journals of my voyage to Loo-Choo, which had provided me with a little extra income in recent years.

But then...*our mutual friend*? What in God's name did Sir Walter have to do with all this?

"I cannot be a part of this," I told Gillies firmly. "Imagine what the authorities would say if I were to be caught with these pages in my possession."

"They *must* be kept safe," he urged. "If they remain with me... Captain, I am unlikely to see British soil again, as I am sure you are aware. I am asking you to trust your good friend Sir Walter, if not me."

I climbed out of the armchair. "I shall have no part in this foolishness. Now, I am afraid I must be off."

We made our way back down the stairs to the hallway, whereupon Gillies once again wrestled with the door. As I made to step over the threshold, he took hold of my wrist.

"What lies within these pages must be protected at all costs," he urged.

Snatching my hand away, I stepped into the alleyway. "Good day to you, Mr Gillies."

I walked across the sun-drenched plaza, pondering over Gillies's revelation. Upon reaching the door of my own lodgings, a thought struck me—or rather, I remembered a conversation that had taken place between Sir Walter and myself when I last paid him a visit at Abbotsford, his stately mansion in the Scottish borders. It had been in June of the previous year, and I recalled arriving at Abbotsford in a jovial mood, having received news from the Admiralty that I was to be offered command of my own ship, and would set sail for the South American station. Sir Walter was quite excited by this and began asking me for all sorts of particulars. Alas, all I knew was that the voyage would take a couple of years and that I would be rounding Cape Horn—as it had been impressed upon me that I should learn as much as I could about navigating the surrounding waters.

I recalled with some clarity how Sir Walter then began talking enthusiastically about his latest novel. "My protagonist must make an urgent journey to Mexico," he had said. "He knows of a ship, a merchant ship as it happens, but how does he go about getting himself on board?"

My reply had been that the character could go as a paying passenger, adding in jest that unfortunately I could not take his protagonist on board the *Conway*, owing to the diplomatic nature of the voyage—the Admiralty would not allow it.

Sir Walter had chuckled at this, waggling his finger at me. "Ah, but you see, my protagonist has connections."

We had left the conversation at that.

And then, three weeks before we were due to set sail from Plymouth, I received a letter from one of my superiors at the Admiralty.

A retired naval surgeon wishes to sail to Valparaiso, the letter had said. *You are to find him a cabin on board the* Conway.

I had been far too busy at the time to give the matter much thought—but, of course, that passenger was John Gillies.

FIVE

Valparaiso, Chile, 22nd March 1821

AS THE CHILEAN summer drew to an end, I was invited to a picnic party in the uplands beyond the port. The invitation came from Mr Henry Kennedy, a retired English diplomat whom I had met several weeks ago at an official engagement in the town hall. Kennedy had been boasting—in an amicable way —that the wine we were drinking was from his own vineyard, and that it was the best in Chile. I was only listening with half an ear at the time, as I was admiring a painting that hung on the wall behind the man's head. It was not until he went on to talk about his house in the hills and how it had a stunning view of the bay and shipping, that I returned my full attention to what he was saying—struck, as I was, with an uncanny feeling that he was talking about the lonely residence I had seen through my telescope upon our arrival in the port. When I questioned Kennedy further, lo and behold it was the very same place. Kennedy was delighted that I was so intrigued by his house, and said that I must pay him a visit when the weather was not so hot.

The invitation duly arrived a few weeks later. It was accompanied by a note from Kennedy informing me that he had taken the liberty of inviting the *Conway*'s surgeon, Mr Birnie, and Captain Spenser of the *Owen Glendower*—another British ship in Valparaiso at the time. A carriage had been arranged for our transportation, and would collect us from the Almendral plaza at nine. As the invitation was extended to *Captain Basil Hall and Guest*, I invited Legge to come along too.

On the morning of the picnic, I waited with Birnie and Legge in the drawing room of my lodgings, which looked directly out onto the plaza. The doctor and lieutenant were dressed comfortably in frock coats, made by the local tailors, and loose linen shirts. I was in my naval attire, as it would not be appropriate to dress casually knowing that Captain Spenser was attending.

So there we were, in the drawing room, biding our time by discussing a piece of news that had arrived in the port two days ago, with the whaling ship *Dauphin*. While still several hundred miles out to sea, the ship's lookout had spied a rowing boat, alone and adrift on the slumbering tide. Drawing alongside the little boat, the *Dauphin*'s crew found themselves gazing over the railings at a rather macabre sight: two emaciated men, with long, straggly hair and skin burnt raw by the sun, lying in the belly of the rowing boat. Though barely alive, they were engaged in a feeble tug of war over what appeared to be a long, slender bone.

"...by all accounts quite oblivious to their audience," the doctor continued. He stood by the window, surveying the plaza. "They just carried on bickering and squabbling, looking for all the world like two living skeletons."

"How long were they adrift?" Legge asked, his eyes wide with interest.

"Three whole months," I said. "At least, according to one of the survivors—goes by the name of George Pollard. He claims to be the captain of the ship that sank, an American whale ship named *Essex*. It is all quite extraordinary. Pollard says they were attacked by a giant whale."

"And so the hunters became the hunted," Birnie said.

"According to Pollard, the whale charged at the ship like a raging bull," I went on. "Tore through the hull, and down she went! The other survivor is a man named Ramsdell. He is in a sorry state, poor fellow—not a clue who or where he is."

That morning, I had attended an emergency meeting held by the town dignitaries. The two survivors were taken to the local infirmary, whereupon Ramsdell began raving like a madman, convinced that he saw Lucifer himself in the eye of the giant whale, as it circled their ship. Naturally, this revelation caused quite a stir among the nurses and patients in the infirmary, and the gossip was already leaking out into the community. We all agreed that this sort of superstitious rumour-mongering could damage the reputation of the port, and the decision was duly made to relocate the two men to the dungeons beneath the fort.

"I was asked to identify the bone earlier this morning," Birnie said, gripping his upper leg with his hand. "It was a femur."

Legge's jaw dropped in disbelief. "A *human* bone?"

"How else do you think they survived all that time out at sea?" I asked him. "They must have…"

I became distracted by an unpleasant squeaking sound,

which seemed to emanate from the other side of the window. "What the devil is that noise?"

"Our carriage has arrived," Birnie said, turning to me with a grimace. "Less of a carriage, I might say. More of a cart."

We left the house and walked across the plaza to where a rather shoddy-looking covered wagon stood waiting with six oxen yoked up front. The driver, having dismounted, was attending to their harnesses.

"Prepare yourselves!" Captain Spenser barked from the back of the wagon. "The Chileans have discovered a new way to torture the foreigners!"

Spenser, a portly, chubby-faced fellow, was dressed for the country in buckskin breeches. I had half a mind to go back and change my clothes.

Peering into the wagon, I saw three women in wide-brimmed hats sitting further inside. Across from Spenser sat a younger, leaner man, perhaps Legge's age. He grinned at me with a mouthful of clean white teeth.

"This is Mr Quinn, my first lieutenant," the captain said, gesturing towards the toothy fellow, whose grin widened a little further still. "And here we have Clara, Maria, and Catalina."

I climbed into the wagon, Spenser shuffling along the bench to make room.

As Birnie was clambering in, I caught a brief glimpse of another of my lieutenants across the plaza. It was Wollaton. He was talking to Gillies's taciturn landlady, and there were two other men with him: Europeans, I surmised, by the way they were dressed. It crossed my mind that they might be passengers on the Italian ship, *Lucile*, which had arrived in the port earlier that morning. They were probably looking for a place to stay.

My view into the plaza was then blocked as Legge climbed up and took a seat. Returning my attention to the company inside the wagon, we all began with our introductions. Clara and Maria, it transpired, were the daughters of a Spanish military officer who was unable to make it to the picnic on account of his health. The two did not look much alike, though they smiled in the same way and had an endearing habit of finishing each other's sentences. The third woman, Catalina, was fair skinned with blond hair. I asked her if she had come to Chile as a passenger on the *Owen Glendower*—at which she laughed and shook her head.

"I was born in Guayaquil, Equador," she said, sweeping aside a stray lock that had fallen in front of her eyes. "But I have lived in Chile since I was a little girl."

"The Guayaquileans are well known for the fairness of their skin," Spencer then explained, looking fondly across at Catalina. "They say it is the moisture in the air."

I nodded politely; the theory was a nonsensical one that I had never subscribed to. Guayaquil was along the shipping route for British ships and well known amongst sailors for its pretty native girls. These sweet, innocent things were all too easily wooed by spirited Englishmen wielding sparkling engagement rings and offering promises of a new life in a thriving foreign city. Unfortunately, these promises tended to sail away on the next favourable trade wind, leaving the poor girls clutching their swollen bellies and gazing hopelessly out to sea.

There was little opportunity to speak further, as the wagon jolted to a start and Captain Spenser's words of caution became abundantly clear: the squeaking was quite unbearable, an ear-piercing scraping sound from the rusty axles, which seemed to come at me from all corners and cling to the cusps of my teeth.

As we trundled out of the plaza, I began to regret having

not taken the journey on horseback. I might have felt particularly sorry for the ladies in our company, except that they seemed hardly to flinch at the noise. I dare say they had become quite used to it: either that, or they were well-practised in hiding their discomfort.

We began our ascent out of the port, up a narrow street lined on either side by a row of single-storey houses. Inside the wagon, we exchanged awkward smiles and glances, any hope of conversation being made quite impossible by the incessant squeaking. In the end, I resorted to staring absently out into the street. This, as it happened, was rather fortuitous, as had I not done so, I would have missed seeing the man who emerged from one of the laneways and ran out into the road.

Seeing who it was, I leapt out of my seat and called up to the driver to stop.

The wagon drew to a clattering halt, and the passengers leant forwards on the seating to see what had caused my sudden outburst. A few long seconds passed before John Gillies appeared through the cloud of dust thrown up behind us, his cane in one hand and a satchel tucked under his other arm.

"Might I..." he managed, arriving quite out of breath. "Might I join you? That is..." He pressed his hand against his chest, wheezing heavily. "I wonder...are you...on your way to Santiago?"

I had not spoken to Gillies since the day of the bullfight, when we rescued the man in the Quebradas suburb—the day of his surprising disclosure.

"This is a private invitation," Spenser told the man. "We are attending a party a couple of hours north of here. And besides that, the wagon is rather full as it is."

Gillies was quite determined. "Captain..."

There was no need for him to explain further. What with the arrival of the Italian ship that morning, and then having seen those men in the plaza conversing with Gillies's landlady, I had already put two and two together. They were not looking for a place to stay.

They were looking for *him*.

"Mr Gillies is a friend of mine," I said, reaching out of the wagon and clasping him firmly by the arm. "Birnie, give me a hand, will you?"

Spenser looked as though he might say something else, but I cut him off.

"Driver! *Vamos!*" I shouted, hoisting Gillies up into the wagon. Moments later, the rusty squeaking recommenced, putting a stop to any further discourse.

The road up the cliffs was narrow and winding, with a sheer drop on one side. On horseback, it might have been a pleasant ride, but inside the juddering wagon it was hard not to think about the state of the rickety wheels as we careered over rocks and around the sharp bends. On one occasion, we passed another wagon coming from the opposite direction and were forced inches from the edge. Our driver yelled something in Spanish as the wagon struggled to remain on the track, scattering stones that went bouncing over the precipitous edge. Quinn began laughing nervously. Catalina exchanged glances with the two other women, and I saw her hands tighten their grip on the wooden seating. Birnie's eyes remained fixed on his book, though I did not see him turn a single page for some time after.

When, to my great relief, we reached the summit in safety; the driver pulled the oxen to a halt on a plateau. Standing close to the cliff's edge, I took in the commanding view of the road we had taken, which wound back down the mountainside. The bay looked quite beautiful, bathed in cool morning sunlight. Looking down from this lofty vantage point at the golden crescent of beach, with its turquoise water and strips of white surf folding onto the sand, I could see why the early explorers had named the port Valparaiso: the Vale of Paradise.

Poor Gillies was suffering terribly from the dust, having spent the entire ascent with his face buried in his handkerchief and stifling his wheezing and coughing as best he could. Unlike the rest of us, he showed little interest in the spectacular view, choosing instead to walk off in the opposite direction with his back to the cliffs and the sea. When I saw him crouch down onto his knees, I became quite concerned and hurried after him. I arrived, however, to find him quite at ease and busy examining the local flora.

"This little lady belongs to the Lamiaceae," he said, plucking a small blue flower from the grass. He handed it to me. "The mint family. Notice how the leaves emerge in opposite pairs, and the flowers are bilaterally symmetrical. Five united petals. Four stamens—two long, two short. I would say we are looking at a species of skullcap."

I inspected the flower. "You are a keen botanist, then?"

"I send specimens back to Kew Gardens now and again for a little pocket money," he said. "Dr Hubbard prefers the pretty ones. Like most men in this world, he is quite blinded by physical appearances."

"While you are interested in their medicinal properties?" I suggested, thinking of his herbal concoctions. "As curatives?"

"I have never been one to ascribe a purpose to a plant," Gillies said, and he began unbuckling his satchel. "Take the belladonna, for example. *La bella donna*, or 'beautiful woman'—so named because, when applied as eye drops, a tincture made from the berries is said to increase a woman's beauty.

It dilates the pupils, you see. And yet, a teaspoon or two of that same tincture in a cup of tea could stop your heart dead."

"Hence its other name," I said. "Deadly nightshade."

"Beauty, and the beast," Gillies said with a smile in my direction. "Yet a plant is neither good nor evil. It is simply as it is intended to be."

Opening his satchel, he withdrew a notebook and a pencil. While he was doing so, I caught sight of something protruding from one of the inside pockets: a collection of papers I recognised immediately as the pages from the Florentine Codex.

Gillies glanced up and saw the direction of my gaze. He said nothing, extending his hand so I might return the flower to him—which I did. I watched him gently place it in his notebook, then snap the book shut.

"They are still safe," he said, without looking at me. "For the time being."

We returned to the wagon.

Thankfully, the remainder of the journey was less of an ordeal. The road became smoother as it cut across sweeping grasslands before diving into a deep green valley. Having crossed a shallow ford, in the centre of which the wagon stopped to allow the oxen to drink, we began the slow climb back up in the direction of the coast. It was then that the house appeared, still a mile or so away, sitting grandly against the hillside. As we drew closer, I could see that it was a white-walled villa with window frames painted red to match the roof tiles. The slopes behind the house were cultivated with what I suspected to be trellises of grapevines. It was, in every way, a welcoming sight.

But then, as we trundled up the long driveway, a cold shiver ran down my neck. I was suddenly overwhelmed by the strangest feeling that I recognised the very moment I was in—

sitting in the wagon with these same eight people on the way to this very house. The feeling intensified into a sense of foreboding. It was as if there was something out there, an event yet to happen, and I was being pulled inescapably towards it.

All this happened in a fleeting moment before the feeling left me, as if my soul had passed from sunlight into shadow and was now back in the sunlight again.

Across the wagon, I noticed Gillies was staring at me intently.

Smiling weakly in his direction, I shook the last traces of discomfort from my thoughts.

We had arrived.

SIX

Valparaiso hinterlands, Chile, 22nd March 1821

MR AND MRS KENNEDY were waiting for us as we drew
into the forecourt, all squeaks and rattles, the sound of hooves
clattering on the cobblestones. Having finished the usual introductions, our hosts took us through the villa to the back of the
house, where a jug of lemonade and a tray of glasses sat waiting
on the terrace. The cool, refreshing drink did wonders to revive
our spirits, and before long the discomfort of the ride was
forgotten, and everyone was chatting and mingling happily.

The view from the house was every bit as spectacular as I
had imagined. The back lawn stretched perhaps twenty yards
from the terrace through a scattering of fruit trees, down to a
low stone wall that marked the boundary of the garden. On the
other side of the wall, the hillside fell away steeply. The
commanding vista that presented itself looked out across the
ocean to the empty blue horizon, and along the rugged coastline north and south.

"You can see the port from the bottom of the garden,"

Kennedy said. "Believe it or not, you can even hear the church bells ringing the oration at sunset."

I told Kennedy that this was the life I dreamed of living one day: a secluded villa with a view of the ocean, far away from the hustle and bustle of society. Somewhere on the Mediterranean coast, perhaps, where the summers were long and the winters mild.

"Time catches up with you sooner than you think," Kennedy said, nudging me with his elbow and glancing in Catalina's direction. "Find yourself a handsome woman and settle down. Raise a family. I am sure you could survive quite comfortably on the half-pension of a retired captain—not to mention whatever you make from those travel books of yours."

"Not much," I said wistfully.

There was no doubting Catalina's alluring beauty. She stood in the dappled shade thrown down by the tamarind tree, absently playing with the lace on her pink and bronze dress. Meanwhile, Spenser and Quinn buzzed about her like two greedy flies. Catalina stole a glance in our direction, as if realising that she was being talked about. I smiled and raised my glass.

Mrs Kennedy came out of the house and announced that the meal would not be ready for another couple of hours. She suggested we might like to stretch our legs and take a stroll to a derelict farmhouse nearby, which had a walled garden full of wildflowers. We all agreed it was an excellent idea.

"But you cannot go romping in the mountains all dressed to the nines," her husband said, prodding the gold trim of my coat with an admonishing finger. "We are all friends together here, Captain Hall. No need to stand on ceremony."

Kennedy continued to chivvy me until I removed my coat and handed it to his groundsman. I confess this came with some relief, as the day was warming up—though I would have preferred to dispense of it myself without quite so much fuss.

The walk took us up through Kennedy's vineyards and along a footpath that led over the hill and down the eastern slope. With the villa now lost from view behind us, there was nothing but miles upon miles of undulating hills: the majestic, snow-capped peaks of the Andes rising from the distant horizon.

As we ambled along in the sunshine, Birnie and I found ourselves some distance ahead of the group. We began discussing the problem of yellow fever, which was rife in the West Indies and a constant worry to European ships sailing to the New World. Birnie had seen many casualties of the disease in his time and once even came down with it himself. Our conversation came, by and by, to the matter of the man in the Quebradas suburb, whom Legge and I had come across through meeting his distraught daughter in the marketplace. I told the doctor how Gillies had at first thought the man might be suffering from yellow fever, but which he later diagnosed as a disease he called *chaoo longo*. I was surprised Birnie had not already heard about this from Gillies himself, but it transpired that the two were not as well acquainted as I thought. At any rate, I filled him in on the details as best as I could remember, including the man's miraculous recovery.

"Mind you, I think it was the bloodletting that did the trick, rather than the herbs," I said, having finished my account. "Gillies gave all credit to you in that respect. He said the two of you discussed the topic on the voyage over here."

"The bloodletting would certainly have helped reduce the fever—with the *chaoo longo*, a high temperature can cook a man in hours," Birnie said. "But I wouldn't discount the herbs entirely."

The doctor went on to explain how, during our passage to Chile, he witnessed Gillies recover from a severe fever on more than one occasion. "All he ever took were those herbs of his. I can vouch for that."

"In which case he could probably make a fortune selling them," I said. "Mind you, I am not so sure our Mr Gillies is that interested in money."

We had reached a stream crossing the footpath. A makeshift bridge made from planks of wood led to the other side.

"I used to spend hours and hours deliberating what sets apart those who succumb to the consumption from those who survive," Birnie said, as he strode across the planks. "Sometimes the sickliest sorts pull through, whilst strapping individuals in the prime of their life wither and die before your very eyes. Then, one day, I realised I was paying all my attention to the physical symptoms, and not enough to the outlook of my patients, their attitude to the disease. Those who survived were often the ones who refused to be beaten by their affliction. They never gave in to death; not because they were afraid of dying, but rather because they saw some greater purpose to remaining here on Earth. A purpose that transcended their disease." He shrugged his shoulders. "Something, someone. I think we underestimate the power of sheer determination as a curative."

"Well, our Mr Gillies is nothing if not determined," I said.

"But for what?" Birnie replied. "I do not believe for a second that he has come all the way here for the fine weather. Nor simply to pick flowers to send back to his friends at Kew. There's something else that drives that man."

I felt sorely tempted to confide in the doctor about the stolen pages from the Florentine Codex. About Gillies's quest to find Aztec treasure, and the two men I had seen in the Almendral plaza earlier that very day.

But I had given Gillies my word not to say a thing.

"So then, what about yourself?" I said instead, crossing the stream to join him. "You survived a severe attack of yellow fever. Were you determined to do so?"

The doctor gave my question some thought as he crouched down and ran his fingers through the water. "When I fell ill, we were already in the thick of it," he said. "The crew were dropping like flies, nearly half of them stricken and not a grimy hammock left in the infirmary. Men crying out in pain all day and all night, the berth deck slippery with black vomit, body after body going overboard with a splash... It was a living hell. Then the headaches and fever began for myself, and before long, I was too weak to get out of my cot. It was the worst thing in the world for me, to lie there watching those around me die when I could not lift a finger to help them. One man after the next breathing his last breath, the stony look of death rolling into his eyes. I remember entering the stages of high fever and becoming quite maddened by my helplessness. I swore that if I lived I would help find a cure for this horrible, horrible disease. I would understand its nature—it is not contagious, whatever others say. I would learn which treatments reduced the symptoms and which did not. Bloodletting, mercury, calomel—these are in my arsenal so far." He shook the water from his hands and stood up. "So yes, I suppose I was determined. And I still am."

"You are a good man, George," I told him, throwing an arm around his neck as we continued on our way. "We are lucky to have you on board the *Conway*."

The path followed the stream around a bend, after which the derelict farmhouse came into view, nestled against the side of a hill. The stone cottage was little more than a shell, the roof having been lost to the elements and the interior overgrown with grass and weeds. There were a few crumbling outbuildings of only passing interest, but around the back of the house the walled garden surprised us all with its splendour. Here, the vegetation was thriving despite the dryness of the summer. Thick green ivy tumbled over the walls, and dense clumps of flowering sweet briar were scattered around the perimeter, providing vibrant splashes of colour. If all that were not enchanting enough, dozens of colourful butterflies fluttered gaily amongst the flowers.

Upon entering the garden, Kennedy requested we remove our shoes.

"The local Mapuche people believe spirits inhabit the garden," he said. "They say that is why it remains so lush and fertile all year round. It is the magic of the dead."

"Or perhaps underground irrigation channels," I said, offering a more rational explanation. "Fed by the stream on the other side of the wall."

We spent some time exploring the garden, enjoying the soft grass between our toes. The women took to picking flowers and arranging them into posies. Enjoying a moment of solitude in such delightful surroundings, I walked the length of the garden, running my hand along the wall to feel its crumbling surface beneath my fingers. I stopped at one point to inspect a sweet briar bush teeming with iridescent green beetles, their shiny bodies covered in pollen.

Reaching a broken section of wall that formed a narrow gap, I spotted Gillies on the other side. He stood with his hands in his pockets, gazing in the direction of the stream and seemingly lost in thought.

Squeezing through the gap, I cleared my throat to alert him to my presence.

"Did you see him?" Gillies said, turning to look at me eagerly.

Glancing around, I saw no one. "Who?"

"The native. He was standing right there in the water."

I followed his eyes to where the stream widened into a deeper pool. A slender tree grew on the bank next to the water. "I am afraid I can see nobody but you."

His voice changed, losing its conviction. "I could have sworn…"

"Perhaps it was one of Mr Kennedy's ghosts," I said, trying to make light of the situation. Poor Gillies must have overexerted himself during the walk.

"His back was to me," he replied, looking quite puzzled. "But then he turned to look your way, and I could have sworn it was…" He trailed off, scratching his mutton-chops.

"A trick of the light perhaps? The reflection of the tree in the water."

While Gillies pondered what he had, or had not, seen, I took in the pleasant scenery, listening to the gentle babbling of water. A bird was singing in a nearby tree.

"You had a couple of visitors earlier," I said at length. "At your lodgings."

Gillies nodded, his eyes remaining fixed on the pool. "So it seems."

I waited for him to say more, and when he was not forthcoming, I pushed the topic further. "Two men, they looked European. I thought they might have arrived on the *Lucile*."

"They are envoys from Florence," he replied. "The Medici household have released their hounds to track me down."

"The Medici?" I stood blinking in astonishment. "Are you telling me those pages you stole—"

"I thought you might have worked it out by now," Gillies said with a casual shrug. "Given that the Florentine Codex"—he stressed the word *Florentine*, as if to make a point of my ignorance—"resides in Florence, which any schoolboy worth his salt knows was ruled by the Medici in the sixteenth century."

"Yes, but that was two-and-a-half centuries ago."

"When the Codex was completed," he reminded me. "1569. It was first presented as a gift to the King of Spain, then passed on to the Vatican, whereby it made its way into the hands of the Medici. The Basilica di San Lorenzo, where the Codex is housed, was built and paid for by the House of Medici. The entire family is buried in its crypt."

I confess, I did not know an awful lot about the Medici family. I knew, of course, that there had been several Medici popes, and that once upon a time they were the most formidable family in Italy, their influence extending into all branches of society: banking, politics, art, science. The House of Medici opened its doors to the likes of Michelangelo and Leonardo da Vinci, and the great astronomer Galileo Galilei.

"I was under the impression the Medici dynasty died out a century ago," I said.

"Families like that never completely die out," Gillies replied. "The pages I took from the Codex were never meant to be discovered by the House of Medici, nor the Catholic Church. They were to remain hidden for as long as it was necessary. Should they ever fall into the hands of the enemy, the consequences would be catastrophic." He had a genuine look of concern in his eyes. "You must help me, Captain."

I shook my head in bewilderment. "Mr Gillies, this entire

continent is in the throes of a revolution, and very soon there will be a rush to strike new trading agreements with the Spanish royalists or the Chilean patriots—whomsoever wins this war of independence. Surely you must see that my business in Chile is of an extremely sensitive nature? I am captain of the first British merchant ship to reach these shores during such a critical time in our history. Imagine what would happen if it got out that I was connected, even remotely, with the theft of pages from a sacred manuscript? Let alone that I was tangled up in a quest to find buried treasure somewhere in Mexico. My reputation would be ruined! And who knows what harm it would cause to British interests."

"I asked you once before to trust the judgement of your good friend Sir Walter Scott, if not my own," Gillies said. "I am asking you again."

"Walter Scott is a brilliant man, but he can be rather foolish at times," I said. "And besides that, he is a novelist—he can afford to entertain himself with wild imaginings. One might even say his career depends on it."

Sir Walter possessed an extensive library at Abbotsford. On several occasions in the past, he had brought me into his confidence—over a solemn oath of secrecy—as to a book he acquired though unlawful means: contraband texts on the occult, the stolen diary of a French monarch, the memoirs of a murdered courtesan...all obtained for substantial sums of money. Stealing pages from an ancient manuscript locked away in a basilica in Florence, not to mention an expedition to find Aztec treasure, would be right up his alley.

"Is Sir Walter financing this entire foolish quest?"

Gillies looked irritated. "Do you think the Medici would send two men to hunt me down if this was all just *wild imaginings*?"

"I really have no idea what to believe."

Gillies hobbled off into the shade by the wall, then signalled for me to join him.

"The pages contain a story about a legendary figure named Topiltzin," he said, as I leant against the wall next to him. "You might recall my telling you that the predecessors of the Aztecs were the Toltecs, who lived back in the tenth century. Topiltzin was their ruler. He was found in the desert as a child and thought to be part man and part god—the incarnation of Quetzalcoatl. He grew up to rule over a magnificent city called Tollan, but an uprising forced him to flee when he was an old man." Gillies looked across at me. "It is all written in those pages. Together with the location of Topiltzin's final resting place."

"The tomb of a lost Toltec king." I shook my head in disbelief.

"Topiltzin was not a king," Gillies said. "He was a wise man, a prophet of sorts. In the Codex, Fray de Sahagún refers to him as *el Divino Sabio*, the Divine Sage."

"And you say he died in the tenth century." I gazed up into the clear blue sky. "Even if you do find this tomb, that leaves nine hundred years for it to have been discovered by looters and explorers."

"Trust me, the golden serpent is still there."

I shook my head and sighed. "Your prized piece of treasure."

Gillies remained silent for a while. "As far as I know, there is only one man who has come anywhere close to finding the tomb. His name was Captain Yañez de Armida, and he went in search of the golden serpent around the time of the Spanish invasion. Yañez spent some time in the city of Tepic, in Mexico, where he was fortunate enough to meet Fray de

Sahagún prior to his death. The sailor was said to have learnt the location of the tomb and organised a small expedition. But alas, he never found it."

"That still leaves about two hundred years."

Gillies shrugged dismissively. "When do you expect to arrive in Mexico?"

I told him that after Peru, the *Conway* would likely return here to Valparaiso before sailing north across the equator.

"It will be a slow hop," I added. "I will be looking for trading opportunities in the towns along the coast. So I doubt we will reach Mexico until the middle of next year."

"We must be in Tepic by next June at the very latest," Gillies said. "The timing is crucial."

"We?"

"You and I, Captain."

I rolled my eyes. "Do you ever give up, sir?"

We returned from the walk to find the dining table had been moved outside onto the terrace. It sat overburdened with crystal and silver: the picnic was clearly going to be a more lavish affair than a few wicker baskets on a woollen rug. Mrs Kennedy's silver-haired grandmother joined us, making twelve in total. We took our places around the table, with our host at the head and myself at the opposite end.

Two native gentlemen dressed in smart red livery brought out each of the courses, starting with a tasty bread soup, then cold dried meats and several rich stews. I recognised one of the men as Kennedy's groundsman; the other, I would say, was his son. They both looked rather uncomfortable in their roles, and I thus forgave them their clumsiness with the plates, and for dripping wine on the clean white tablecloth as they refilled our glasses.

While we ate, Spenser and Quinn enlightened us all with

their opinions on the coming revolution, and how they believed freedom from Spain would doom the continent to being once again ruled by heathens and warring tribes. The two men spoke to the ladies in our company as one might speak to children, unaware that the womenfolk in Chile were generally better informed about politics than the men. I could see Catalina biting her lip under the brim of her hat. The old grandmother seemed to pay little attention to any of the conversation, passing the time between courses engrossed in her knitting. As she barely spoke a word, I was not entirely sure she understood English.

Dessert arrived as a generous serving of plump figs, picked from the trees in the garden, accompanied by a sweet muscatel wine brought up from Kennedy's cellar.

"I was wondering who plays the fiddle?" I overheard Legge asking Mrs Kennedy, as the last of the plates were being cleared. "I saw it in your parlour."

"It was Roger's," she said, her face softening as she glanced at her husband. "Our son. He died a few summers ago, and I have not the heart to pack the thing away."

"Our lieutenant is an accomplished violinist," I said. "You should hear him play."

Mrs Kennedy's face brightened as she looked fondly at the lad. "Oh, would you? It would mean so much to me."

"I would be honoured," Legge said.

Rising from her chair, Mrs Kennedy hurried back into the house and returned with the violin. The lieutenant, having tuned the instrument to his ear, played a melody that I was quite familiar with. He often practised in the evening after dinner, when the crew were drinking rum and drowning out his sweet music with their sea shanties and raucous laughter. I would be sitting eating my dinner in the Great Cabin, or writing at my bureau, and the sound of the violin would travel up between the boards and catch my attention. I might have boasted that I knew Legge's entire repertoire were it not for the tune he played next. It was a haunting melody, the notes drawn out in long strokes of the bow while the lieutenant stood with his eyes closed, his lean frame swaying gently in time with the music. The women sitting around the table, Mrs Kennedy, Catalina, Clara and Maria, were quite bewitched. They appeared to know the words and began quietly singing along in Spanish. Even the old grandmother was murmuring under her breath.

When the tune came to an end, Legge opened his eyes and bowed his head in the way musicians do. We filled the air with our applause. Glancing across the table, I saw Mrs Kennedy pull out her handkerchief and use it to dab her eyes. The grandmother, too, seemed quite moved by Legge's performance. Lifting herself out of her chair, she shuffled across the paving stones in her black shawl and clasped the lieutenant's hands tightly.

"He played a traditional Mapuche song," Catalina said, leaning towards me. "I have heard it sung many times, but never has it sounded so enchanting."

The lieutenant entertained us with one more song, a jig this time, then returned the instrument to Mrs Kennedy.

"Your son loved this fiddle," he said. "One can feel these things when one plays."

She appeared quite overcome by these heartfelt words and embraced the lad warmly. "I think you would have liked Roger," I heard her say, "and he you."

I smiled at Legge, feeling rather proud of my young lieutenant. Not just because of his exquisite playing, but also because he was by all accounts such a kind and decent sort. I noticed Catalina was smiling at him too, and our eyes met. Encouraged by a little light-headed drunkenness, I asked her if she might like to accompany me on a walk around the villa.

"I thought you would never ask," she replied, then adding under her breath. "I need rescuing from Captain Spenser's anecdotes."

We excused ourselves from the table. Having taken a turn about the garden, I suggested we go and admire the jasmine vine I had glimpsed earlier, climbing up the north wall of the house. The vine was in full bloom and quite magnificent, almost entirely covering the wall with its dense green foliage. Releasing my arm, Catalina began picking the delicate white flowers.

"Charles Legge is disarmingly handsome," she said, lifting her palm to inhale the sweet fragrance of the flowers. "Clara and Maria melt like butter when he looks at them with those romantic blue eyes of his."

"Does my lieutenant not beguile you too?" I asked in amusement, leaning casually against the wall.

"I favour darker features on a man," she replied. A coy smile stretched onto her lips. "Might I ask how old you are?"

"Thirty-two."

Catalina placed her hand on her bosom and opened her mouth in mock surprise. "Without a single grey hair on your head? You must live a charmed life, Captain Hall."

"I suppose I have been lucky enough," I said. "Though I have worked hard to get where I am."

Tipping the flowers into the pocket of her dress, she took hold of my hand and began inspecting it. "Soft as silk. And no sign of a wedding ring. There is no Mrs Basil Hall back in England?"

"I am not really the marrying type," I said. "At least, not yet."

"Then a betrothed, perhaps?" She turned my hand over, running her finger along one of the lines on my palm. "I can see her now, practising her needlework. Patiently awaiting the return of her dashing, dark-eyed captain."

"I do have...a friend," I confessed. "Her name is Margaret. Lady Margaret Hunter. And I can assure you she is not the type to waste time on idle pursuits such as needlework. She is quite the social butterfly."

Catalina took my arm and we recommenced our walk, passing through a stone archway that led to front of the house, then crossing the forecourt. A chestnut-skinned boy was tending to one of the horses, and when Catalina walked over to pet the beast, the boy stood with his shoulder lodged against its neck, holding the bridle tightly.

"Do you write to her?" Catalina asked, stroking the horse's nose. "This Lady Margaret Hunter?"

"When I can." I joined her in petting the horse, running my hand down its sinewy neck. "Although I am often home before my letters arrive. If they arrive at all."

"Do you love her?" Catalina turned to look me straight in the eye. When I did not answer immediately, she drew a breath. "You paused."

"We are not that well acquainted as yet," I explained. "But yes, I suppose one day I might love her."

"That sounds awfully practical," she scoffed.

"I do not believe in romantic love."

"And *I* do not believe that for a moment." Catalina's hand slowed its stroking movement until it rested, motionless, on the horse's nose. The animal remained perfectly still, breathing heavily through its nostrils as if drawn into a trance.

"One can learn a lot by following a man's gaze," she then said. "I was watching you at dinner. Those dark eyes of yours."

I caught a glimpse of my distorted face in the unblinking eye of the horse. "And what was it you learnt?"

Snapping out of its trance, the horse threw its head about playfully. Catalina smiled at me, but not as wholeheartedly as before.

"I think he is telling me to be quiet," she said.

SEVEN

Valparaiso, Chile, 22nd March 1821

AT FOUR O'CLOCK, the wagons were ready to depart, Kennedy having impressed upon us it would be unwise to make the passage back down the cliffs after dark. While Captain Spenser and his lieutenant helped Catalina, Maria and Clara into the wagon, I turned to look for Gillies. He was standing a little further back, by the stone archway, cane in one hand and satchel in the other.

It had not escaped me that the two men who arrived on the Italian ship would be waiting for Gillies back in the port. What was he planning to do? I found his story about the Medici family being involved somewhat hard to swallow. Perhaps there was a more rational explanation I was overlooking: Gillies might have swindled a business associate out of a large sum of money or some such. Perhaps he had committed a murder? Perhaps there was a price on his head?

But then why on earth would he make up such an elaborate

lie? Breaking into a basilica in Florence in the dead of night and stealing pages from an ancient text, and that they were some kind of treasure map leading to an ancient tomb... Why draw attention to himself like that? Surely it would be more sensible to lie low. And what about his connection with Sir Walter Scott? Why had he asked me to take the pages into my safekeeping? I had to admit, they seemed genuine enough when I saw them in his lodgings; but then again, having seen his artistic talents, it was not entirely out of the question that he had crafted them himself.

It was all very puzzling. Was I missing something glaringly obvious?

Although I did not entirely trust Gillies, neither was I ready to see him thrown into the hands of his enemies. After all, there was still the possibility that he was telling the truth. I decided the only solution was to quiz him some more and see if I could find any holes in his story. If it remained watertight, then I would have to submit to believing him—however improbable it all seemed—until I found evidence to the contrary. And if I believed him, I decided, I would help him get away from those men.

But all this required more time—and to that end, I had an idea.

"Would you be averse to having guests for the night?" I asked Kennedy, who was standing beside me. "Mr Gillies tells me he has business in Santiago tomorrow. He plans to travel there from the port, but it has just occurred to me that if our driver were to return here at sunrise, he could pick Gillies up, take him to Santiago, and be back here by tomorrow afternoon. I would very much enjoy a night in the countryside, if it is not too much of an inconvenience."

"Oh, but you *must*," Kennedy insisted. "We have four

guest rooms, so the doctor and your lieutenant are welcome to stay as well."

While Kennedy went to persuade Birnie and Legge, I walked over to Gillies.

"It is not safe for you to return to the port," I said, my eyes drifting to his satchel, where I knew the stolen pages were tucked away. "I have arranged for us to stay the night. The wagon will take you to Santiago in the morning and return here afterwards."

Gillies blinked in surprise, then smiled at me. "Yet again you have come to my rescue."

"And for the very last time."

We watched the wagon clatter away down the driveway; the groundsman having given the rusty axles a good greasing to stop the awful squeaking.

Once it was out of sight, Kennedy led us back through the archway to the terrace. Our convivial afternoon thus continued, drinking wine and puffing on fat Cuban cigars while the sun descended through the trees and the long summer shadows drew across the lawn.

Gillies sat slightly apart from us, on account of the cigar smoke irritating his lungs. Reclined in a deckchair at the edge of the terrace, he appeared to be paying little attention to our conversation; his eyes turned inwards, as one who is engaged in the world of his own thoughts. Was he dreaming about his lost tomb? I recalled the passion in his voice when he first told me about the Franciscan friar, Bernardino de Sahagún, and his great manuscript, written to save a dying civilisation; and the steely look in his eyes when told me: *What lies within these pages must be protected at all costs.*

I suppose in a sense I admired the fellow. Was he not the daring adventurer every boy dreamed of being?

"Do you hear it?" I heard Kennedy say, and snapping back into the conversation, I saw his hand was cupped around his ear. "It never ceases to amaze me how far the sound travels."

At first, I heard only the wind rustling through the tamarinds. But then, as I trained my ear, I caught something else; the faint tolling of bells—the sunset oration ringing in the church belfries of the port. Excusing myself from the table, I crossed the lawn and walked down through the orchard to the low wall at the bottom of the garden. Far below, the rows of houses skirting the bay were bathed in a golden twilight. In the dusty streets, the mules and horses would have stopped instinctively, so aware of the hour that there was no need to wait for advice from their riders. As the chimes ceased, I knew that the cobbled laneways and plazas would now have fallen silent, and the men and women would be standing with their heads bowed in prayer.

I heard someone approach—it was Legge. He stepped onto the wall and stood for a while with his hands in his pockets, gazing out across the ocean at the tangerine sun, which sat balanced upon the horizon.

"It is just so beautiful," he said with a sigh. "We take so much for granted, we sailors. Sunsets like this. The freedom in our lives."

"Enjoy it while it lasts," I said, joining him on the wall. "I expect orders from the Admiralty to sail north in the next week. From the reports I am hearing about the revolution in Peru, we might not have the time to savour the sunsets for a while."

"Then we must commit this moment to memory," Legge said. "The radiance of the sun tonight, the colour of the sky. The silhouette of the headland." He lifted his chin and closed his eyes. "This warm breeze."

I placed my hand on his shoulder. "Always the romantic, Charles Legge."

Standing together in a comfortable silence, we watched the sun sink into the ocean, sending a river of golden light across the darkening water. The stray wisps of cloud lingering over the horizon were set alight with a fiery glow.

"We must share a secret," I announced, seized by an impulse. "A secret spoken in the sacred minutes between the tolling of the bells, when the world beneath us is in prayer."

Legge liked the idea. He pointed towards the golden rays of light stretching from the horizon into the sky. "When I was little, I used to sit at the end of our garden, watching the sunset," he said. "I thought those sunbeams were caused by light being drawn back into the sun at the end of the day, making it so heavy that it sank. Then one day my father explained to me that although it looked like the sun was sinking, it was an illusion, and what was really happening was the world was spinning." The lieutenant chuckled to himself. "I didn't believe him. My own theory was far easier to understand."

Legge nudged me with his elbow. "Now you, sir."

I already knew what I wanted to tell him, and I fixed my eyes on the tiny silhouette of the *Conway*, anchored in the bay amongst the other ships.

"It is a confession of sorts," I said. "The day we arrived in the port, I was quite against you taking part in that swimming race, despite what Mr Gillies told you. But when I saw you splashing through the water, then running recklessly through the surf, naked as Adam, I became quite envious. You see, I have never done anything like that in my life. Not once."

"Then why not do it?" Legge said. "The ocean is not going

anywhere, and there are deserted beaches down there waiting for you."

"Yes, I suppose there are; but that is just it, Charles. As much as I yearn to do these things, to do something reckless, to say, 'To hell with conformity and rank and what the world expects of me,' I feel this opposing force forever holding me back." I shook the lad's shoulder warmly. "Forgive me for sounding like an old fool. The wine has softened my brain."

"We all feel it," Legge said, shrugging beneath my grasp. "The heart and the head doing battle with each other."

"And with you, Charles, it is the heart that prevails."

The distant tolling of the bells returned, signalling the oration had come to a close. The lieutenant and I continued to talk for some time, watching the stars prick one by one into the sky. Behind us, the moon rose in the southern quarter, throwing its silvery light over the hills.

"I think I might take a walk back to the abandoned garden," I said, idly scratching the back of my head. "I imagine it will look enchanting in the moonlight."

"What an excellent idea," Legge said. "Might I come with you? Unless, of course..."

"I shall enjoy it all the more with your company," I said, and jumped down from the wall. "We should steal a bottle of wine from Kennedy's cellar."

We made our way back towards the house, passing Gillies as he stood in the centre of the lawn with his neck craned, gazing up at the heavens. Pointing up at the sky, he drew our attention to an unfamiliar pinprick of light that sat between the red star Aldebaran and the bright white Sirius.

"It has been there for five nights," he said. "A foreboding sign, if the ancients are to be believed."

"Well, I never. A comet!" I had not noticed it until then;

with us being ashore, there had not been the usual necessity to monitor the stars.

"Comets upset the harmony of the cosmos," Gillies said. "They tear through the sky, bringing destruction and upheaval in their wake."

"Then it is well timed for the revolution," I told him. "You should write a letter to the Royal Society of London."

"I have tried that once before," he said. "A discussion on the identity of the forbidden fruit in the Garden of Eden. They dismissed my letter, calling it unsubstantiated nonsense."

"Then you must send the letter directly to my father. I will vouch for you. Rest assured it will be recorded as a genuine astronomical observation."

Gillies smiled. "I shall leave that to you, Captain. Your father will, I am sure, trust your word more than my own. Now, I am afraid I must bid you good night. I am an early riser and I like to be in bed by nine."

He began walking back to the terrace. Realising that I might not see the man again, I hurried after him.

"I have been thinking about your treasure map," I said, catching him up on the porch. "You told me that Bernardino de Sahagún not only compiled the Codex but led the transcription of the Nahuatl language into its written form, and also its translation into Spanish."

Gillies stood with his hand on the door handle. "Go on."

"Who is to say the two versions are identical? If Fray de Sahagún was to mistranslate the Nahuatl, who would know? It would have to be someone literate in both Nahuatl and Spanish."

"And someone with the time to search through two thousand five hundred pages looking for anomalies." Gillies glanced over my shoulder towards the terrace. "Stray words and phrases that must then be decrypted before they reveal their true meaning."

Following his gaze, I saw Birnie and Kennedy getting up from the table. Legge was still stargazing on the lawn. "Then there is hidden information within the Nahuatl text?"

Gillies nodded. "When Fray de Sahagún began compiling the Codex, the Aztec elders already knew their civilisation was doomed. Four centuries before them, their forefathers, the Toltecs, had died out. Now it was to be their turn—but this time, it was far worse. The entire history of these ancient people, many centuries of knowledge handed down from generation to generation by word of mouth, was in grave danger of being lost forever."

"So, being an illiterate people, they needed to find someone who could write things down," I said. "Someone they could trust. They chose Fray de Sahagún."

"But what was the friar to do?" Gillies replied. "If there was so much as a whiff of heresy in the Codex, he would be burnt at the stake, his precious manuscript with him. He very nearly was, in fact. The Catholic priests never entirely trusted Fray de Sahagún—after all, this man had spent his entire life living amongst the Aztecs, and there was little doubt he deeply loved these native people. One morning, the friar was dragged from Mass and thrown to his knees in front of his accusers, most of whom were his brothers in the Church. In the trial that followed, there were one or two monks who could read Nahuatl, and they could find not a shred of evidence for heresy in the Codex. If anything, it was quite the latter. Fray de Sahagún frequently wrote of how the Aztecs were a fallen people in need of salvation. He told the court that the Codex was to be used as a physician would use a medical text to cure his patients of a disease."

"The other monks were protecting him?"

"Not at all. Fray de Sahagún was alone in this. He was a man of tremendous courage, Captain. A man who believed in himself, though his beliefs were at odds with everything he had been taught, with all his holy brethren who surrounded him, and even with the will of the Almighty God he served. Yet he never wavered in his resolve, devoting his entire life to compiling his masterpiece." Gillies smiled at me. "Because it is in every sense a masterpiece. A gift from a man betrayed to those who betrayed him."

"The friar knew all along that his manuscript would end up in the hands of the Catholic Church," I said. "That was his intention, was it not—to hide forbidden knowledge within a Catholic stronghold, in plain sight?"

Gillies turned his gaze towards the porch lamp, where a cloud of moths flew in dizzying spirals. "Imagine a beautiful tapestry, hundreds of feet long and a half century in the making: that is what the Florentine Codex is, Captain: an extraordinary tapestry, with its thousands of pages of pictorials and text. Now, imagine that somebody told you the tapestry was woven for an entirely different reason than you might suppose. Not for its craftsmanship, nor its beauty, nor to document great triumphs or great defeats in history. Imagine instead that amongst the warps and the wefts, a single piece of yarn of great worth lay concealed. A golden yarn that had the power to bring down the royal family to whom this great tapestry was given as a gift."

"That 'royal family' being the Catholic Church?" I asked, struggling to put all this together. "If those pages you stole are this golden yarn you speak of, then are you suggesting that the discovery of Topiltzin's tomb poses a threat to the Church?"

Gillies stepped towards the lamp. "These poor creatures,

flying around and around in circles without cause or meaning, banging their little heads against the glass. They yearn to get closer to the light without knowing what leads them in their desires." He removed the cover from the lamp. The moths hurtled into the flames, igniting into bright orange sparks as their incinerated bodies rose into the air amid wisps of smoke.

"We are taught that only death reveals the mysteries of the afterlife," he said, turning to me with a wild look in his eyes. "But what if there were another way to find out what lies beyond? A back door into the divine? What then?" He stared at me for a moment, then replaced the glass cover, and a host of new insects arrived to recommence the dizzying dance. "Goodnight, Captain."

A back door into the divine?

I was still standing on the porch scratching my head when Birnie and Kennedy arrived on the step.

"The doctor and I are turning in for the night," Kennedy said, stifling a yawn. "Mr Legge wishes to stay up. You and he can sleep in the downstairs bedrooms at the back of the house."

The two men went inside, and I turned to see Legge wandering back from the lawn.

"Tonight is turning out to be quite a night for revelations," I said to him. "Perhaps we will catch a glimpse of those native spirits Kennedy mentioned, wandering about in the walled garden in the moonlight? Watering the plants and what have you."

EIGHT

Valparaiso, Chile, 1st May 1821

THE DAY of our departure from Valparaiso saw the *Conway*'s crew in high spirits. The men lined up along the gunwale, draped in the flower garlands they had been given as parting gifts, while their new friends and lovers crowded the wharf, waving handkerchiefs and shouting their fond farewells. As I watched this romantic scene unfold, I thought of the many times I had witnessed it before: different sailors waving to different girls in different ports.

Lieutenant Darby was standing next to me on the quarter-deck, his elbow hooked casually over the wheel, his white shirt billowing in the breeze. "I will miss this place," he said. "So many pretty ladies, and so little time to enjoy them."

We had spent four and a half easy months in the port, during which time I enjoyed success in my duties to protect British trade interests, whilst still having plenty of time to rest and relax, and soak in the charm of the town. Indeed, life had become quite habitual. On days when I was not engaged in official business, I rose late and took a long walk along the head-land to a secluded cove I had discovered. It was a beautiful spot, hidden from sight and accessed only by a difficult scramble down the cliffs. There was a natural cave there, which emptied and filled with the tide. I would while away the hours reading a book or sleeping in the shade, now and then stripping off my clothes and dashing into the cool, turquoise water for a swim.

"Yes, I dare say I shall miss the place too," I said with a sigh. "But we will be back soon enough."

"I did not see Señorita Catalina on the wharf." Darby was gauging my reaction carefully. Since the picnic in the hills, Catalina and I had attended several parties together. I had little doubt that the nature of our relationship was the subject for gossip for the *Conway*'s crew.

"We said our farewells last night," I told the lieutenant. "Her father is ill."

"But she awaits your return?" Darby raised a thick black eyebrow in my direction. "Perhaps intending to sail back to England with us, as the future Mrs Basil Hall?"

"We are just friends," I said, laughing. "Nothing more."

To which the lieutenant shook his head in dismay. "Well, that is a tragedy. She is the prettiest girl in the port—and by all accounts the cleverest too."

I leant back against the railing. "Romances at sea are meant to be fleeting," I said, gazing up at the clear sky above the masts. "Farewells should be given without melancholy. After all, both parties have been saved from the shackles of more permanent arrangements."

"One has to marry eventually, sir," Darby replied. "What is a man in his old age without companionship?"

"We are not old men yet, Lieutenant." And with that, I

turned my attention to the main deck, yelling, "All hands make sail!"

———

Our passage north could not have been smoother. A steady wind blew the *Conway* effortlessly up the rugged Chilean coast, leaving the men with little to do but enjoy the glorious weather. Much of their free time was spent lying out on the deck tanning their backs, or taking part in boyish wrestling matches, or sometimes a noisy game of leapfrog.

We took frequent stops, trading and negotiating with local merchants in the towns and ports along the coast. While at sea, I spent most of my time in the confines of my cabin, arranging my affairs. It was now common knowledge that General San Martín, who led the southern thrust of the independence movement, was preparing to seize Lima. If he was successful in his attack, then—as the first British ship arriving in the port—I would be an ambassador for King and Country. The responsibility of negotiating new trade agreements caused me some anxiety. Buried in paperwork, I surfaced only now and then to stroll on the deck and clear my lungs of the stuffy cabin air.

One afternoon a couple of weeks into our passage, Birnie arrived at my cabin door with a troubled look on his face.

"We have a problem," he said, "concerning Mr Legge."

I ushered him inside. "What about him?"

Birnie walked to the long window at the far end of the Great Cabin, gazing out through its lattice of square panes. "I caught the men having a cruel joke at his expense. That bird he has been looking after."

A week ago, Legge had found a young albatross hopping about on the deck with its wing outstretched and unable to fly.

Having rescued it, the lieutenant kept it in a chicken cage in his cabin, hoping its wing would heal. The bird had become quite tame, and the lieutenant often brought it up on deck so that it could enjoy some sunshine and sea air. I had even allowed it in my cabin while he wrote the ship's log, as was his duty. The little thing would perch on the edge of a chair, cocking its head and looking at me with its black pearl of an eye. Every once in a while, it would let out a contented squawk.

"What have they done to the poor creature?" I asked.

"I'm not exactly sure," the doctor replied with a grimace. "Charles arrived back at his cabin this morning to find the cage door open. There's a rumour going around that the cook has killed it and intends to serve it up in tonight's stew."

I felt a surge of anger—not so much because of the fate of the bird, but because this was downright insubordination by the men involved. It was a deliberate attempt to undermine Legge. I had seen this sort of thing before and despised it.

"A lieutenant *must* be respected by his men," I snapped. "I need names, George."

Birnie shrugged. "I was on deck this morning when Mr Legge took the watch. That odious deckhand, Slick, was up there with his gaggle of cronies—I'm sure you know who I mean, mostly the weaker boys, who are afraid of him. When Charles walked past, one man let out a noise that was quite clearly meant to imitate a seagull."

"Very well. I shall deal with this," I said, regarding my reflection in the mirror as I tied back my hair. "I will not tolerate this sort of divisive behaviour on board my ship, George. Mark my words—this matter *will* be nipped in the bud."

Later in the day, I was down on the gun deck talking with Mr Leonard, the bosun, when I overheard the shrill cry of a gull. I promptly excused myself and climbed the ladderway up to the main deck, and was just in time to see Slick throw a bedraggled creature, flapping and squawking in a cloud of loose feathers, onto the deck. Sure enough, it was the young bird, its neck and rump plucked down to the pink flesh. Still unable to fly, it ran helplessly about the deck, darting amongst the men's feet as they tried to catch it.

"What the devil is going on?" I yelled.

The men shrank away and the bird plunged into a corner, hiding itself amongst the barrels and ropes. Just at that moment, Legge appeared from below deck looking terribly flustered. Hearing the muffled cries of his pet, he hurried over and picked up the sorry thing. It seemed to calm down in his care, burying its little head in the safety of his armpit.

"Enough of this! Back to work, the lot of you," I shouted, then took Legge aside, lowering my voice. "Charles, you cannot allow these men to challenge your command like this. Give them half a chance, and they will make a mockery of you."

"Sorry, sir, I..." The lieutenant's jaw tightened in anger.

I followed his eyes across the deck to Slick, who was standing by the bulwarks with a mop and bucket, and a spiteful grin on his ugly face. "Is he at the centre of this?"

"I'm uncertain, sir."

"You might not be certain, but do you *suspect* it was him?" I said. "Come along, you need to make a decision. And quickly."

Legge bit his lip, then nodded.

"Mr Allen, get over here!" I shouted. "And be quick about it!"

Slick walked sullenly across the deck. He stood in front of us, gnawing at his dirty fingernails.

"Cap'n?"

"Mr Legge has informed me that you are the ringleader of this...this act of wilful insubordination," I said. "I have given him permission to administer punishment. Two dozen lashes."

Slick ran his hands through his oily hair. "Mr Legge is mistaken, sir. See, I wuz—"

"If my lieutenant tells me you took the bird, Mr Allen, then you took the damned bird! *Do you hear?*"

Slick threw a desperate glance in the direction of the quarterdeck. Following his gaze, I saw Wollaton standing by the railing scratching his beard.

"Did you witness this, Mr Wollaton?" I called out.

"Afraid not, sir," he replied with a shrug. "I were looking the other way at the time. Just turned when I heard all that commotion."

I turned back to Slick. "Strip off your shirt. And if you so much as *open* your mouth, it will be three dozen lashes instead of two."

Having ordered the Master at Arms, Mr Trickett, to tie Slick to the grate, I took Legge to fetch the cat o' nine tails from its nail.

"You must deliver this punishment yourself," I said, taking the bird from him. "And make sure you put some elbow into it."

We returned to the grate, where the men had gathered to witness punishment. Slick's sinewy back glistened with sweat as he tensed his muscles. Turning his neck, he shot Legge a black look.

A good lash of the cat should tear cleanly through a man's flesh. I saw only five of the two dozen that Legge administered release any blood, but I decided it would suffice: Slick would think twice before challenging Legge's authority again.

"If the fair weather continues, we will be in Peru in two

weeks," I called out to the crew, handing the bird back to Legge. "And judging by the news I have received, we may face tough times in the days to come. It is therefore an absolute necessity that we work together, remembering first and foremost that we are here to protect the interest of Great Britain and the futures of our families and friends back home. No more of this silly business. You all know the rules and regulations of His Majesty's Navy, so there is no excuse for insubordination, or contempt, or misbehaviour of any kind. And for those of you who have forgotten these regulations, I shall gladly lend you the copy of the Articles of War on my bookshelf so you might remind yourself. Take note of Mr Allen's mistake and learn from his foolishness, because from now on, any man who flagrantly disobeys the ship's rules—by so much as a letter —will face a severe punishment."

I looked around at the men, most of whom were staring silently at the deck. Except for Wollaton, that was: his narrowed eyes bore down on Legge.

Not that the young lieutenant noticed this, as he was preoccupied with stroking the bird.

NINE

Callao, Peru, 2nd June 1821

WE SAILED into Callao to find the bay heavily blockaded. With the revolution in Peru well underway, the port was being fiercely guarded to stop the Spanish royalist ships from gaining access to Lima. Standing on the quarterdeck, I surveyed the harbour through the eye of my telescope: it was a thoroughly miserable sight. All along the seafront, the houses were blackened with soot, many having been destroyed by fire. Jetsam littered the thin strip of beach.

There was none of the usual excitement on deck. I watched a dozen men lumber around the capstan, winding in the anchor to moor the ship. Today, there were no sea shanties being sung, no encouraging shouts. The rest of the crew looked glumly across the bay at what was to be their home for the coming weeks—if not months. One thing was for certain: there would be none of the festivities and frivolities of Valparaiso here.

We rowed ashore in the longboat under sullen grey skies. A

handful of people were standing on the quay, but they remained lurking around a pile of empty crates with their hands in their pockets, and hardly gave us a second glance as we climbed from the boat. We left the quay in a telling silence, making our way into the town to find the people equally unfriendly. Passers-by ignored us when we greeted them in Spanish, turning their heads away as if affronted by our very presence. Everything looked as though it was falling into ruin: the streets were filthy, a foul stench filled the air, and the inhabitants were dirty and dishevelled.

"San Martín has his army wrapped around us like a snake," a town dignitary said to me in a tavern later that day, his office having been destroyed by fire. "The general is cutting off all our supplies and squeezing Lima of its power, while his ally, Lord Cochrane, sweeps the seas clean of royalists." Gulping down the rest of his ale, he slammed his tankard down on the table. "There is no way back now. This country is to regain its independence, whether these people like it or not!"

As there was nowhere to stay in the port, the crew returned to the ship that night—and then each night thereafter. During the long days that followed, we did what we could for these disillusioned people, but our goodwill was only ever met with suspicion and ungratefulness. We gave them our food and clothing, only to be told it was not enough. We spent our money in their taverns, only to find the patrons heading for the door or retreating into the corners to talk in whispers. Whenever I attempted to make business arrangements with the local merchants, my appointments were snubbed or cancelled at the last minute. It soon became quite obvious that neither the Peruvians nor the Spanish had any use for us until the revolution had succeeded or failed in its efforts.

I decided instead to focus my efforts on the diplomatic side of things. In this regard, I achieved some success, having managed to arrange an interview with none other than José de San Martín himself, who stood to take Lima for the independence movement. The appointment, I should say, cost me a considerable sum of money. It was to take place in Lima, which was less than an hour's ride from Callao on horseback.

I arrived in the capital to find it in as equally a sorry state as the port. The streets were piled with rubble, and there were signs of looting everywhere. Doors were barred, window shutters closed, and the few people I came across in the streets looked agitated and in a hurry to get away. Having located the government buildings, I thought at first that I had been swindled out of my money: the entrance doors were barred with planks of wood. San Martín, however, had sent a man to meet me outside. He led me around to the back of the building to a door guarded by two soldiers. These rude and abrasive men subjected me to what was by all accounts an interrogation before, with a haughty flick of his chin, one of them took me through the door and up a winding stairway. Having ushered me into an empty room, save for a single chair by the window, he told me to wait and then slammed the door shut. I was then left looking out across the rooftops for nearly two hours before the guard returned and said that San Martín was ready to see me.

My meeting with the general took place in a lavishly furnished dining room on the next floor up. San Martín sat in a cloud of cigar smoke at one end of a long table, with papers strewn all about him. He stood up as I entered the room, and I saw that he was tall and well proportioned: a handsome, olive-skinned Argentine with a strong aquiline nose, jet-black hair, and bushy whiskers extending across his cheeks. Right from the start, San Martín put me at ease with his relaxed manner and cordial disposition. During our interview he reclined comfortably in his chair with his knees wide apart, sucking on his cigar as he watched me carefully through his piercing jet-black eyes. I confess, I was rather nervous to begin with, but as the minutes ticked by, the general's natural power to engage calmed me.

We spoke for some time on matters of trade, San Martín listening earnestly while I canvassed British interests. When we then began discussing the revolution, I could not help but be impressed by the general's passion for independence and his unwavering determination to rise above the disharmony that surrounded him.

"I have no ambition to be the conqueror of Peru," he announced at the end of our interview, fixing me with his penetrating gaze as he snubbed out his cigar. "What use would Lima be to me if the inhabitants were hostile? None whatsoever! That is why I intend to take this city by winning the respect and hearts of its people."

I should think it was no coincidence that, following the interview, I suddenly found it easier to conduct business in the capital. My diary quickly became filled with appointments, and I took lodgings in the city to save coming and going from the port. Two whole months passed before orders finally arrived from the Admiralty, and what wonderful news—we were to sail back to Valparaiso! I could not have been more overjoyed, and returned to Callao that same day to tell the good news to the *Conway*'s crew.

I have never seen the men work so eagerly to ready a ship for departure, and two days later, all was set. I paid one last visit to Lima to finish up my business with the merchants, returning to my lodgings late on that last night. I must have finally crawled into bed at around two in the morning.

Plunging immediately into sleep, I found myself in a lucid

dream in which I was lying on my back, squinting through the sunlight at a tatty canvas sail flapping idly against a flimsy mast. I could hear the gentle slopping of water around me, and even as I dreamt, this tranquil scene struck me as strangely familiar. Propping myself up on my elbows, I looked around: I sat on a makeshift raft wearing only my breeches, which were rolled up past the knee. The raft was adrift upon the horse pond, in the grounds of our family home, Dunglass Castle, where I lived as a child. The grey walls of the Scottish baronial mansion rose up from across the paddock, its windows glinting in the sunlight. On the edge of the pond stood a dark-haired boy with tanned skin. He waved his arm in the air as if to get my attention, or perhaps to say farewell—I was uncertain which.

I was awoken from the dream by a steady thumping sound: someone knocking determinedly on the front door of the house. I made my way down the stairs in my nightgown and opened the door to find one of my midshipmen, Mr Ryley, standing there. He was dripping with sweat, bent forwards with his hands on his knees and heaving in the night air.

"There's... There's a man dead!" he exclaimed, struggling to catch his breath between words. "In your cabin, sir... An intruder. Mr Legge, he shot him, and then he was attacked himself, sir. They said I was to come and get you, sir, quick as I could."

"Slow down, Ryley." I stepped out into the street. "Who is this dead man? And you say Mr Legge was attacked?"

"Aye, sir. Stabbed in the back." Ryley straightened up and put his hands on his hips. "No one knows who the dead man is, sir."

"Legge has been *stabbed*?" I asked, aghast. "How bad is it?"

"Very bad, sir. He was the colour of death when I seen him."

"But he is *alive*?"

Ryley nodded, then wiped his forehead with his arm. "At least, when I left the ship he was. I don't know much more about what exactly happened, sir. See, I was woken by the gunshot—like we all were. Mr Darby came to fetch me, seeing as I'm quick on my feet."

I returned inside and dressed as quickly as I could while Ryley untied my horse. Riding back to Callao at a gallop, we arrived to find the town enshrouded in a thick sea fog. It was impossible to see more than a few feet ahead, and we slowed to a walking pace as we made our way through the streets to the harbour. When we finally arrived at the wharfs, a man emerged from the fog to greet us—Mr Percy, the *Conway*'s bosun.

"It ain't looking good for Mr Legge," he said, taking me along the quay to where the gig was waiting.

"Ryley told me an intruder was killed," I said. "Have you any idea who he is?"

Percy held his lantern out over the water so I could climb down into the boat. Below me, two men sat ready with the oars. "We never seen him before, sir."

The oarsmen navigated through the fog towards the ghostly tolling of the ship's bell; and all the while, I sat on the thwart with a sense of dread filling my stomach. How serious was Legge's injury? I went over and over what Ryley had said. What was this intruder doing in my cabin? How the hell did he get on board the ship?

When at last the *Conway*'s dark silhouette appeared out of the fog, we could not have been more than twenty feet away.

The men took in the oars, and the boat slid up against the ship's hull. Grabbing the rungs of the ladder, I climbed up the side.

Darby was waiting for me on deck.

"Tell me what happened," I demanded.

Before the lieutenant had time to answer, Birnie emerged from below deck. He walked towards me with slumped shoulders. His sleeves were rolled up and dyed red with blood.

"Charles is badly injured," the doctor said. "He might not live."

The ship's infirmary was a dingy, windowless room aft of the berth deck. The operating table stood grimly in the centre, and Legge was stretched out with a grimy cushion under his head. His hair, untied from its ponytail, hung down over the sides of the table. His face was ghostly white. I glanced at the bloodied surgical instruments lain out on a cloth next to him—scissors, lancets, knives.

"He has lost a lot of blood," Birnie said, lifting the sheet to reveal a gash in Legge's side, criss-crossed by thick black stitches. "I've seen to the wound as best I can."

As the doctor replaced the sheet, Legge moved his head and opened his eyes. "I am not in a good way, Captain," he managed drowsily, giving me a weak smile.

"Birnie here has sewn you up a treat," I reassured him. "You will be just fine, Charles. But for now, you must rest." Taking out my handkerchief, I wiped the beads of sweat from the lad's forehead. His eyes closed again.

"He needs daylight," I said, scowling at the gloominess of the infirmary. "And fresh air. You must bring him up to the Great Cabin, George. I shall move the dining table and fetch a bed. This hole is no place for him."

Birnie put his hand in his pocket. He seemed about to withdraw something, but then noticing the men standing behind us in the doorway, appeared to change his mind.

"We have not moved the intruder's body yet," he said, after a pause. "We thought it best to leave him where he was until you came."

One of the men in the doorway spoke up. "We saw a boat in the water, sir. But they escaped into the fog."

"They? How many were there?"

"We dunno, sir."

Birnie gave me a look. There was something he did not wish to say in front of the crew.

"Mr Birnie," I said, snatching a lantern, "accompany me to the Great Cabin, if you will."

We left the infirmary and crossed the berth deck, the hammocks creaking in the darkness as their occupants turned to watch us walk by. Climbing the ladderway to the gun deck, I could see the door to the Great Cabin standing ajar at the far end. The lamps were lit within.

The cabin had been turned over. The drawers to my bureau were open, and their contents lay scattered across the floor. Books from the bookshelf had been tossed onto the dining table. A window was flung open to the night, and a broken vase lay in pieces on the floor.

The intruder lay face down near the open window, his stony eye staring into the beyond, his outstretched hand still clutching his pistol. I loosened the weapon from his grasp and placed it on the floor. The man had a swarthy complexion and thick black hair. His shirt and trousers were well tailored—not sailor's attire, nor that of a common thief.

I rolled the corpse over. He had been shot square in the chest.

"Who is this man?"

Birnie closed the cabin door. Reaching into his pocket, he handed me a folded piece of paper. "It was in his pocketbook. No one else has seen this yet."

It was a letter, dated the 25th of March of that year.

My Dearest Walter,

I write in haste, as the hounds are hot on my trail. Two men arrived on the Italian ship Lucile *on Saturday morning, and were it not for a serendipitous turn of events, the game might well have been over. I have managed to escape to Santiago and intend to make my way further into the interior until it is safe to return to the coast. Since my departure from England, there have been several intriguing developments that I am unable to explain in this brief correspondence, but suffice it to say that my premonitions have continued, and I firmly believe that H is who we think he is. I have as yet been unsuccessful in persuading him to join us, but the alignment of coincidences has been quite remarkable. H sails for Mexico later this year! I have made arrangements for the pages to be delivered to him—do not think me foolish. We must continue to trust the path of serendipity. In the event of my untimely demise, he will need them to find the Way.*

I will write again from Tepic.
Your faithful servant,
John Gillies

P.S. Today is the equinox, but a quarter turn from the solstice. Wish me Godspeed!

"Tell me what you know," I said, glancing about the ransacked room.

Birnie walked to the open window and looked out into the foggy night. "Charles was up late writing the ship's log in his cabin. He was returning the logbook here, when he noticed a light flickering under the door. He said at first he thought it was you—that you had returned from Lima. But then as he approached, he heard voices speaking in a foreign language."

"Who was on watch?"

"Mr Allen, and—"

"Slick," I hissed. "Who else?"

"Mr Garvey. He said he was at the heads at the time."

"And where was Slick?"

Birnie shrugged. "Charles said he was up on deck. He saw him peering down through the main hatch on his way here. When he realised there were intruders in your cabin, he went back and called up to Slick, but the man did not answer. So Charles returned to the cabin on his own. He said he pushed the door open an inch and saw two men looting the place. One was at your bureau, going through your papers. The other was at the bookcase."

Birnie's gaze turned to the dining table, which was littered with books. "There was a pistol lying on the table. Charles must have acted on an impulse. He rushed in and seized it, then yelled at the intruders to stay where they were, lest he shoot. This man"—Birnie nodded in the direction of the corpse on the floor—"still had his gun in his belt, so Charles marked him, which gave the second man a chance to make his escape out of the window. The man left behind raised his hands in surrender and pleaded with Charles not to shoot—but then all at once reached for his own gun. Charles took him down.

"I'm not sure what happened after that. I suppose Charles was probably in shock, having never killed a man. All he remembers is someone hooking their arm around his neck, then feeling the knife go into his side. He said he fell to his knees and heard the cabin door slam shut behind him."

"The man returned on deck?" I said, feeling the anger rising inside me.

"We all came running when we heard the gunshot," Birnie said.

"And where was Slick in all this?"

"Mr Darby found him three sheets to the wind, slumped against the mizzenmast and reeking of rum."

I was standing on the rug with my feet inches from a deep red stain. Reaching down, I ran my fingers through the sodden fibres. This was Legge's blood.

"What was their business here?" I said, while trying to figure this out for myself. Walking anxiously around the cabin, I inspected the damage more thoroughly. The silverware was still in the sideboard, and the crystal remained untouched in the cabinet. "It does not look like a common robbery."

"In the letter," Birnie said. "The H is you, is it not?"

"I suppose it could be," I said, returning my eyes to the note. "We are destined for Mexico. But there are plenty of others who might be 'H' on board this ship—Horatio Darby, for one. Besides that, I have little idea what any of this means." Standing over the dead man, I studied his face. Was this one of the two men I had seen in the Almendral that day?

"Did Gillies try to persuade you into something?" Birnie then asked.

"Not that I recall." I closed the window. "But you know what Gillies was like, difficult to follow at times. What about Mr Wollaton? Where was he when all this was going on?"

"I suppose he was asleep like the rest of us."

"Does he recognise this man here?"

The doctor looked puzzled. "I'm sure he'd have said so if he did. Why do you ask?"

I shook my head. "No matter. Now is not the time." Walking to the cabinet, I snatched a bottle of rum and poured myself a stiff drink. I offered one to the doctor, but he refused. "This all makes as little sense to me as it does to you, George."

Birnie's frown remained as he stood pondering. "Back in March, when we went for the picnic in the hills. I did wonder at the time why Gillies seemed in such a hurry to get out of the port. Then...later that day, you arranged for us to stay overnight so that the wagon could take him to Santiago."

"What exactly are you implying?" I asked, challenging him with a look before knocking back my drink. "That I deliberately assisted Gillies in his escape from these men, whoever they are? Is that what you think?"

"I'm just trying to figure things out," Birnie said, then sighed heavily. "But you're right. This is not the time." He glanced at his bloodstained sleeves. "If you will excuse me, I must attend to Charles. I'll make arrangements to move him up here in the morning."

"They will hang for this, George," I said, pouring myself another drink. "Mark my words. We will find out who did this, and they *will* hang!"

The doctor turned to me as he reached the door. "If only that would help Charles recover," he said. "But it will not, sir. Not one bit."

TEN

HMS *Conway*, Callao, Peru, 5th August 1821

MORNING BROKE across the damp and foggy deck. Having ordered all hands to witness punishment, I waited at the quarterdeck railing, tapping my foot impatiently while the men gathered under the main hatch. They looked up with blurry eyes from the gun deck; I doubted any of them had slept much. Slick had been stripped of his shirt by two of my midshipmen, and now they tied him to the grate. Looking down at him, I despised every inch of his wretched body. His back still bore the ugly red scars from his previous flogging. His lank, oily hair hung about his face. I could tell he was still drunk.

Slick put the knife into Legge. I was certain of it. With all the men arriving on deck after they heard the gunshot, why had not a soul seen an intruder making his escape? Because the man who stabbed Legge and left by the cabin door was one of the crew—that was why. And that man had to be Slick. I suspected he had taken a bribe from the intruders; he was just the vile, conniving sort who would do such a thing.

I could just see it now. Slick, sitting in a sordid little tavern in the port when those men approached him. *See to it that the window to the Great Cabin is left open*, they would have told him, slinging a few grubby coins in front of him. *Keep an eye out for a rowing boat in the water on your watch. You are to send us a signal when the coast is clear. A whistle.*

And then, of all people, it was Legge who was to foil their plans. Legge, whom Slick envied and despised. My grip tightened about the railings as I became swept up in the blackest thoughts. In my mind's eye, I saw Slick creeping down the ladderway and following the lieutenant as he made his way back to my cabin. I saw him lurking outside the cabin door while events unravelled within. Then an opportunity to take the lieutenant down presented itself, and Slick seized it.

I had no proof, of course, but neither did I want any. With hard evidence that Slick had committed such a traitorous act, it would be a matter for the authorities to deal with. I would be duty-bound to hand Slick over without inflicting so much as a scratch on his repulsive body.

"For drunkenness and neglect of duty, five dozen lashes will be administered!" I yelled, striding across the deck and climbing down the ladderway. The men parted to let me through. "And another two dozen for insubordination," I seethed, kicking his feet apart. Up close, Slick stank of stale sweat. "And let us say a dozen for uncleanliness."

I surveyed the crowd, looking for Wollaton. He was standing further back.

"Step forwards, lieutenant."

Wollaton looked worried as he shuffled through the crew—and so he should. Only an hour ago, I had summoned him to my cabin to view the corpse. Oh, he knew the man, all right; I could tell by the guilty look on his face while he lied to me. But

I could not punish a lieutenant without evidence for his disobedience. The crew would lose all respect for my command—and if word got out, I could be reprimanded severely, even stripped of my rank. Nevertheless, I would show Wollaton what becomes of traitors on board my ship.

I called the Master at Arms forwards to administer the punishment.

"Mr Wollaton, you are to count the lashings," I said, looking the lieutenant fiercely in the eye before turning my attention back to Slick. "Mr Jacob Allen, in neglecting your duty and acting in a manner wholly unsuitable for a sailor on board this ship, you will be given eight dozen lashes. Do you have anything to say in your defence?"

Slick did not speak. The muscles on his back twitched in agitation.

"Does any man aboard this ship stand in defence of Mr Allen?" I yelled out.

The deck remained in a blurry-eyed silence.

"Mr Wollaton, have you not a thing to say in Mr Allen's defence?"

"No, sir," the lieutenant mumbled into his beard.

It was then that I heard Slick mutter something under his breath. Wheeling around, I glared at Mr Dawson—one of the midshipmen who tied Slick to the grate. "What did he just say?"

"I am not so sure," the lad replied nervously. "Birds of a feather...? I didn't catch the rest, sir."

Rolling up my sleeves, I held out my hand to the Master at Arms. "I shall administer this punishment myself," I said, snatching the cat from him. "And for your additional insolence, Mr Allen, I shall add another dozen lashes. Which makes it one hundred and eight."

There was an audible gasp from the crowd of onlookers.

"Do you hear that, Mr Wollaton? One hundred and eight!" I shouted, feeling the anger churning inside my breast. "I want to hear your count on *each* and *every* crack of this whip!"

Leaning forwards, I put my mouth to Slick's ear. "And you can rest assured, Mr Allen, I shall give as much thought to your suffering as you gave to Mr Legge's."

I remember the first strike. I twisted my body and held my hand high, throwing my full weight behind the swing. The knotted cord came down upon Slick's left shoulder with a crack, tearing through his skin as if it were made of paper. He cried out. I watched the claw marks in his flesh begin to leak blood.

"Mr Wollaton? I did not hear you!" I yelled.

"One," he called out.

It was the most severe lashing I have ever given a man. With each sweep of my arm, I fell deeper into a black cloud of rage, until it wholly consumed me. I thought of the spiteful grin on Slick's face as he threw that young albatross onto the deck. I thought of Legge lying injured on the floor in my cabin.

"Thirty-two..." I heard Wollaton call.

I despised the life out of this man. This worthless dog.

"Forty-six..." came Wollaton's call.

Every lash was released with force. I barely took notice of Slick's ragged torso in front of me. What did I care? I hated him; I hated this wretched, miserable port, and I hated the ungrateful people who walked its filthy streets.

"Sixty-five..."

Why on this last night? I thought, as I belted on. *We would have been out of here by daybreak. Why did this happen on the very last night in this godforsaken place?*

On the count of eighty, Birnie stood forwards. "Captain, the man is—"

"Stay back!" I roared, casting my eyes in Wollaton's direction. "Continue the count, lieutenant."

"Eighty," he called.

The stupefied faces of the men, the raw and bloodied state of Slick's back, Birnie's desperate look—all these things were lost to me in my rage. It was just the crack of the whip and the burning soreness in my arm.

"Ninety-three..."

I stopped to pull the knotted cords through my fingers, removing the clots of blood. Slick was hanging limp against the grating. Every inch of his back was torn to shreds.

Working the fingers on my hand to release the tension, I gripped the shaft of the cat once more.

"How many, Mr Wollaton?"

"One hundred an' four...sir," he said, his eyes averted.

I delivered the remaining four lashes in quick succession, then threw down the cat.

"Mr Allen is no longer in the employment of His Majesty's Navy," I said. "Take him back to the wharfs. I care nothing for his fate, only that it is no longer tied to my own."

The men stood aghast.

"Do you hear me?" I shouted.

"Aye, aye, Captain!" they said in unison, but with no enthusiasm in their reply.

———

We weighed anchor the very next day under clear skies and with a favourable wind. The fine sailing conditions required little effort from the crew, but I allowed no idling on board the

Conway, no time to sit around dwelling on the dark events that had taken place in Callao. I kept the crew busy with an endless list of tasks: tarring the decks, mending the rigging and sails, painting the window frames, preparing charts, stowing the hold. I was not belligerent in my command—I had no intention of being a tyrant. Never once did I reach for the cat, nor was there ever a need to. The men worked from daybreak to dusk without complaint. At the end of each long day, I instructed Cook to double the rations; and for an hour after supper, I allowed the rum to flow freely from the barrels. The men worked, and they ate, and they drank—and after that, they retired to their hammocks and fell sound asleep.

Legge remained on a bed in the Great Cabin. Shortly after our departure, he had come down with a fever. When his condition worsened, Birnie took to sleeping on the long seat beneath the cabin window. Each night, I would lie awake tormented by the lieutenant's groans and cries. When at last I fell into a restless sleep, I was haunted by the same recurring dream, time and again.

I was standing at the helm during a terrible storm. Rain lashed against the sheets and lightning cracked through the sky. All at once a great wave would surge up over the side and sweep across the deck. Legge was always standing by the mainmast, and each time I would see the wave take him slipping and sliding helplessly overboard. Running to the railings, I would catch sight of the lieutenant flailing his arms and crying out my name before he disappeared beneath the heaving surf.

Awakening from this nightmare, drenched in sweat, I would press my ear against the cabin wall and listen for Birnie's caring words as he reassured the lieutenant that he would soon be well again.

"Drink this down, Charles. It will help ease the pain."

And while the laudanum pulled Legge back into its shadowy embrace, I listened to Birnie speak to his friend of better times. Of their expeditions on horseback into the Chilean countryside and the dances and parties they attended in Valparaiso. When Birnie's voice ceased, I would light a candle to chase away the guilt that clawed at me in the darkness. Pouring myself a whiskey, I would sit in a chair and read a book, write in my journal, recite poems from my youth. Anything to keep my mind preoccupied until the rays of the morning bled through my porthole.

ELEVEN

Valparaiso, Chile, 31ˢᵗ October 1821

WE SAILED into Valparaiso harbour nineteen days later. Having fired our welcome salute, I watched a longboat filled with uniformed men row towards us. As it drew close, I recognised Captain Spenser of the *Owen Glendower* sitting in the front of the boat.

"You are to sail immediately for Conception," he informed me, climbing aboard and handing me my orders. "A journey of three days south, if this fair weather holds. There's been some terrible business down there—a traitor, turned pirate, turned... warlord, is cutting the heads off our officers."

I read the details from the Admiralty. Conception was under attack by a man called Vicente Benavides, a Chilean soldier who had become disillusioned with his fellow countrymen and now fought for the indigenous people. In command of his new army, who were equipped with only knives and spears, Benavides had taken to capturing British and American ships and holding their officers hostage. The resourceful outlaw did not know the first thing about sailing, and so he forced the crew of these captured ships to remain on board, commanding them to sail wherever he wished or else the kidnapped captains and officers would be put to death. I was instructed to take the *Conway* to Conception and assist the British and American fleets in any way I could.

"My lieutenant must be taken ashore," I said. "He is badly injured and remains in a high fever."

Upon hearing it was Legge, whom Spenser had met at the picnic party in the hills, the captain agreed to take the lieutenant in his longboat. As a further show of goodwill, he arranged for the surgeon from the *Owen Glendower* to sail with us so that Birnie could remain with Legge until we returned.

An hour later, we were on our way. Our passage south was a frustrating one, slowed to a snail's pace by scattered winds that were difficult to harness. Arriving at Conception, we spent the first few weeks guarding the port with the other ships, the inhabitants of the town needing protection from future attacks. Then news arrived on an American man-of-war, informing us that one of the kidnapped ships had been set ablaze, but another was successfully rescued with most of the crew still alive. Benavides was nowhere to be found, having taken his army inland with the kidnapped officers in tow. Rumour had it that the pirate intended to take the capital, Santiago. It was a grandiose plan with little chance of success; but then again, Benavides had already proven himself capable of the extraordinary.

Determined to make myself more useful, I volunteered to take the *Conway* south to Arauco, an Indian settlement where Benavides had been based—and where two American officers were apparently still being held hostage. Upon our arrival at

Arauco, however, it was clear that we were too late: the town was in flames and deserted; it being the custom for the Indians to burn their settlements before fleeing. Needless to say, there was no sign of the officers.

Turning the *Conway* around, somewhat disappointed, we sailed back to Conception to continue the task of keeping guard with the other ships. An uneventful month went by, and then the good news arrived that Benavides and his army had fallen at the inland town of Chillan, and that several British officers had been found alive. With Conception no longer in any immediate danger, I was finally permitted to return to Valparaiso.

After witnessing so much wretchedness in the face of war, it was such a relief to sail around the headland and see the sunny harbour once again, filled with merchant ships and wharfs bustling with life. Casting the eye of my telescope along the bay, I tried to instil in myself a sense of optimism. I must take advantage of the coming days in this happy and vibrant town. Life was good here—at least for now.

I was, of course, eager to learn of Legge's wellbeing, and no sooner had I placed my boot upon the quay, than the answer came in the form of a boy carrying a crate of chickens. Upon seeing the stripes on my coat, the lad stopped in his tracks and stared at me wide-eyed, his mouth slightly parted as the thoughts collected on his mucky brow. Feathers were drifting out from between the bars of the cage as the birds clucked and squawked inside.

"'Scuse me, sir," he said cheerily. "You'd be Cap'n 'All, would you not?"

I greeted him with a nod.

"I had the pleasure of meetin' your lieutenant, sir. Mr Legge. I was in the 'ospital with him." The boy placed the crate on the ground so he could tip his cap, then hoisted up his slops to show me a badly stitched wound on his calf. "It goes right the way up to me knee, sir."

I threw him a good-humoured grimace.

"Fell off the yardarm, sir," he went on. "Mr Latham had to fix it afore it went gangreenious."

"Gangrenous," I corrected him. "Mr Latham has done a good job, and you should thank your lucky stars you get to keep that foot. Now, how is my lieutenant?"

"Alive an' well, sir. Convalescing at an 'ouse up in the 'ills. I remembers the day he left. The gentleman who came to fetch him were very kind, sir. A Mr..." The boy rubbed his eyebrows. "I forgotten his name."

"Kennedy?"

"Aye, sir." He nodded enthusiastically. "That were him."

Filled with a tremendous sense of relief, I thanked the lad and tossed him a coin.

"Alive and well," I repeated, as I walked along the quay. "Charles Legge is alive and well."

I strolled into town whistling a tune.

———

Rising early the next morning, I found myself a horse and set off on the winding track that led up through the cliffs and into the backlands behind the port. Upon reaching the high ridge that separated the coastline from the undulating hills beyond, I stopped to enjoy the breathtaking view. It was a glorious day, with not a cloud in the sky. Down in the crescent bay, the sun sparkled on the turquoise water. Tightening the reins, I turned the horse's nose away from the coast and nudged her into a steady gallop. It was an exhilarating ride, racing along the grassy hilltop with the Andes in full view, then plunging down through rich and verdant countryside into the valley below. Having splashed through the shallow ford in the valley basin, I galloped up the neighbouring hill with my eyes fixed on the solitary house settled into the side of the mountain. When finally I pulled the horse to a halt in the gravelled forecourt of the villa, her neck was glistening with sweat. Tossing the reins to the stable lad, I turned to see Kennedy walking my way.

"What wonderful news," I said, striding to him with an outstretched hand. "You cannot imagine my relief when I..."

It was only then that I took in how forlorn Kennedy looked. His shoulders were slumped, his eyes leaden.

"We are close to the end," he said, shaking his head gravely.

When one is prepared for good news and the opposite is delivered, the body and the mind remain, for a time, at odds with the change in situation. Racing across the hills on horseback, I had pictured the lieutenant sitting on a deck chair in the garden, his curly blond hair untied about his shoulders and a book in his lap. I imagined spending a long, sunny afternoon with him under a tamarind tree, drinking cool lemonade while I explained why those men from Italy had broken into my cabin. I had the letter with me, and I intended to show it to Legge, then tell him all about the pages Gillies stole from the Florentine Codex. Legge's piercing blue eyes would grow wide with excitement as I told him that the pages were some sort of treasure map, and that Gillies was on a quest to find the tomb of a lost Aztec ruler. And then, in the most heartfelt way, I would say how deeply sorry I was that he had become entangled in the whole affair—and that I would use every ounce of my position to ensure the man who escaped through the cabin window that night was found and hung by his neck.

But standing there in the courtyard as Kennedy continued

to talk, my mind was confronted with the prospect of a different future. One I had not dared to face.

"In all my years as a soldier, I never saw a man so courageous," Kennedy said, lowering his voice as we entered the house. "The doctor will fill you in on the medical details. He has fought hard to save his friend."

I felt numb as I followed Kennedy down the narrow, wood-panelled corridor that led to the back of the house. Birnie emerged from the room at the end of the passageway. He looked dreadfully tired, his eyes carrying heavy shadows beneath them. When we shook hands, he was quick to release his grip.

"We heard news of your return," he said. His voice was soft and dispirited. "Charles is eager to see you, but what I've agreed to is against my better judgement."

Birnie and Kennedy exchanged a glance. Without explaining further, they left me in the corridor.

Wiping the beads of perspiration from my brow, I reached for the doorknob.

TWELVE

Valparaiso, Chile, 1st November 1821

CHARLES LEGGE SAT in an armchair by the window, dressed smartly in his naval attire: a white cotton shirt and breeches, a waistcoat with a gold-laced neck and gold buttons, and a cravat knotted about his neck. He was gazing out into the courtyard, his face bathed in the afternoon sunlight.

"Captain!" he said, turning to me as I walked into the room. "I knew you would come this day. I told George as much."

As I went to greet him, Legge sat forwards out of the beam of sunlight. It was only then that I saw how gaunt he looked.

"How are you, Charles?" I said gently.

"I have been better, sir."

Sitting down in the chair facing him, I was crushed to see how weak and sickly my lieutenant had become. His blistered lips were drained of colour. His skin, a bloodless yellow-white, was drawn tight against his cheekbones. His hair had been cut short and lay like straw upon his scalp. Only his eyes remained as before, shining brightly in their hollow sockets as if defying the sickness that was squeezing the life out of him.

"The *Superb* has arrived in the port," I said as cheerily as I could muster. "In a month, she sails for England. I intend to arrange a cabin for you."

Legge considered this as he gazed out of the window. "England seems so far away," he said. "My life there. My family. It is all so distant."

I watched an affectation of sadness steal across the lieutenant's face. He knew there would be no happy return to England. He knew he was to die here, in this foreign land, with nothing familiar around him. And when he looked me in the eye then, with such honesty, with such innocence, I felt as if my heart would break.

This was all my fault.

I wanted to speak to him, I wanted to explain, but the words were stuck in my throat.

"Tell me of your voyage to Conception," Legge said, before coughing hoarsely into his hand. "Did you rescue the English officers?"

"It was rather a wasted journey."

Glancing down at the floor, I became distracted by the sight of a silver bowl filled with bloodied bandages, tucked beneath Legge's armchair. I recalled Birnie's words before I entered the room; is this what he'd meant? Charles wishing to look like this, all dressed up in his uniform, no matter the severity of his illness, no matter the discomfort, no matter how thinly veiled his disguise. Was this all for me?

"At any rate," I went on, still struggling with this realisation, "I hear Mr Birnie has looked after you well."

"Oh, George... He has been my saviour!" Legge's chest wheezed as he drew in each breath. "I would have gone long ago if it had not been for him. Do you know, his very presence has the most welcoming effect. If I am feverish and hot, I feel suddenly comfortable when George enters the room." He lifted his arm to wipe his brow. "We have seen quite the battle, he and I."

It was then that I caught sight of a thick red stain beneath his waistcoat. The lieutenant dropped his arm quickly, pulling it tightly against his side. A cloud crossed his brow, the corners of his mouth struggling to maintain his smile. "Let us talk of better things," he said. "Tell me of life on board the ship."

We continued talking for a while on matters that were of little consequence, though I found it difficult to engage fully in the conversation, conscious of the ever-growing stain on Legge's shirt. After a time, the lieutenant's attention began to drift. His gaze returned to the window, his eyes moving to and fro as if he were following an insect trapped against the glass.

It was time to call for Birnie.

"You must rest," I told him, making to get out of my chair. "We can talk more later."

Reaching out with his hand, Legge felt along the sill. He retrieved a book that had been concealed behind the curtain. "I have been meaning to return this to you."

It was *Kenilworth*, by Sir Walter Scott. I had lent the book to Legge on our passage to Peru—but now, there was something lodged within its pages.

Legge handed me the book, watching me intently as I opened it.

"How...how did you come across these?" I said, suddenly taken aback as I laid eyes on the stolen pages from the Florentine Codex.

Legge blinked heavily as he fought to steady his gaze. "Mr Gillies... He asked me to look after them."

"Charles, when was this?" Leaning forwards, I touched his hand. It felt unnaturally cold, as if made of porcelain, not flesh and blood. "Did Gillies come here to the house?"

"It was the day before we set sail for Peru," Legge said, closing his eyes and perhaps conjuring up the memory. "Someone was tapping on my window—and I looked up and saw him there, standing in the pouring rain. He told me I was not to tell a soul. '*Swear upon your life,*' he said. '*You must keep these hidden until the time comes.*'"

"And you are sure of this?" I squeezed his hand gently. "You saw Gillies last March, in the port?"

"As sure as sunrise," Legge said dreamily, his eyes finding their way back to mine. "The day before we set sail. He told me about the lost tomb, and the treasure. And those men who are after him... He said I must give the pages to you, when the time comes...but you would need convincing. I asked him what he meant by *when the time comes,* and all he said was I would know. I would just know." His gaze turned to the book. "So I hid them in there."

I ran my hand through my hair, stricken by the realisation of what he was saying. The pages had been with us on board the ship when the intruders broke into my cabin.

"He knew," Legge said, his eyes clouding with tears. "*This* is the time he meant, this day, this moment—and ever since I have been here, I have known it too." His breathing was becoming shallow and rapid, his lungs rattling with every breath. "That is why I knew you would come. You had to come, do you not see?"

"Charles, I—"

"The golden serpent!" he cried out. "We must find it before they do!" The lieutenant took hold of my sleeve. His eyes were burning furiously. "Gillies is on his way to Mexico...

He will wait for you in Tepic. He said if anything happens to him, you have the pages now. You must find the way, that is what he said. You must find the golden serpent. It is the way between worlds!"

I tried to calm him. "Charles, you must not exert yourself like this. Let us talk about this later, when you—"

"There is no later. I am dying, sir. I am dying..." Legge sank back into the chair, the burst of life in him suddenly spent.

"You must not speak like this," I said, taking his hands in mine. "I am going to fetch Mr Birnie."

"Stay with me, Captain." Legge took away his hand and searched between the cushions of the armchair. He withdrew a small green medicine bottle and gently pulled out the stopper, his hand shaking as he did so. "It does not smell so bad," he said, bringing the rim of the bottle to his nose. "It will be just like drifting into sleep."

I took the bottle from him and placed it on the sill. "Whatever is in there, do *not* drink it. I will fetch George and—"

"George has suffered enough," Legge said, his eyes searching mine. "I would have taken it sooner, but you see, I knew you would come. I always knew it."

A breeze blew into the room and the curtains billowed against the window frame. When I reached to close the window, Legge caught my wrist.

"Please, leave it," he said quietly. "I shall miss the wind."

We sat for a while in silence. I was leant forwards in the chair, my elbows on my knees, my head bent low, and a feeling of utter desperation welling inside of me. I could not think of what to do, or what to say.

I felt the lieutenant lift his arm and place his hand on my head. He began stroking my hair. When I looked up, I saw his eyes were filled with tears.

"Might I ask you one last favour, Captain?"

"Anything..." I replied. "Anything you wish."

"Would you hold me, sir?"

Climbing out of my chair, I took Legge's languishing body into my arms. He felt so delicate, so terribly frail, that I feared even the slightest pressure might crush the life from him. Holding him in that silent and tender embrace, I listened to his laboured breathing, desperately wishing that the warmth and vitality of my body could enter his.

"You must not leave me," I said softly. "Do you hear?"

"Promise me," he replied in a whisper. "Promise me you will find the golden serpent. Keep it safe."

I would have promised him anything in that moment. I was his captain, and I had failed him in every way imaginable.

"You have my word," I whispered. "But let us find it together. Let it be *our* quest. Only do not leave me, I beg you. I cannot do this alone."

He did not answer this time. I thought perhaps that he had lapsed into sleep, as his grip around my waist loosened and I felt his weight fall against my own. Holding his head with my hand, I rocked him gently, listening to the clock ticking on the mantelpiece and the wind rustling through the tree outside the window. Legge shifted slightly, his head rising so that his lips touched my ear.

"Death is nothing to fear," he whispered. "We are entangled souls, you and I."

THIRTEEN

Valparaiso, Chile, 1st November 1821

THE BACK GARDEN was bathed in evening sunlight, the long shadows from the tamarind trees stretching out across the lawn. Birnie and I walked down through the fruit trees to the low perimeter wall. Across the sea, a crimson sun smouldered above the horizon.

"We took lodgings in the Almendral," the doctor began. He looked exhausted. His chin was thick with stubble, and his eyes carried the heavy shadows of countless nights without sleep. "Charles remained in a high fever. His wound refused to heal. When Kennedy came to visit us, he was quite insistent that Charles be brought up here to the villa where he would be afforded better comfort. I told him at first that it was too much of a risk to move Charles, but when after a week his condition showed no signs of improving, I changed my mind. I thought being out in the country amongst those who care for him would do him good."

"It was the right decision," I said.

"The Kennedy family have treated him as if he were their own son. He remained quite sick after we arrived and was suffering from a terrible pain in his side." The doctor placed his fingers on the bottom of his ribcage. "I located a lump, just here, which continued to grow over the next week or so. In the end, we were left with no choice but to reopen the wound."

"We?"

"I sent for help," Birnie clarified. "Mr Neil, the surgeon from the *Creole*, assisted me in the operation. There was an abscess on the outside of his liver, and when I lanced it, a foul discharge was released." He closed his eyes for a moment. "Charles was in terrible pain, but he never cried out. Not once, despite all of our heavy-handed butchering. And when he did speak, when we paused to wipe the sweat from our brows, or blot away the blood that obscured the abscess, his words were only ever to encourage us. 'Dig deeper, George,' he would say to me. 'Dig deeper.'"

Birnie fell silent for a while. He took off his spectacles and rubbed his eyes.

"And do you know, I thought perhaps his suffering had been worthwhile. The next few weeks saw him regain his appetite, and the fever diminished. I began to see the old Charles return. I even entertained the thought that we were winning our battle." Taking a deep breath, he then sighed heavily. "But what foolish optimism that was. Two mornings ago, I walked into his room carrying breakfast on a tray, and found him upright in bed, clutching his side. 'Something is terribly wrong,' he said to me. I told him to stay calm and to let me take a look. When I attempted to move his hands, he was reluctant to let go."

Birnie swallowed hard. "I sat on the bed, and began to prise his fingers apart, repeating that he must stay calm, and to trust me. Then all at once he released his hand and the wound broke open. It began leaking foul-smelling, blackened blood. I thought I might faint. Charles must have seen the horror in my eyes, because he withered instantly. *This is it*, I thought to myself. *My friend is about to die*." Birnie kicked the toe of his boot against the wall. "And in many ways, I wish he had died there and then."

Though I wanted to comfort the doctor, I felt curiously detached, as if the man he spoke of was but a distant acquaintance, a man I hardly knew. I understood the gravity of Birnie's words, but somehow they failed to reach me.

"You did all that you possibly could," I found myself saying, my words sounding cool and removed. "Charles could not have had a more caring and skilled friend by his side."

"I did no more than my duty." Birnie looked at me with reddened eyes. "But if ever the bounds of that duty could have been extended, it would have been for Charles. He is the purest soul I've ever met. And this family loves him as much as I do." He glanced up towards the house. "I've watched Mrs Kennedy dress his wounds and boil his bloodied bandages, even though she knows it's of little use—she knows that beneath the surface, the infection rots his insides, and there's not a thing any of us can do to stop it. I have lain awake at night listening to her husband praying for Charles—and to what end? Where are all the saints with their miracles? And the old grandmother, every morning she makes her way to that abandoned garden in the valley, come rain or shine, against untold aches and pains, to bring him fresh flowers for his room. And why? Because of a silly superstition that the garden is blessed by spirits." His voice began to crack. "Well, where are they now, these spirits? Where are the blessed angels when a man who is *not a thing* but good suffers more pain than I've seen any man suffer?"

I placed a hand on Birnie's shoulder. "This has been very hard for you."

"Hard for *me*?" he said, shrugging off my hand and stepping away. "I care not for *myself*."

"You must not torture yourself like this," I said. "You have done all you can, and Charles has those he loves around him—"

"Aye, he does," Birnie turned to me with anger brimming in his eyes. "Although I rather think you speak of something you know precious little about."

I was taken aback by this remark. "What?"

"How many times did you sit with Charles when he lay wounded in your cabin?" he went on, raising his voice.

"George, perhaps this is not the time to—"

"*Not once*. That's how many," Birnie snapped. "Yet you would have heard him call your name night after night. And why was it that you remained for so long in Conception, on your—your *quest* to save others, when the very man who has been most loyal to you lay here dying?"

"You speak of matters you do not understand," I said, trying not to become roused by this sudden burst of insolence. Birnie and Legge were close; it must have been devastating for the doctor to have seen his friend go through so much pain and suffering, let alone have to operate on him. Taking in a deep breath, I let the comment pass.

Birnie stood glaring at the ground with his arms folded tightly against his chest. I watched him as he stood in anguish, tapping his foot on the grass irritably, perhaps fighting against whatever was welling up inside him. When he next spoke, his words came out slow and deliberate. "Captain Spencer from the

Owen Glendower came to visit a few weeks ago," he said, his eyes narrowing and unable to meet mine. "He assured me that you were instructed to return to Valparaiso less than a fortnight after your arrival in Conception—that the *Conway* was of little use once his ship returned there. But he said you would not listen—quite adamant, as you were, that you should remain, despite Spencer being the captain of a forty-gun warship, and you, sir, being the captain of—of a *merchant vessel* that is not even a ship of the line! Why would he do this? I asked myself. Why would Basil Hall choose to remain in Conception unnecessarily, when his most valued lieutenant lay dying but a day's journey away?"

"I do not have to explain my actions to the ship's surgeon!" I yelled at him. "Who the hell do you think you are?"

"Let me tell you why," he said, defying me with his eyes. "You stayed away because you hoped that Charles would be dead before you returned. Because you wanted him out of your sight and out of your guilt-ridden mind."

"Get a grip of yourself, man!" I ordered, the anger burning in my chest. "We were detained in Conception and—and I do not feel obliged to explain to you why that was. Now, I suggest you go back to the house and get some rest before—"

"Why not just tell me?" Birnie cried. "Just *tell me* the reason you were detained, and we can be done with this. It is simple, is it not?"

"No, George!" I shouted. "It is *not* simple, and I suggest you refrain from saying another word until you have controlled yourself."

"I will not *control* myself!" he shouted back at me. "Why should I? I'm not like you! I *feel* things. Whereas you—you stand there as dry as a desert. You have no heart, sir. You're a monster."

With that, I lunged at Birnie and struck him clean across

the jaw. He reeled but managed to remain standing. His eyes bore down on my clenched fist.

"Go on, hit me again," he said, his voice choked with anguish. "But make sure to knock me out cold this time."

"Your impudence will cost you more than a punch in the face, Mr Birnie. Do you know, I could—"

"You could what? Flog me?" Birnie whipped his arm into the air. "Aye, go ahead, flog me, just as you flogged Slick. Give me a hundred lashes. Tear the flesh from my back—and I assure you I'll not feel even a *measure* of the pain that Charles has endured these last few weeks! Nor will your actions relieve an ounce of your shame. You left Charles to die because you were afraid—because you're a heartless coward."

I hit him again, harder this time, and he went sprawling to the ground. He climbed slowly to his feet, wiping the blood from the corner of his mouth.

"That is enough!" I announced. Turning my back on him, I fixed my gaze on the fiery horizon. "Good night, Mr Birnie. We are done."

But Birnie was far from done.

"I was there," he said. "At the old farmhouse. All the food we had eaten, the coffee we drank—I couldn't sleep. I took a bottle of wine from the cellar and decided to join the two of you. I was but half an hour behind."

His words shocked me to the core. I relaxed my fists, consumed by an overwhelming sense of dread that numbed my entire body and took the wind out of my lungs.

"I saw you with my own eyes," Birnie said, more calmly now. "You and Charles, together."

The world about me seemed to be rocking. I became dizzy, and nauseous, and wanted to be sick. Suddenly I felt as though

I was standing on top of an enormous chasm, and down below there was nothing but darkness and dread.

"My room was above his," Birnie continued. "Do you think I can't recognise the sounds? The muffled groans, the rhythmical creaking. Did you think I was oblivious to what was going on?" His eyes bored into mine. "I know what you are."

Unable to move, unable to turn around, I watched the last traces of the sun disappear into the ocean. Everything around me seemed to darken. The birds stopped singing. The wind fell. It was as if the whole world was steadily fading away.

"What is it you want of me, George?" I said, my voice having lost all its strength. "A confession?"

Closing my eyes, I felt the words I wanted to say forming on my tongue. I longed to speak them but was barred by a resistance from within, a rising panic that froze me like an icy wind. My mouth moved silently, but the words were stuck fast in my throat.

Then, through the dull thump of my heartbeat in my ears, came another sound, the faraway tolling of bells. The sunset oration had begun. I looked down at the lights of the port, tapering in thin lines into the dark ravines, and thought of the people standing silently in the streets. I thought of the prayers they whispered. Prayers of hope. Prayers of thanks. Prayers for forgiveness. And I might have prayed myself, had I not known that Birnie was right. There were no saints listening. No angels to save me.

"I am...an abomination," I said through clenched teeth. My hands were trembling as I gripped my hair. "There, you have it. My soul is blackened, George. It has cast a shadow over Charles. I stayed away for his sake."

I could hear Birnie walking towards me, but I could not make myself turn around. I could not face him. I could not look him in the eye and face the revulsion and hatred that would stare back at me.

"Let me tell you something, Captain," he said, standing right behind me. "Up there in that house, there's a man who sees not a thing but good in you. A man who is dying and whose only wish is that you might show him just a little of the love he so desperately needs to see. So by all means, keep your bitter remorse. Punish your soul if you must—but not his. Let Charles die as he lived, with honour and integrity. Let him die with a noble heart."

I watched Birnie walk away through the trees, then sat down on the wall with my head in my hands. I felt a terrible pressure in the centre of my chest, as if something cold and heavy as iron was growing there.

I sat like this, in a stunned silence with my mind reeling, until the sound of the bells signalled the oration was at an end. Then, fighting against the lethargy that weighed down my limbs, and against the shame and despair that was consuming me, I rose to my feet and made my way back to the house.

A single lamp was lit in the passageway. As I walked with heavy steps towards the door at the far end, the floorboards creaked beneath my feet. The door stood ajar. In the room beyond, I could see Mrs Kennedy and her grandmother kneeling on the floor, their hands closed in prayer. Mr Kennedy stood by the bed with his head bowed low. Over by the window, Birnie crouched by the lifeless body of Charles Legge, still slumped in the chair with his head fallen to one side.

The window was open. The curtain billowed in the breeze.

I watched the doctor lift Legge into his arms, as a father might move a sleeping child. He carried him across the room and gently laid him down on the bed, crossing the lieutenant's hands over his thin white chest. I watched as he pulled up the bedsheet as if he were tucking him in at night. I watched as he closed his friend's eyes.

Then, with his hands over his face, George Birnie broke down in tears.

I did not approach the bed. Instead, I went to close the window, retrieving the little green bottle that was hidden behind the curtain, now emptied of its contents. Reaching down to the floor, I picked up the book, *Kenilworth*, and without uttering a word, I left these good people to their mourning.

FOURTEEN

Valparaiso, Chile, 7th November 1821

THERE WAS no Protestant church in the port, and as Legge was an officer of rank, I obtained permission for him to be buried in the Fort of San Antonio, which guards the harbour on the western side. An early morning funeral was organised so as to avoid the heat of day. Having spent some time rehearsing the service, I made my way down the hill to the town. The market-place was empty and silent. I remembered how busy it had been on the day Legge and I came across the little girl in need of help.

The graveyard in the fort was enclosed on three sides by fortifications, with the remaining side open to the cliffs. Lines of wooden crosses stretched across the grass. Gazing out across the bay, my eyes settled on the *Conway* moored in the cobalt-blue water, her flag hung at half-mast out of respect.

We were gathered in the far corner, in a spot drenched in morning sunlight. Legge's coffin was draped in the Union Jack, and a fresh mound of soil sat piled on one side of the grave.

I surveyed the crowd. In addition to the crew of the *Conway* and sailors from the two American vessels in the port, there were people whom I recognised from the frequent walks Legge and I had taken into the poorer quarters of the town. Men and women who used to stop and talk, and knew Legge by name. I caught sight of the man we found suffering from *chaoo longo*. His face was clean-shaven, his hair tied into a neat plait. The little girl who had tugged at Legge's sleeve in the marketplace stood beside him in a pale blue dress, clutching the lieutenant's embroidered handkerchief in her hand.

For all the faces I recognised, there were many more that were unfamiliar: women in black dresses, men in ponchos, officers in uniform, Indians in animal skins strung with tassels.

"In twenty years, I have never seen the like," the reverend remarked. "Your lieutenant has touched many hearts."

The bell in the tower tolled, and the murmuring crowd fell silent. Looking down at the coffin, I stood for a while listening to the low rumble of the waves as they broke against the rocks below.

"Lieutenant Charles Legge died at peace with all mankind, and they with him," I said, commencing the eulogy that I had rehearsed by heart. The words flowed from my mouth without my needing to attach to them, and I was free to look around at the solemn faces. I saw Mr Neil, the surgeon who had assisted Birnie with the operation. Next to him stood Captain Mackenzie from the *Superb*, the ship that was to take Legge back to England. Behind the captain stood a line of men from the *Conway*. Wollaton was there, sullen-faced and looking down at his feet, and next to him was the Master at Arms, Mr Trickett. My eyes drifted from face to face, and all the while my voice spoke on:

"...his sense of humour hardly ever deserted him. Nor his playfulness of manner, which shone through all his sickness."

Catalina was there, shoulder to shoulder with Captain Spencer of the *Owen Glendower*. She wore a veil covering her face. I noticed she was holding the captain's hand.

"...and when I write to Lord and Lady Legge," I continued on, feeling a growing pressure in the centre of my chest, "I will be sure to inform them that, in his last moments, Charles was surrounded by his friends. I do not imagine it possible that he could have been better cared for in his dying days than by the Kennedy family, who took him into their arms and became so much attached to Charles that their time and their thoughts became entirely devoted to him." My eyes fell on Kennedy, and his wife, and the old grandmother, who stood along the edge of the open grave. Mrs Kennedy was sobbing. The old woman held a small bouquet of sweet briar.

Birnie stood next to her.

"... Latterly, when he kept to his bed, the lieutenant threw himself entirely on Mr Birnie's care," I said. "George was not only his physician, but his nurse, his valet, and his cook—his unceasing companion. And though his skill was too weak to cope with the disease, it appears..." My voice began faltering. I stopped to take a breath. "It appears quite clear, that, as far as any human aid could go, Mr Birnie supported life and maintained his patient's spirits to the last—thereby giving Charles the best chance of recovery."

I looked at Birnie, but the doctor's eyes remained fixed on the coffin. We had not spoken since Legge's death. "Will you say a few words, George?"

Birnie nodded, still averting his eyes from mine. Reaching into his pocket, he withdrew a folded piece of paper.

"Charles was my best friend," he said. "Early after our first acquaintance, our similarity of talks, studies and pursuits made us companions. The more I knew Charles, the more I loved and esteemed him for his candour and his independent spirit. He was a good man, rich in all that does honour to human nature. And in his dying days, few could stand the test that he did—for whether in sickness or health, no cloud ever obscured his humour, nor his tender affections." The doctor wiped the tears from his eyes with the back of his hand. "And I claim no merit in having paid a few small attentions to such a person with whom I'd spent many happy days, and whose confidence and affection I enjoyed. Every moment I spent with Charles is a moment I'll treasure to the last. I've never witnessed any man more beloved or respected, or one whose heart and mind were so entirely pure and virtuous." Folding up his piece of paper, he looked down at the coffin. "I'll miss you dearly, my friend."

Birnie's words moved me to the core, and I struggled to finish my eulogy.

"On November the first of this year, eighteen twenty-one, Lieutenant Charles Legge passed from this world and into the next. Charles suffered without complaint. He died at peace with all mankind, and they with him."

As Legge's coffin was lowered into the grave, the reverend stepped forwards and spoke the final sombre words, "In sure and certain hope of resurrection to eternal life through our Lord Jesus Christ, we commend to Almighty God our brother Charles William Legge, and we commit his body to the ground. Earth to earth. Ashes to ashes. Dust to dust."

I heard then the sound of wooden pipes being played. I recognised the music immediately as the haunting melody Charles played on his violin on the day of the picnic. The native song that had captivated every man and woman about the table. I located the musician in the crowd, an old man in a red poncho, moving the tapering lengths of hollow wood to and fro under his lips. Many of the crowd were singing along.

I was overwhelmed by the tenderness of the moment. In my mind's eye, I saw Legge standing with the fiddle pressed against his neck, his eyes lost within the staves of the melody as he drew the bow back and forth across the strings. It was only then that it struck me, truly struck me, that I would never hear him play again. Never hear his laughter. Never again look into his pale blue eyes. He was gone.

When the musician lowered his pipes, I felt exhausted with melancholy. My mind was swimming, and a dizziness overcame me that made me fear I might collapse. Crouching down, with one hand on the ground to steady myself, I picked up a handful of freshly dug earth.

"I made a promise to you," I whispered, tossing the soil into the grave. "A promise I shall keep."

PART TWO
THE GOLDEN SERPENT

FIFTEEN

HMS *Conway*, Valparaiso, Chile, 15th November 1821

"Farewell and adieu unto you, Spanish ladies,
Farewell and adieu to you, ladies of Spain,
For we've received orders, for to sail for old England,
An' hope very shortly to see you again!"

THE *CONWAY'S* crew stood in a line along the bulwarks, bawling out the old sea shanty while their raven-haired sweethearts crowded in the rowing boats below, clutching pocket watches, handkerchiefs, and other parting gifts that had been bestowed upon them. Overhearing a deckhand sing, *"An' there ain't too much chance that we'll see you again,"* I gave him a clip across the ear. We were leaving for good this time—and not for "old England," but northwards, back to Peru.

As we sailed from the harbour, I cast a parting glance at the row of white houses that stretched along the sandy bay, and at the Fort of San Antonio perched upon the promontory.

"Farewell and adieu," I whispered, listening to the wind

whistling through the lines and the crying of the gulls above the topgallants. Reaching into my pocket, I felt for the pages of the Florentine Codex. Since Legge's death, I had kept them with me at all times.

My orders were to return to Lima where the revolution had triumphed, the independents having freed the city from Spanish rule. Sailing at a pace up the western coast of Chile, we dropped anchor in Callao some thirty-two days later—it now being mid-December—and found the flag of independence flying high upon the castle turrets, and ships crowding the bay.

Four months ago, we had left the harbour blockaded and empty. Now we returned to a thriving port, with merchant ships from every corner of the globe eager to negotiate trade. The streets were clear of debris, and the plazas were bustling marketplaces. Faces that previously eyed us with hatred and disdain now wore beaming smiles. Voices that once cursed and swore at us now called out cheerfully for us to join them in the noisy taverns.

"The Great Protector—that is what we have named General San Martín," said one gentleman, speaking of the very man these people had despised on my last visit. "He has chased those royalist bastards into the hills and freed us from tyranny. Let us drink to his good health!"

Though in full support of the independence of Peru, I was astonished by how rapidly the loyalties of these people had been reversed. Was the past so quickly forgotten? They had been angry with San Martín because he closed off the port, choking their only source of income and forcing them into poverty. Now, the port was open for trade once more—and a roaring trade at that—and there was not a trace of bitterness towards the officers who had caused them so much misery, men whom only weeks ago they had sworn to be their irreconcilable enemies.

Walking through the streets, I felt as if I was surrounded by actors who had, in my absence, been paid to perform new roles. Townsfolk chatted merrily in the laneways as if their former unhappiness was of no consequence and had no bearing on the parts they were now to play. And yet for myself, I could not shake the deep animosity I harboured for this port. No amount of sunshine and merriment would erase my bitter regret of the night Legge was attacked.

Fortunately, my diplomatic business was upriver in Lima, and I welcomed the opportunity to stay away from the port as much as possible. Negotiating trade agreements was a slow process, and to pass the time I accepted the many social invitations that were extended to me. Though I found it difficult to engage in the frivolities and merrymaking, I nevertheless attended parties and dances that went on well into the night. Being around others was far better than lying awake in bed, staring up at the cracked ceiling in my hot and stuffy room. For the first time in my life, I found myself visiting the brothels. Sometimes, it was the bawdy, buxom dames I sought, all fleshy thighs and pretty curls as they giggled and squirmed on the bed and whispered obscenities in my ear. Other times, I chose a slim young thing with pale skin and fair hair. With her face pressed into the pillow, I would ask her not to speak, not to utter a sound until we were done. Then, as the rays of morning sun broke over the city, I returned to my lodgings and flopped onto my bed, hoping to fall into a dreamless sleep.

But these night-time distractions—for that was all they were—did not last. At length, I tired of the parties, and I tired of the brothels, realising that I could not shut the atrocity that occurred in Callao from my thoughts. And thus, one afternoon, when I was freed from my duties, I returned to the port to see if there was any information I could gather about the intruder who escaped through my cabin window all those months ago.

My search took me to the rougher side of town, where I gave money to the less reputable members of society in exchange for anything they could tell me. I soon learnt that two European gentlemen had been in the port back then, one of whom matched the description of the man Legge had shot. The other was described as taller and leaner, with a crooked nose. My mood darkened when I found out that they had been seen in the company of a greasy-haired English sailor, in a nearby tavern known for its whores and its reputation as a gambling den. The sailor was said to visit this same tavern each night to drink himself into a red-eyed stupor.

Dressing informally in old clothes, I made my way to the insalubrious establishment. The place was filled with scruffy, boisterous men, shouting over each other to be heard. A few slovenly women threw themselves from one jiggling knee to the next. Many of the occupants were English and American sailors—but disreputable sorts, with grimy shirts and toothless grins.

Sometime around ten, the man I was waiting for, a man I would have been happy to never lay eyes on again, walked through the tavern door.

Slick.

He glanced shiftily around the room—I covered my face and looked down at the table. Walking to the bar, he sat on a stool and called out to the bartender.

I stood behind him as he drummed his fingers impatiently on the bar. The barman glanced at me as he handed Slick his drink, but I shook my head. I waited until Slick curled his dirty fingers around his tankard before I said his name.

"Mr Allen."

Slick looked over his shoulder.

"You," he snarled, his voice filled with loathing.

I withdrew my pocketbook, slipping several notes onto the bar. It amounted to a year's salary for a deckhand.

"To sustain your drunkenness," I said coldly.

Slick's eyes feasted on the pile of money. "I s'pose this ain't charity."

"The men who paid you to get on board. Tell me their names."

He shrugged his shoulders. "What men?"

It sickened me just to be talking with this vile weasel. "Do you want the money or not?" I said. "You took a bribe and helped two Italian men steal aboard the *Conway*. Who were they?"

Slick took a long swig of his drink, the ale spilling down his chin. He wiped his mouth with his sleeve. "I ain't about to incriminate meself."

"You have my word this will go no further," I said. "Tell me what you know, and I will leave you in peace."

"In peace." Slick spat as he spoke. "You ain't giving me no peace. You ruined me."

"You ruined yourself the moment you took that bribe," I said. "Take another now, and you might have some semblance of an existence. Or would you rather we leave it?"

As I reached for the notes, he slammed his hand down on them.

"They never said who they wuz. Said you were hiding papers belonging to a royal house in Italy," he hissed. "That you wuz a thief, and they'd prove it. See? I ain't as rotten as you think."

"You endangered your ship," I said, controlling my anger.

"You endangered your fellow men and meddled with matters you knew nothing about—because you saw profit through your greedy eyes. Let us not waste time debating your virtue." I forced my hand down on his. "If you want this money, tell me what happened that night."

Slick curled his lip. "I hardly remember."

"Oh yes, you were drunk," I said. "That must have impressed your employers no end."

"I weren't drunk then," he seethed. "Just once I knew I wuz in for a beating. That's when I hit the grog."

"You mean once Mr Legge foiled your plans. That is why you attacked him, is it not? Because he spotted you. You meant to silence him."

"You got that wrong," Slick hissed. "I never did it. I never done that to any man. Not even one like him—that I hated."

"Then who did?"

"Some 'un else."

"*Who?*" I demanded, digging my nails into the back of his hand. "One of my men?"

Slick winced and pulled his hand away. "I never saw."

Blood leaked out across his knuckles.

"Take the money." I slid the pile of notes towards him. "Just give me the name of the man who attacked Mr Legge."

Slick looked daggers at me. "Maybe it were the Almighty himself. Hand of God, smiting the sodomite for his sins."

It took everything in me not to strike him in the face, not to strangle his grubby neck with my hands. "A name, Mr Allen. Then we are done."

Gulping down the rest of his drink, Slick slammed his tankard on the bar and let out a belch. "We are already done," he said, snatching up the notes. "This here is payment to say nothing more about those papers you got hidden away." He stuffed the notes into the pocket of his tattered waistcoat. "And a word of warning, Cap'n, which I'll give you out of the kindness of me own dear heart." His mouth stretched into a wicked grin. "You had better watch your back."

That night, I listened to the sounds in the street with my pistol tucked under the pillow. When he came for me, this man from Italy, he would find me ready. I returned to Lima the next day, and over the nights that followed, I lay awake, rehearsing what I would say to the Italian before I killed him.

But the nights in Lima passed one by one, and the only time I ever met my adversary was in the dreams that tormented me.

And even then, I failed to kill him.

SIXTEEN

Galapagos Islands, Pacific Ocean, 10th January 1822

OUR BUSINESS in Peru having reached its conclusion, I received orders to proceed north to Panama. While rallying the crew together to prepare for our departure, I found out that Mr Darby was missing. A rumour was already spreading in the port that the lieutenant had deserted, escaping into the hills with a native girl. When there was still no sign of Darby two days later, I urgently requested that an experienced officer be transferred from another ship and take Darby's position as first lieutenant. The last thing I wanted was Wollaton stepping up in rank. Alas, the Admiralty transferred a young man from another ship who had only held a lieutenant's post for a year. I complained, of course, informing the Admiralty that we were already one lieutenant down, having lost Legge.

"You will have to make do," an official told me upon introducing Mr Wood, the pimpled, naïve looking fellow who was to take Darby's place. "You have a lieutenant you can promote, and besides that you'll be sailing back to England in a few months."

"Mr Wollaton is not first lieutenant material, sir," I told him.

To which the official rolled his eyes. "Well then, you had better *make* him so."

We set sail the very next day, following the sunburnt Peruvian coastline north under the watchful eye of a great volcano, before swinging west and out to sea. Our destination was a cluster of uninhabited volcanic islands known as the Galapagos. In addition to Mr Wood—who, I might add, turned out to be a proficient officer despite my initial reservations—there were other new faces on board the *Conway*. Our old cook, Ellis, had taken his pots and pans to another ship. His replacement was a welcome addition, as he was more adventurous with the spices stored in the hold, and managed to make the food palatable. Five sailors had deserted during our time in the port, no doubt tempted by the prospect of fortune now that Peru was under new rule; two had been caught and punished and now skulked around the ship like guilty dogs. We bade farewell to another two crewmen who were deemed unfit to sail owing to poor health, including our schoolmaster, Mr Kelly—a gangly legged Irishman who used to claim, rather dubiously, to have once taught at Eton—and our much-valued carpenter, Mr Dunn, who had lost his leg to gangrene.

The voyage to the Galapagos was a welcome distraction from my diplomatic duties. I had been granted permission from the Admiralty to conduct a small geological survey to assist the research of my father, Sir James Hall, and his academic colleagues in the Royal Society. The study involved taking regular readings from an instrument known as the invariable pendulum, which can be used to determine the contours of the planet through the measurement of gravity. Having arrived at one of the larger islands, we located a suitable landing place and hurried to construct our makeshift observatory.

The experiment was conducted with some haste, as there was only a week available for the purposes of scientific experimentation. We experienced little comfort during our pursuits, as the midday heat on the island was oppressive, lasting until late afternoon when the torrential downpours sent us scuttling for cover beneath a flimsy layer of leaking canvas. My greatest regret was that this left little time to survey the fauna of the islands, which were unlike any I had seen. Among the many peculiar animals, there were enormous swimming lizards, a peculiar flightless bird that resembled the European cormorant, and a gigantic species of land tortoise that weighed several hundred pounds.

During our stay, we happened to fall in with the *Constellation*, an American frigate under the command of Captain Charles Morris, with whom I had become acquainted in Valparaiso. Morris, a hulking specimen with sharp blue eyes and thick lips, had by all accounts been a handsome man in his youth. Now in his fifties, he had gained a considerable amount of weight, and years of stooping below deck had bent his back. Nevertheless, he retained his reputation as a skilled commander renowned for chasing and sinking pirates and privateers who were interfering with American commerce. Since seeing him in Valparaiso almost a year ago, the *Constellation* had sailed to Mexico to deal with some trouble in the waters off San Blas. Having succeeded in sinking two privateer schooners that were attempting to raid merchant ships in the region, the captain and his crew were now returning south at a more leisurely pace.

I invited Morris to dine with me one evening on the

Conway, and it was then that I heard a piece of interesting news.

"I gave a ride to an acquaintance of yours this year," the captain said, wielding his fork in my direction. "Went by the name of John Gillies."

I placed my knife and fork down and stared at him. "Gillies?"

"Funny little bugger," Morris said. "Somewhat reminded me of a fox. Bright-eyed and bushy-whiskered, and a clever fellow at that."

I had presumed Gillies was dead, the men from Italy having finally caught up with him in Chile. It seemed the most rational explanation as to why the corpse lying in my cabin was carrying Gillies's letter in his pocketbook.

"He is...well?" I asked, still somewhat in disbelief.

"As well as can be expected with that illness of his," Morris said, cramming a piece of meat into his mouth. "A little wobbly on his legs, but still standing all the same—at least he was when I left him. He saved my life, you know." The captain turned to the boy who was waiting on us. "By God, this is good. What is it?"

"Tortoise, sir!" the boy said enthusiastically.

Chewing voraciously, Morris took a large swig from his wineglass. "Finest stew I've had in a long time."

"The island's full of 'em, sir. Great big creatures an' all," the boy said, beaming. "Takes four men to lift a single one."

"Well, I never. Better get our cook to stock up on a few." Morris winked at the boy. "What do you call a collection of tortoises? A pack? A herd? Certainly not a flock." Draining his glass, he tapped the rim with his fork. "Now come along, don't let an old man die of thirst."

While the boy filled our glasses, I prompted Morris back to our topic of conversation.

"Where exactly did you meet Mr Gillies?" I asked. "And when?"

"Acapulco," the captain said, his eyebrows knitting while he thought. "Let me see, we sank the *Ria* on the eighteenth of November last year, so it would have been around…early December when we dropped anchor in Acapulco. That's where I came down with the bloody brain fever. Caught it from a local girl. Mmm. She died, the poor little treasure."

The captain appeared to be genuinely saddened by the memory, albeit only for a moment. "Goddamn worst disease I've ever had, let me tell you. Hell's bells, those headaches— thought my old noggin was going to explode. Mmm. I thought I was a goner. World went black and I swear I took a few steps into that tunnel between the here and the hereafter—until I woke up strapped to the bed with a rag in my mouth and stinking of piss and vinegar. They coat your head in the stuff— vinegar that is, not piss."

Morris took another slurp of his wine and wiped his mouth with the back of his hand. "Still no idea how he found me. Gillies, that is. But there he was, standing over me like an angel of mercy, sticking his fingers into my mouth and humming and hawing in that way of his. Next thing I knew, he was pouring some god-awful concoction down my neck. Left a taste on my tongue like I'd been pleasuring an old whore— mind you, it did the trick, whatever it was." Again he wielded his fork in my direction. "So I said to him, *'Name your price, my good fellow!'* After all, he saved me from the sharp end of the Grim Reaper's scythe—I'd have given him my left bollock if he'd asked! At any rate, we settled on a free ride to San Blas. He was very eager to get to Tepic, our funny little friend. Not that I blame him. Lovely place. I have half a mind to retire there one day."

I sat blinking in astonishment. Gillies had made it to Mexico!

"Did he tell you how he got to Acapulco?" I asked.

"Hitched a ride on the *Superb*," Morris said, mopping up the gravy on his plate with a piece of bread.

"And when did you arrive in San Blas?"

"Mmm. Three weeks ago." The captain wiped his mouth, and then his forehead, with his serviette. "Last I saw of him, he was haggling with a Mexican on the wharfs, trying to convince the man to take him out on his whaling ship. Of course, I took him aside and warned him never to trust a whaler—let alone a bloody Mexican! I said no sooner were they out of sight of the mainland, than the swindler would grab him by his collars, have his crew swing him upside down, and they'd shake the coins out of his pockets. Then they'd toss him overboard and sail away without so much as a backward glance."

"Do you have any idea where he was headed?"

Morris chuckled. "On a fishing trip, by all accounts." Pushing his plate aside, the captain released an unwholesome belch. "Not that I believed a word of it—like I said, peculiar fellow." He threw his serviette at the serving boy. "Wake up, lad! We're all finished here. Time for some dessert."

When Morris finally left, it was well after midnight. Clearing aside the plates, I spread the stolen pages out on the dining table. I had more or less managed to translate the columns of Spanish relying on my rudimentary grasp of the language. Three of the pages bore the heading *de los Tultecas*. They told the story of the Toltec ruler, Topiltzin—which Gillies had mentioned in Valparaiso. Topiltzin was found in the desert by a tribe of nomads, who believed him to be the incarnation of their benevolent god, Quetzalcoatl—and here there was an illustration of a child in a lilac cloak, sitting beneath a tree. The illustrations on the pages that followed were of Topiltzin as a grown man, ruling over the city of Tollan: preaching on the steps of a temple, sitting on a throne while men and women brought him stems of corn. Finally, there was an illustration of the temple in flames—the Spanish text alongside spoke of the uprising that saw Topiltzin banished by his people.

As for the remaining four pages, they looked as though they might have been torn from different places within the Codex, as the handwriting differed on each. There was the page that bore the illustration of Quetzalcoatl, with the serpent wrapped around his leg and the resplendent quetzal bird flying over his head—*Dios de la Estrella de la Mañana*, as was written underneath. The other side of the page bore the illustration of Tezcatlipoca, *Dios del Cielo Nocturno,* in his lilac headdress and with the obsidian mirror strapped to his knee.

Then there was the page containing an illustration of a gigantic tree, and no accompanying text whatsoever. The canopy of the tree was filled with animals, birds, and flowers. Naked figures climbed the trunk and wandered across the branches. The text on the reverse said the tree was called a world tree, and the figures were human souls climbing to Paradise. The roots of the tree grew down to a starlit cavern—the Underworld, I presumed, as Tezcatlipoca was there, seated on a throne.

Another of the pages was on Aztec craftsmanship, and contained an illustration of men working stone slabs beneath a rocky cliff. The text spoke of how the Aztecs were skilled at stonemasonry, carving figures to decorate their temples or to trade with other tribes. On the reverse side, there was an illus-

tration of women weaving baskets and making pots, and of a
mother cradling her child.

And then there was the page bearing the illustration that
first caught my eye in Gillies's room that day: the human sacrifice, *Tonatiuhtiz*. Gillies had said the word translated to *He
will become as the sun*.

"Death by snakebite," I mused, knocking back a whiskey.

Although the snake in the illustration was not coloured at
all, I was quite convinced that it was the golden serpent that lay
at the heart of this whole mystery. For a start, the regal figure in
the purple cloak, holding the snake above the victim, looked to
me like Topiltzin. Then there was the ceremony itself: the
Spanish text said that during *Tonatiuhtiz* the Chosen One
received a bite from a deadly snake. I recalled Gillies having
told me that the victim's soul was then transformed into a ray of
sunlight, so that it could cross between worlds. And on the day
Legge died, the lieutenant said something similar—that the
golden serpent was *a way between worlds*. If the golden serpent
was used in the ceremony, by Topiltzin, then perhaps it was
buried with him in his tomb? But then what was this golden
serpent? It could not be a living creature; no animal could
survive three centuries locked inside a tomb. I suspected it
might be a ceremonial artefact of some sort. A bite from the
golden serpent could relate to the way this implement was used
to kill the victim. Sharp fangs used to tear open his throat. Or
perhaps they were impregnated with poison?

"Gillies, Gillies, Gillies," I muttered, refilling my whiskey
glass. "Where the devil are you, my friend?"

And what about the pencil marks? On the four pages that
had been torn from different sections of the manuscript, several
lines of Nahuatl text were underscored. I could not recall
having seen these annotations when Gillies showed me the

pages in his lodgings, in which case they must have been added since.

I drained my glass. One thing was for certain: there was not a hope in hell of my finding Topiltzin's tomb until I found someone who could translate Nahuatl.

Better still would be to find Gillies—who I now knew might yet be alive.

SEVENTEEN

Panama, 1ˢᵗ February 1822

HAVING FINISHED the experiments on the invariable pendulum, we set sail from the Galapagos Islands in the direction of the mainland. The tropical calms slowed our passage considerably, and it was not for two weeks that we caught sight of the coastline, and then two days more before the town of Panama came into view, sitting high upon the cliff tops.

A local fisherman guided us through the scattered reefs to a beautiful little bay fringed with plantain and coconut trees, where a group of negroes stood waiting at the landing place. Rowing ashore, I was quite surprised to hear them speaking fluent English—a result, I was later informed, of their constant dealings across the isthmus with Jamaica.

The Panamanians had a relaxed and cheery disposition. The trade negotiations I attended were informal affairs, taking up the entire day and closing with an invitation to a social engagement. The nights were hot and humid, and I spent them gazing up at the shadow of the candle flame dancing on the ceiling, plumping up my pillow and turning onto my front, then turning restlessly onto my back again, my mind forever preoccupied with thoughts of the golden serpent. More often than not, temptation would win out, and I would climb out of bed and sit at the desk by the window with the stolen pages spread in front of me.

My orders to continue north arrived a few days later, delivered to me in a plushly furnished office in the town hall by a high-ranking official of the Admiralty. Handing me a pile of paperwork, he informed me that the *Conway* was to sail first to the town of Acapulco on the southwest coast of Mexico, and then onwards to San Blas.

"Tepic is two day's ride inland from San Blas," he said, lighting up his cigar. "You'll find it an interesting place. Rather quaint, what with its gardens and terraced walks." Leaning on the windowsill, he puffed a ring of smoke towards the ceiling. "The merchants there are a wealthy bunch and keen to trade directly with England. More's the point, they have a million pounds in gold and silver at their disposal to buy English goods. And you"—he poked the air with his cigar—"dear fellow, shall be taking that bounty back with you on the *Conway*."

News such as this should be music to the ears of any captain of a merchant ship, since one per cent premium was paid out on the transport of gold. Given the million pounds of treasure that the *Conway* was to carry in her hold, I would be due ten thousand pounds. Enough money to buy that villa on the Mediterranean coast I dreamed about.

Except that my dreams had changed, and instead I felt my heart sink. The trade deal meant our stay in Tepic would be brief, and we would have to return immediately to England—there would be no time to go in search of Topiltzin's tomb.

Leaning over the paperwork with the ink pen between my fingers, I felt my promise to Legge fading before my eyes.

"Come on, man, smile a little," my superior said. "Ten thousand pounds by the time you arrive at Plymouth docks—that's a small fortune."

Forcing a smile, I signed the paperwork.

EIGHTEEN

Tehuantepec, Mexico, 24th February 1822

ACAPULCO LAY fifteen hundred miles to the north. Instead of creeping, as it is called, along the coast, I decided to swing the *Conway* out to sea so we could enjoy a full view of the Andean mountain range as we sailed; the weather having remained clement for weeks. One evening, eighteen days into our voyage, I stood on the forecastle watching the sun setting with astonishing splendour. Having descended towards the horizon unimpeded by clouds, it became a deep blood-red as it touched the water. The sea was as smooth as glass and dyed a lurid crimson by reflection from the sky, which looked more ominous and threatening than any I had seen.

In spite of the fine weather, I was made uneasy by the sight of this eerie spectacle. Consulting the barometer, I saw that it was falling rapidly.

"All hands, shorten sail!" I called out.

Many of the crew were on deck witnessing the sunset, and they sprang into action on my command. High up in the crow's nest, the lookout began yelling out and pointing to the eastern horizon.

Striding across the deck, I gazed out over the railings. A bank of thick black cloud was rolling towards us at great speed.

The wind picked up, and the sea began to swell and churn with unease. The *Conway*'s crew leapt to the ratlines and climbed the rigging—but before their tasks could be fully accomplished, a furious gale was upon us, splitting our sails and breaking the lines as if they were cobwebs. Had it not been for the great exertions of the crew, we might have lost a mast.

By midnight, the full force of the storm was upon us, and a deluge of rain fell from the sky. We battled every minute of every hour, riding the wild and heaving sea in a desperate attempt to keep the ship afloat.

The onslaught remained cruel and unabated for three whole days. The men worked in shifts throughout, changing over every four hours when the ship's bell rang out against the howling gale. Those whose turn it was to take some rest would sit hunched about the mess table, cramming food into their mouths and clinging to their tankards against the constant corkscrewing of the ship. Meanwhile, water flooded down between the decks, soaking the hammocks and extinguishing the lanterns.

By the time the storm finally began to loosen its grip, the black clouds quietening to a sullen grey, we were all thoroughly exhausted. The *Conway* was left in tatters. Two of the mainsails were torn, and the mizzenmast yardarm hung like a broken wing. The bowsprit had a long crack that ran up its length, and the slightest exertion might have snapped it clean in two.

But we were still afloat, and not a single man had been lost.

The storm had swept us some distance out to sea, but with

the ship in such a wretched state, our only choice was to head back to the coast. Once in sight of the rocky shoreline, we looked for a break in the cliffs so that we might obtain wood to mend the masts. By my reckoning, we had been taken to a place near the top of the Gulf of Tehuantepec, where the continent tapers into a narrow waist at the southern tip of Mexico.

We arrived at length at a sandy beach sheltered by a ring of rocks that broke the waves into white foam. A line of trees skirted the beach, and thin trails of smoke could be seen rising up behind them.

Through the eye of my telescope, I spied a group of natives standing by their canoes at one end of the beach.

"An aboriginal tribe," I said, handing my telescope to Wollaton. "I would say their village lies just beyond the trees."

"Look like savages to me," he muttered, with the glass to his eye.

"They are coastal natives." I said. "There is no record of animosity towards European sailors by such people—at least not these days. Send orders to take a boat ashore."

"Even so, best be well armed." The lieutenant glanced down at the main deck. "A pistol for each man?"

"Absolutely not!" I said, snatching back the glass. "That will only make them nervous. Mr Wood and Mr Percy can take theirs, and if there is any trouble they can always fire a shot in the air."

I selected a dozen men to accompany me in the longboat, leaving Wollaton in charge of the ship. The sea was choppy, and in rowing to the shore we took in a good deal of water— more than once, we were forced to clamber over each other to stop the boat from capsizing. Seeing our clumsy struggling, the natives came to our assistance, positioning their canoes around the longboat to steady it.

Having dragged our boat up onto the beach, I was approached by an elderly man who appeared to be a figure of authority within the tribe. His leathery skin hung loose upon his old bones, and he wore a straw hat adorned with crimson flowers and colourful feathers. I introduced myself with a cordial smile and an outstretched hand, at which point the old man began speaking enthusiastically in an aboriginal tongue. We were now in Mexico, and it struck me that he might be speaking Nahuatl, it being the language of the indigenous people of the country. With a pang of excitement, I felt into my pocket for the stolen pages from the Florentine Codex, which never left my person. These tribal people would almost certainly be illiterate, but if by any chance Fray de Sahagún's written language was a phonetic transcription, they might understand the words if I were to read them aloud.

The old man signalled for us to follow him as he began retreating up the sandy beach. Leading the way, he took us through the trees to a small settlement on the other side of the wood. The huts were built with wattled canes and thatched with palm leaves, and sat around a central area with an enormous tree towering in one corner. A pack of mangy dogs with lolling tongues lay amongst its sinewy roots.

Despite the dishevelled appearance of the settlement, the inhabitants were cheerful and generous. They offered us hairy coconut shells filled with coconut milk, and a thick stew served in folded leaves and accompanied by a sweet corn paste. As the day was heating up, we retreated to the shade of the tree to eat. All the while, the old man stood next to me chattering away in his peculiar tongue.

My eyes fell upon the feathered skin of a little bird with blue plumage, which was attached to his knee.

"*Ket-sal*," he said, straightening his back and puffing out his bony chest.

Unstrapping the bird from his leg, he placed it in my hand. So this was the quetzal. It was a magnificent creature, with a crimson breast and a crown of gold feathers on its tiny head. Although its plumage had faded somewhat, its wings still carried an iridescent blue sheen. Little wonder the Aztecs had named a god after it.

I tried pronouncing *quetzal* the way he did, then made an undulating motion with my hand, at the same time saying, "Coatl," the Nahuatl word for snake—which Gillies had also taught me.

The old man placed his hand on his heart to show reverence. "Quetzalcoatl."

Returning the little bird to him, I glanced around at the crew—they were still eating and trying to talk with the natives. Taking the old man aside, I removed the stolen pages from my pocket and handed him the page with the image of Quetzalcoatl.

I pointed to the Nahuatl writing. "Can you by any chance read?"

His puzzled look was a clear indication that he could not.

I placed my finger on a word that I knew how to pronounce. "*Topiltzin.*"

He poked his chest and held his chin high. "*Tolteca.*"

"You are a Toltec descendent?" I said, lowering my voice. "This is a story about Topiltzin." I pointed to the figure wearing the purple cloak in each of the illustrations. "I am looking for someone who can tell me what this writing says."

The old man inspected the pages, the puzzled look returning to his countenance. I tried pronouncing a few more of the words: some he recognised and would repeat enthusiastically, but with most he just stared blankly back at me. He then became quite animated upon seeing a comet in one of the illustrations.

"*Citlalin popoca*," he said, and pointed up at the heavens.

"Yes, there was one in the sky earlier this year," I said. Turning to the page with the illustration of the sacrificial ceremony, I tried another word. "*Tona-tiuh-tiz.*"

The old man stood blinking at me in astonishment.

"You know of this ceremony?" I drew his attention to the man lying upon the stone slab with shards of sunlight entering his chest. "This man is bitten by a snake. He is transformed into sunlight."

He grinned and nodded. "*Tonatiuhtiz!*"

"And this is Topiltzin, leading the ceremony?"

He continued to nod eagerly, placing his finger on the snake that Topiltzin held in the air. "*Teocuitlacoatl.*"

"The golden serpent," I said in a hushed voice. "I am looking for this. I have come a long way."

He stared at me for a moment, his eyes still filled with astonishment. Then, handing back the pages, he beckoned for me to follow him and hurried away between the cane huts. I caught up with him outside a dwelling with a veranda of sorts out the front. Hanging from the poorly thatched roof were strings of seashells and pieces of bone, which made a tinkling sound as they knocked together in the breeze. The door was a flap of dirty white canvas, which looked as though it might once have been a sail.

The old man called out, and moments later a tatty-looking woman appeared in the doorway. She was a petite thing with a weathered face and matted grey hair. Dressed in animal hides, she wore a necklace of tiny skulls and fangs, and another of bright red seeds.

As the two began chatting away in their strange language, I heard my name being called. I turned to see Birnie and Wood approaching.

"She's a shaman," Birnie said, stepping onto the veranda. "A medicine woman, and the tribe's spiritual advisor."

The woman became quite insistent that I crouch down so that we were of equal height. Up close, I could smell her sour, stale odour. She began caressing my cheek with her hand—I might have found the whole thing more uncomfortable were it not for the look of serenity in her deep black eyes.

"I'd be careful," the doctor said. I glanced up and saw the worried look on his countenance.

The woman returned to the entrance of her hut, lifting the flap slightly and gesturing with her hand that I should go inside. She waggled a finger at the others to indicate they were not allowed in.

"She seems to like me," I said, peering into the gloomy interior. "I shall not be long. This is too good an opportunity to miss."

"Captain, I must advise against it," Birnie said. "Shamans practice black magic."

"I thought you did not believe in such nonsense."

"I don't," he said. "But there are plenty who do, and if rumours were to spread on board the ship—"

"Oh George, stop being such an old spoilsport." I smiled at Wood. "We can trust the lieutenant here not to tell the crew. Is that not so, Mr Wood?"

If the truth be known, I had already surmised that the woman must be a shaman by her curious attire, and by the way the old man responded to her with an air of respect. These people were highly regarded amongst the indigenous tribes.

The dingy hut was lit by candlelight and smelled quite

rancid. Hanging from the ceiling, there were countless more strings laden with shells, bones and feathers. Grimy animal skins lay on the floor beneath my feet.

While I looked around, the woman became preoccupied with lighting a small bundle of dry herbs from a candle. It flared alight with a crackle, and she quickly stubbed out the flames. Having walked the perimeter of the room, she then circled me, wafting the smouldering bundle in front of my face, under my arms and between my legs as it poured white smoke into the air. I recognised the aroma as sage, and was unsure whether this act was to mask the unpleasant smell of the room, or whether it was my own odour she disliked.

When the task was done, she ushered me down onto one of the animal skins. Lowering myself to the floor, I watched her scuttle over to the wooden bench on the other side of the room, whereupon she removed her necklace of red seeds, snapped the leather cord, and proceeded to pull the seeds off one by one. Having crushed them with a stone, she then added the powder to a copper pot that sat close by, and poured in liquid from a jug. Stirring the pot, she began muttering a stream of unintelligible words to herself.

The stirring continued for a few minutes while I sat patiently on the floor with my arms folded. Picking up a ladle, she transferred some of her concoction into an earthenware vessel and brought it over.

"I am afraid I must decline," I said, raising my hand politely.

The shaman frowned and shook her head, uttering something in a scornful tone. Sitting down beside me, she drank from the vessel in heavy gulps then offered it to me, still half full.

"I suppose that is to convince me it is not poisoned," I said.

It struck me that this might be a customary drink and I was being rude in declining. Perhaps if I drank it, she might then be willing to take a look at the pages from the Florentine Codex?

Taking hold of the vessel, I glanced across the room to where a thin beam of sunlight was streaming in through the cracks around the doorway. Birnie and Wood were still outside; I could hear them struggling to make conversation with the old man.

"Oh well, bottoms up!" I said, raising the vessel to my lips.

The drink was quite disgusting, but the shaman was not satisfied until I had finished it. After this unpleasant task was done, I took out the stolen pages and handed them to her. She flicked through each one in turn, all the while gabbling away to herself. Upon reaching the illustration of the ceremonial sacrifice, I spoke the word that had been sitting on the tip of my tongue since I entered the hut.

"*Tonatiuhtiz*."

The shaman's black eyes grew in wonderment as she ran her wrinkled finger over the illustration.

I pointed to the snake in Topiltzin's grasp. "This is what I am looking for. The golden serpent."

"Tezcatlipoca," she said with a toothless grin, then gestured to the empty vessel from which we had drunk. She continued chattering away incomprehensibly, pointing at this and that on each of the pages as she laid them out on the floor in front of us. It was then that I realised I was beginning to feel lightheaded. My first thought was that the liquid she poured from the jug must have been a strong alcoholic beverage. Looking down at the pages in front of me, I noticed the colours in the pictures seemed strangely vibrant—and whilst the columns of Spanish writing remained clear and easy to read, the Nahuatl columns were blurred. I blinked heavily. The lines of words had begun gently undulating like ocean waves.

Realising things were quickly getting out of hand, I sought to get up and leave—but when I tried to move my limbs, nothing happened. I could not move! Only with the greatest effort could I turn my head and look at the old woman sitting beside me, her black eyes boring into me.

Seized by a wave of panic, I tried to call out to Birnie—but my lips were stuck fast. I was trapped within my body, and at the mercy of this terrifying woman. My heart thumped wildly and there was a high-pitched ringing in my ears.

Reaching forwards, the shaman placed her hand upon my chest.

"El corazón," she said, shocking me with her Spanish. "Libera tu corazón."

I tried again to cry out, but then was seized by a wave of nauseousness. All of a sudden, my stomach churned violently and I vomited a slimy green liquid down my shirt.

I felt myself falling backwards.

After that, the world turned black.

NINETEEN

I FOUND myself standing on a sandy beach hemmed in by steep red cliffs. It was evening time. Across the ocean, the sun had already set beneath the waves, leaving a sky painted with the mauves and soft blues of twilight.

The place seemed at once familiar, as if I had been here before, perhaps many times—standing just as I was now, with my feet in the wet sand and the tide sliding up between my toes, gazing out upon this same tranquil scene.

Further along the beach, I caught sight of a lone figure standing in silhouette. Seeing him raise his hand in greeting, I walked towards him. The man was tall and muscular, with chestnut-brown skin and black hair that fell down his back. Dressed as a chieftain or warrior, he stood bare-chested with his hands placed masterfully on his hips. He wore a jaguar pelt slung around his shoulders. A decorated loincloth fell between his legs.

As I neared him, I saw within the lilac feathers of his head-dress, a strikingly handsome face, painted with a black and yellow stripe across his broad, flat nose. I had never laid eyes on a man so beautiful. Everything about him was exquisite, every inch of his body carved to perfection.

I glanced at the object strapped to his leg—a mirror made of polished black stone.

"I know who you are," I said.

Tezcatlipoca held out his hands. "And am I not sublime?"

It was only then that my mind began to question where I was, and how I had got to be on this strange and lonely beach. I could vaguely recall sitting on the floor in the shaman's hut—though this in itself seemed to be little more than a dream, a fading memory that came only as fragments and flashes—the earthenware bowl containing the vile tasting drink, the pages of the codex laid out on the floor, the old woman's toothless smile and black eyes.

Those words she spoke, *Libera tu corazón*.

There was a part of me that realised I must be in the grip of a powerful hallucination. Yet, at the same time I could not believe this, as everything about me looked, and felt, and *was*, as real as real could ever be.

"Where am I?" I asked him.

"You journey in the soul," Tezcatlipoca said, and then his mouth broke into an ivory white smile. "And your journey has brought you at last to me."

I looked around the deserted beach. There were no footprints in the sand save for my own.

"Is this real?" I asked, glancing up at the palm trees on the cliff tops, their long fronds swaying in the breeze. "Or is this all in my mind?"

Tezcatlipoca shrugged his muscular shoulders. "You waste your time asking questions that are of little importance."

"Am I dead?"

"Not yet," he replied, his eyes searching mine. They were

deep, penetrating eyes, and I felt as if he was looking into the very depths of my soul. "But I can set your soul free from its shackles. You have only to ask."

"And then what will become of me?"

He smiled. "As becomes of every living thing. Every flower that wilts, every deer that falls to the lion, every mortal whose heart ceases to beat. You will be released and returned."

"I cannot die yet," I urged, recalling again that other place, that other existence, where I lay intoxicated in a dingy hut with the stolen pages laid out on the floor. "There is a promise I must keep. You must send me back."

"But there are no promises," Tezcatlipoca replied, placing his hand on my cheek. "All is illusion. The seas you sail upon, the night sky you wonder at, the sunsets that capture your heart. It is the Great Deception, the labyrinth in which souls become lost."

He placed his hand on my shoulder, and with only the slightest pressure my knees gave way and I crumpled onto the wet sand. And I lay there, barely able to breathe, with the tide sliding up over my body and my heart pounding in my chest.

Crouching beside me, Tezcatlipoca began slowly unbuttoning my shirt. "What you seek cannot be found by one whose heart is trapped in sticks. One to whom fear clings like chaff and straw."

"Why must you torment me?" I said, my voice barely more than a whisper.

Because I *was* tormented: I did not want this, to be helpless to his beauty, to be burning with desire for him; and yet as he laid his hand upon my belly, I felt my whole body surrendering to his touch.

Reaching out, I locked my fingers between his. "I cannot fight you..."

Tezcatlipoca leant forwards and pressed his lips against my ear. "It is not I with whom you fight," he whispered. And then, leaning forwards, he kissed me on the mouth.

I tasted the sea on his lips. I caressed his beautiful face and stared into his dark eyes.

The Lord of the Night Sky lowered himself onto me, and I surrendered. I wrapped my arms about him, I ran my hands over his muscular back, I became lost in the movement of his body and the strange language he spoke in a voice as soothing as the gentle roll of the ocean. When I wept, he kissed away my tears. And afterwards, I was filled with a feeling of calm unlike anything I had ever known.

We lay in silence for a while.

"Beyond here lies a world of peace," he said at length, turning to look at me. "A world where everything is known, where everything is whole, and the light is pure and white." He took a handful of sand, allowing it to slip through his fingers onto my chest. "This realm, it is as a diamond that splits the light. Only within the diamond can the colours manifest. Only here can you experience beauty, and love, and sorrow, and joy."

Climbing to his feet, the Lord of the Night Sky filled his lungs with the sea air. As he exhaled, he released a sound: a deep, resonant hum that made the world about him shimmer as if it were a mirage. I watched in astonishment as the deity transformed into a being that was both terrifying and beautiful. His body became translucent like golden glass, and his hair became a nest of writhing golden snakes, which licked the air with their crimson tongues. Within his skull I could see a whirling galaxy of stars.

"It is the greatest gift," he boomed, his voice echoing about me. Throwing back his head, he exploded into a cloud of glittering golden dust, which danced for a moment in the evening sunlight before scattering to the wind.

I was alone then.

Tezcatlipoca's jaguar pelt lay next to me alongside his headdress of lilac feathers—and, half buried in the sand, the obsidian mirror.

I sat for a while running my fingers through the sand and listening to the gentle slopping of the waves. Then, wiping the surface of the mirror with my sleeve, I gazed into its smoking depths.

TWENTY

Tehuantepec, Mexico, 25th February 1822

I AWOKE IN MY COT. Birnie was sitting in a chair next to me, reading by candlelight. I lay there for a while, still heavy with sleep, comforted by the doctor's presence and the familiarity of the cabin surrounding me. I felt tremendously relieved to be back—from wherever it was I had been. When I shifted slightly, my body felt heavy and unfamiliar. My fingers and toes were at first numb, then began tingling as I moved them.

Upon seeing my eyes were open, Birnie put down his book.

"How long have I been out?" I asked groggily.

The doctor checked his watch. "Eight hours. I had no choice but to declare you temporarily unfit to command. As first lieutenant, Mr Wollaton is in charge."

It struck me then that the ship was moving—we had set sail.

I propped myself up in bed. I felt weak, drained of strength, and my mouth was bone dry. "I... I remember the drink," I said, rubbing my temples. "Being unable to move.

Then after... George, it was... I am not quite sure how to explain it."

"Mr Wood and I found you in a stupor," Birnie said, filling a glass with water from a jug. "In a pool of your own vomit with your eyes rolled up into the back of your head. That woman was next to you in a similar state."

"I—I went somewhere, George. And now I feel..." I trailed off, unable to find the words. It was as if a fresh wind blew through me, a sea-change, bringing with it a sense of release, and a lightness in my heart.

"You were out cold," the doctor said, handing me the glass of water. "Intoxicated by whatever it was you drank. I tried to bring you to your senses while the lieutenant went off to fetch help. When the others arrived... The way it looked inside that hut, and the stench of the place... The men were convinced she was some kind of witch. They were cursing and shouting, and arguing about what to do. Then all of a sudden Mr Percy took out his gun and put the barrel between the old woman's eyes. So I broke in and began shouting that they must calm down, and drew their attention to the commotion outside. The villagers had surrounded the hut but seemed afraid to enter. I said if we showed any signs of animosity, the whole settlement might attack us." He took off his spectacles and stared at the candle flame. "With a single gun between us, our only chance was to leave peacefully. Thank God they listened to my advice."

"George, I am indebted to you," I said, though noticed Birnie did not look at me. "I know what I did was terribly foolish. If I had known—"

"I'll inform Mr Wollaton you are fit to resume command," the doctor said, and stood up. "The men will be relieved to hear it. Drink plenty of water. There's more in the jug."

He made for the door.

"There were some papers..." I called after him.

Birnie turned wearily. "You mean those old pages? They're in the drawer of your bureau."

Within an hour, I was back on the quarterdeck and feeling much revived. The sea was calm, the stars were out, and a steady breeze lifted the sails as we cut through the night. Standing at the helm, with my eyes upon the glittering band of the Milky Way, I tried to comprehend what had happened to me while under the spell of that powerful drink. It was no dream, of that I was certain. No dream could be so real. No dream could feel how that place felt, in every way so wholly indistinguishable from the waking moment. So then could I have gone somewhere beyond the boundaries of earthly existence? Had I journeyed in the soul?

Shortly before daybreak, I returned to my cabin to get some sleep. I was restless, though, and after an hour of tossing and turning, I found myself at my bureau, pulling open the drawer that contained the stolen pages. I took them out and spread them on the table. In less than a month, we would be in San Blas. I would ride immediately for Tepic and use every moment of my spare time to track down Gillies. Even if he was gone from there, even if I found out he was dead, those men from Italy having caught up with him, I still had the pages, did I not? All I needed was to find someone who could translate Nahuatl.

TWENTY-ONE

Acapulco, Mexico, 25th March 1822

WE RACED northwards across the cobalt-blue ocean, a trail of white foam churning at the stern of the ship. Through the eyes of a passing seabird it might have looked as if all was well on board the *Conway*: the hands clambering up the ratlines and shuffling along the yardarms, the air filled with the oily fragrance of fresh tar, and the sound of hammering and sawing as the men repaired the ship.

Yet, the rats scurrying about in the darkness below deck would know that all was not well on board. They would have heard the whispers that leapt from hammock to hammock once the oil lamps were turned out. Whispers about how the captain was acting strange, always with that faraway look in his eye; how he paced back and forth in his cabin at night, muttering to himself; how sometimes he would stand in the moonlight, staring out across the water for hours on end. Aye, something was not right about the captain—and it was ever since those queer happenings at the Indian settlement.

But these were rumours I neither knew nor cared about, such was my obsession with the task I had set myself; and no sooner had we dropped anchor in Acapulco, than I began looking for someone who might be able to translate the Nahuatl writing in the stolen pages.

The town comprised fewer than fifty stone townhouses, surrounded by a large suburb of reed huts. The inhabitants of this sprawling settlement were mostly negroes who, having mixed thoroughly with both the natives and Spanish alike, were the most handsome of races: tall men and women with chiselled cheekbones and thick lips. Many spoke Spanish, and a few could manage a smattering of English.

I was soon to learn that the aboriginal Indians remained away from the harbour, preferring to live in the mountains. These people were very different to look at, being slender in build, with coppery skin and long, straight hair. They visited the harbour on market days but kept mainly to themselves. Any attempts I made at conversation with them gained little more than vacant looks: either they failed to understand my poor Spanish, or simply pretended not to understand to avoid answering my questions.

We had been in the port for a few days when my enquiries eventually led to a man called Joseph Lyle, an elderly missionary who lived in a village in the foothills, a day's journey inland. Father Lyle had spent his life amongst the local tribes teaching literacy in a small school. I learnt that he often travelled to the coast to see his grandson, a wealthy merchant in Acapulco—and as luck would have it, he was in town during our stay.

Acapulco did not receive many ships in its harbour, and it was easy enough for me to gain an invitation to meet with the merchant at his house—a whitewashed brick building at the end of the row of townhouses along the seafront. The merchant arranged a dinner party, and I arrived to find eight other guests in attendance.

Upon entering the drawing room, I immediately spied the reverend standing by the fireplace. He was the oldest person in the room by several decades, with snow-white hair sprouting from his scalp and dressed in a navy-blue jacket that was a few sizes too big for him. Despite his rather dishevelled appearance, however, the old man carried the ease and familiarity of a privileged person; and watching the way our host attended to the needs of his grandfather, I could tell he was extremely fond of him.

During dinner, I made sure that I sat next to the reverend, and over the course of the meal he told me about his earlier days as a missionary in the Yucatan. Having taken the voyage from Ireland in 1762 as a young man, some sixty years ago, Lyle had spent his life among the native people, teaching them to read and write. His story reminded me instantly of Bernardino de Sahagún, the Spanish friar who compiled the Florentine Codex—though that would have been more than two centuries earlier. When I remarked on this to the reverend, he appeared to be quite flattered.

"The world has yet to realise all that Fray de Sahagún accomplished," he said, raising an eyebrow in my direction. "If not for the Florentine Codex, we might remember the Aztecs as little more than a tribe of savages who built pyramids and indulged in human sacrifice. Their knowledge of agriculture and astronomy and medicine would have been lost and forgotten."

"I have an acquaintance who has seen the Florentine Codex with his own eyes," I said, glancing around the dinner table to make sure no one was listening to our conversation.

"He believes the friar's motives for writing the manuscript were not quite what they seemed."

"Spend a little time at any of the monasteries further north and you will hear all sorts of stories," Lyle said, lowering his voice to a hush. "Many believe Fray de Sahagún swore his allegiance to the Aztec people and secretly worshipped their gods."

I contemplated telling the reverend more of what I knew, but remained cautious. "And what do *you* think, Father? Do you think he was a heretic?"

Lyle reached for his glass and took a sip of wine. "I think it takes great courage for a man to follow his heart. Especially when it means he must cast aside the very values he has built his life upon. Great courage and great faith—in oneself."

Our conversation was interrupted by the appearance of dessert. As it was being served, Lyle took hold of my wrist. "It brings joy to my heart to hear a young man like yourself speak of Fray de Sahagún and the Florentine Codex. I rarely hear mention of either these days."

For the remainder of the evening, there was little opportunity to speak privately with the reverend. Upon leaving the house some hours later, however, I was in the hallway talking to one of the other guests when I saw him slip through a door into another room. Politely excusing myself, I hurried after him and found myself stepping into a small library.

Lyle was lowering himself into a chair by the hearth. He seemed quite unsurprised to see me, nodding his head and smiling as I ventured into the room—I wondered if perhaps he was expecting me to follow him.

"I have something I would like you to take a look at," I said, reaching into my pocket.

The reverend took out his reading glasses when he saw the

pages I was holding. I felt for a brief moment unsure as to whether I should give them to him, a little nervous even, having kept these treasured pages on my person for many months now without letting a soul near them. Lyle gave me a reassuring smile, as if he could see the doubts I was harbouring.

"I shall treat this in the strictest confidence," he said, holding out his hand.

I gave him the pages, and the old man cast an eye over each in turn. "Many years ago, I spent some time at the Colegio de Santa Cruz in Mexico City," he said, his gaze straying to the painting that sat grandly over the fireplace: a battle scene, with cavalrymen clashing swords and a fallen horse struck with a look of terror in its eyes. "The school was built by the Franciscan Order of the Catholic Church back in the early fifteen hundreds—not long after the Spanish conquest—with the intention of preparing young native men for the priesthood. The friar we spoke of earlier, Bernardino de Sahagún, was one of the founding scholars at the school. He taught the boys to read and write in Latin, Spanish, and their own language, and how to paint in the European style of the time. The manuscripts written by Fray de Sahagún and his students have a familiar style: two columns of text, one in the original Nahuatl, the other a translation into Spanish, and then accompanying pictorials." He looked at me over the top of his spectacles. "Might I ask how you came across these?"

"They were entrusted to me by a friend," I said. "For safekeeping."

"Stolen, by the looks of it." Lyle ran his finger down one of the torn edges. "Or, if they are forgeries, then they are very good ones."

"I believe they are the genuine article. And yes, they were stolen."

The reverend continued to regard me over his spectacles. "From the Florentine Codex, I suspect, by your question earlier about the friar's motives in compiling the manuscript."

"I was hoping you might be able to translate the Nahuatl writing," I said, cutting to the chase. "I am intrigued to see if it matches with what is written alongside it in Spanish."

Lyle's eyes returned to the pages in his hand. "Nahuatl cannot be directly translated, as it is very different from the Latin languages—a single word can carry the meaning of an entire sentence. And this writing is very old. But let us see what we can do."

I watched the old man's wrinkled finger slide from one Nahuatl word to the next, his lips moving silently as he did so. Every now and again he would stop and gaze up at the painting on the wall. After what seemed like an eternity, but was probably only a few minutes, the reverend rearranged the order of the pages, nodded in satisfaction, and looked up at me with a smile. "The two columns say more or less the same thing, although—as I'm sure you have noticed—the Spanish side contains most of the illustrations, so there is a little less detail." He held up three of the pages. "These three contain a narrative about the Toltecs. I shall translate as best I can." Returning his finger to the page, he cleared his throat.

"Long ago, there lived a tribe of men who roamed the ancient lands, following the winds and the animals they hunted. Their prophesies spoke of…of a promised land, I suppose. But after many years of wandering, they knew only the desert winds that threw sand in their eyes and the barren plains that stretched endlessly in all directions. Until one night they saw a bright star fall from the Cloud Serpent." Lyle glanced up at me. "It was their name for the Milky Way."

"They saw a shooting star," I said.

The old man nodded, then continued reading. "It fell towards the dunes in the east, and the nomads walked all night across the sands, never taking their eyes from the spot where it hit the earth. As the sun rose into the sky, they arrived at a lone tree, and beneath its bows sat a child dressed in finery. A little boy."

The reverend drew my attention to the illustration of the infant in his purple cloak, sitting beneath the tree. "The child was unlike any they had ever seen. His skin was as pale as milk and his eyes were the colour of the emeralds they dreamed of in their sleep. The tribesmen fell to their knees, for they knew the child was sent by the gods to lead them. And they swore themselves unto him, and named him Cē Ācatl Topiltzin Quetzalcoatl." The reverend thought for a moment. "Cē Ācatl is an auspicious date in the Aztec calendar. It translates to *one reed,* and returns in a cycle of fifty-two years. Topiltzin means *Our Prince.*"

"And Quetzalcoatl was one of their chief gods," I added. "The Plumed Serpent."

Lyle nodded, then began reading once more. "Topiltzin grew up to be very wise, and the people came from afar to listen to him. He taught them how to master nature so that their crops grew tall. He taught them how to make dyes that were as radiant as the quetzal, and their fabrics were sold throughout the land. He showed them how to craft pots so beautiful that their potters were said to have taught the clay to lie. And so the people prospered under the wise Topiltzin, and a mighty city grew in the desert. It was named Tollan, and its inhabitants, who were craftsmen and artisans and scholars, were known as the Toltecs. In the centre of the city, a great temple was built in honour of Lord Quetzalcoatl, and upon its completion Topiltzin disappeared within its walls and there began a life of solitude, spending his days in meditation and prayer. So connected was he with the spirit world that no food touched his lips, and he needed only to bathe once a day in sunlight and drink water from a holy spring."

Lyle began chewing his lip as he pondered something. He tapped his finger on the words written beneath one of the illustrations of Topiltzin. "*El Divino Sabio*," he read. "The Divine Sage." It was the illustration of Topiltzin sitting on a throne before his people. The reverend's brow remained in a deep furrow for a moment longer; then, shaking the thoughts from his head, he turned to a new page and continued reading.

"For many years the Toltecs lived in a time of peace, where no blood was shed in human sacrifice and only butterflies and snakes were given as offerings to the gods. But life with such wealth and good fortune had made them a conceited race of men. They considered themselves above other races and forgot how they were once a lowly tribe of nomads. The leaders of the city were the children of the children of those first people. They did not like being ruled by an old man who hid himself away, forbidding the wars that would make the Toltecs richer and stronger, and human sacrifice that would please the Lord of the Night Sky, Tezcatlipoca, and bring them victory in battle."

Lyle's finger rested on the illustration of the temple in flames. "And so one night, the temple was taken by storm. Men with burning torches searched the corridors and catacombs, and the priests were dragged out onto the walls and beheaded before the crowds. But Topiltzin was nowhere to be found. Helped by those still faithful to him, he fled to the shores of the ocean where a raft had been made for him. Topiltzin sailed away into the sunset, vowing one day to return and bring an end to the darkness his people had fallen into."

"He fled across the ocean!" I said. "So that is why Gillies—"

I was interrupted by a knock on the door. Hurriedly tucking the pages into my pocket, I turned to see the merchant standing in the doorway.

"What are you two conspiring about?" he said jovially.

I scrambled for an answer. "We...we were—"

"I was just in the process of persuading this young man to accompany me on my morning walk tomorrow," Lyle said, coming to my rescue.

The merchant smiled at me apologetically. "I am sure Captain Hall has business to attend to, Grandfather."

"He has already agreed, so long as I have him safely back by ten," Lyle replied, with a glance in my direction. "I rise at six, so shall we say...seven o'clock, Captain? We can continue with tonight's intriguing conversation along the way."

TWENTY-TWO

Acapulco, Mexico, 26th March 1822

THE FOLLOWING MORNING, Father Lyle arrived at my door dressed in a poncho and a straw hat with a yellow band around its brim. For a man in his eightieth year, he was in remarkably good shape. We walked the dusty road that led out of the town, arriving at length at the remains of a former Jesuit College—a derelict, quadrangular building with neat cornices and high mouldings. The college stood two stories high, and Lyle informed me it would have had a third, had it ever been completed.

I was curious to explore the place further, but the reverend was eager to continue our walk before the heat of the day was upon us. Having skirted around the building, we took a narrow trail that wove through dense scrub, then waded through a field of long grass to the ruins of an old church.

Stepping through the crumbling entrance, I was immediately struck by the tranquillity of the place. The roof of the church was long gone, and the inner walls and remaining

pillars of the colonnade were matted with creepers and brilliant flowers. Along the uneven ridge of the eastern wall, a row
of thin saplings sprung up in a wild and unnatural way.

"I come here to escape all the fuss," Lyle said as we walked
down the grassy nave to what must once have been the chan-
cel. "My grandson is a good man, but he forgets sometimes that
I live an independent life."

Upon reaching the far end of the church, we sat down on a
weatherworn slab.

"Right then," Lyle said, polishing his spectacles on his
handkerchief. "Shall we get down to business?"

I removed the stolen pages from my pocket.

Having spent some time examining them, now and again
reshuffling their order, the old man handed three of the pages
back to me. "We discovered last night that these contain a
version of the story of Topiltzin."

"Then you know of other versions?" I asked, casually
glancing at each of the pages, and the illustrations of the
Divine Sage in his purple cloak: as a child sitting beneath the
tree in the desert, then as a grown man preaching before his
people, and seated on his throne as they brought him offerings
of corn—*he taught them how to master nature so that their crops
grew tall,* I recalled Lyle having read—and then finally the
illustration of an older Topiltzin fleeing from a burning temple.

"Topiltzin is a legendary figure in Aztec folklore," Lyle
said. "And what legend does not have countless versions?" He
looked puzzled for a moment. "It is curious that there is no
mention of Tezcatlipoca here..."

The reverend went on to explain that in the versions he
knew, Tezcatlipoca arrived in the city and tricked Topiltzin
into drinking an alcoholic drink made from the maguey plant.
"In his drunken state, Topiltzin looked into Tezcatlipoca's

smoking mirror and saw himself as a decrepit old man—he then fled believing he had lost his divine powers," Lyle said. "And there is another version where the maguey unleashed his sexual desires, which was forbidden for Toltec priests."

Lyle turned his gaze to the illustration of Tezcatlipoca, dressed in his feather headdress and wearing a jaguar pelt, the obsidian mirror strapped to his knee. "He might not be mentioned, but I have a feeling the Lord of the Night Sky has an important part to play in this."

I felt a flutter of nervousness as I laid eyes upon the illustration of the dark god in his starry realm, a black-and-yellow stripe across his face and the obsidian mirror strapped to his leg. Was I to tell the reverend about my encounter with this divine entity? How I could still remember the taste of the sea on his lips?

I realised then that Lyle was watching me closely. As eager as I was to confide in the old man, I could not risk doing, or saying, anything that might jeopardise my chances of learning what was written in those pages he held. Not after I had come this far.

I smiled at him, but it was half-hearted. The smile Lyle returned was warm and genuine. "Perhaps it is time you told me about the thief who stole these pages?" he said.

"His name is John Gillies," I said. "He was a passenger on board my ship."

"And these pencil markings in the Nahuatl text. They were made by Mr Gillies?"

"They were not there when I first laid eyes on the pages a year ago," I said with a shrug. "Gillies was journeying to the New World to better his health and to study the native flora— or so I believed."

"Or so you *believed*?"

"Until one afternoon in Valparaiso when he invited me to his lodgings," I explained. "Gillies revealed he was planning to journey to Mexico on a quest, and that the pages were some sort of map for lost Aztec gold. He tried to persuade me to look after them for him." Removing the letter from my pocket, I handed the folded piece of paper to Lyle. "We have a mutual friend back in England—Sir Walter Scott. Gillies wanted the pages delivered to him. He tried on more than one occasion to get me to join him on his quest, but I refused."

"Which makes you the mysterious H." Lyle cast his eye over the letter. "What was it that changed your mind?" He looked up. "Or who?"

"I... My lieutenant," I said, caught a little off guard by his question. "He died rather tragically. I made a promise to him— to find something that lies within Topiltzin's tomb."

Lyle nodded. "I see. And what precisely are you expecting to find?"

"A piece of treasure. It is called the golden serpent." I drew his attention to the illustration of the sacrificial ceremony, and to the snake that Topiltzin held in the air. "I have a feeling it might be a ceremonial artefact, used to kill the man who was to be sacrificed. Gillies spoke of it—and my lieutenant too, on the day he died. It is supposed to have magical powers, the ability to transform people into sunlight." I laughed, somewhat awkwardly. "It all sounds so preposterous when I say it out loud like this. Exactly the sort of thing I would scoff at if I heard it from another man."

My mind drifted back to that day in Gillies's lodgings when he first showed me the stolen pages. I remembered how I leant against the fireplace puffing on my cigar while I told Gillies that treasure maps were for fools. "And yet here I am on a fool's quest," I muttered, rubbing the palm of my hand uneasily. "Perhaps it is not a promise I am bound to curse."

Lyle placed his hand on mine and gave it a comforting squeeze. "This lieutenant, he meant a lot to you."

"Yes. Yes he did," I said. "Charles... He meant the world to me."

I told Lyle about the two men from Italy mentioned in the letter, and how Gillies had said the Medici household had sent them to track him down. I went on to say how these two men had stolen on board the *Conway*, looking for the stolen pages, and how Legge, having sprung the intruders in my cabin, shot one of them before being stabbed with a knife by an unknown person who stood behind him—then, too, how we had found the letter on the intruder's corpse. It was a great relief to unburden myself of this secret. "Charles had the pages all along, in his own cabin," I said. "He was meant to give them to me." Leaning forwards with my elbows on my knees, I began recounting the painful memory of Legge's death. "He clung on," I said, burying my face in my hands as I struggled to hold back the tears. "All those weeks, and through all that pain. I shall never forget the look in his eyes when he spoke of the golden serpent. I made a promise that I would go in search of it. It was his dying wish, Father. I cannot fail him."

Composing myself, I sat up straight and inhaled deeply. "I apologise—I have no one to confide in."

"There is no need for apologies." Lyle patted me comfortingly on the back. "No need whatsoever, my son."

We sat in silence for a while.

"And you say Mr Gillies was studying the local flora?" Lyle then asked.

I nodded slowly. "He was collecting plant specimens to send back to the Royal Gardens at Kew, in London."

Lyle shook his head. "There we have it," he announced, then continued to mutter to himself. "I did wonder last night... The part about him bathing in sunlight and drinking water from a spring...and the friar calling him the Divine Sage. But I thought, *Surely not.* Then of course the name, Topiltzin...and now it is revealed that Mr Gillies is a botanist. A botanist. It *has* to be."

"What is it, Father?"

The old man's eyes were glittering with excitement. "This is not about buried treasure, Captain. The prize here is far more valuable than pieces of gold."

"You must speak plainly. What—"

"Forbidden fruits!" he gasped, locking his skinny hand about my wrist. "Sacred plants that unlock the secrets of the divine and have for centuries been banished by Christianity." The reverend continued in a hushed voice, as if fearing someone might be eavesdropping on our conversation. "There is a tale among the Nahua people that when Hernán Cortés first met King Moctezuma in the great Aztec citadel of Tenochtitlan, the two leaders spoke amicably about the prospects for trade between their countries—and for several weeks, Cortés and his men remained as guests of honour in the king's palace. Then, one evening, and while thoroughly drunk, the king boasted to the conquistador about the sacred plants the Aztecs possessed. There was a vine, a cactus, a mushroom, and several species of flower, each bestowing upon those who consumed them the knowledge of the gods. Each plant imparting its divine knowledge in a unique way."

Lyle's deep blue eyes widened. "Knowledge of the realms that exist beyond our world and the entities that inhabit them. Knowledge of what lies in our future—mankind's triumphs, our greatest discoveries, and the terrible disasters that will befall us in the years to come. Knowledge of the cosmos. Knowledge of time itself!" The old man glanced down at the pages in his hand. "Cortés listened to this revelation with great interest, and the very next day he sent word of these magical plants back to the King of Spain, Charles the sixth. Upon receiving the news, King Charles sought council with his ally, Pope Leo the tenth, who ruled over the Papal States at the time. The Pope decreed that the plants belonged to the devil himself and all those who sought to use this evil magic were to be trialled as heretics of the worst kind."

He nodded grimly. "And so began the invasion of Mexico. Hernán Cortés's original plan to negotiate trade with the Aztecs was replaced by an expensive and bloodthirsty conquest, its singular aim being to subjugate and conquer this forsaken civilisation. So the story goes, Cortés was under strict orders to seek out the sacred plants and destroy them all, erasing all knowledge of their magic."

"And Fray de Sahagún knew this," I said, my mind scrambling to put the pieces of the puzzle together. "So he hid information about the sacred plants in the Florentine Codex, concealed within the Nahuatl text. A manuscript he intended all along to become the possession of the Church."

"What better place to hide a great secret than in the very hands of those from whom it must be hidden," Lyle said. He gazed absently down the nave to the remains of the belfry at the far end. "There was one plant called pipiltzintzintli. The Aztecs were said to have inherited it from their forefathers, the Toltecs, who themselves received it as a parting gift from a travelling stranger who lived amongst them for a time. This stranger, whoever he was, told the Toltecs that the plant must be protected, as it bore the sacred flower that was stolen from Paradise in their legends." Lyle's gaze returned to the pages in his lap. "There is no mention of pipiltzintzintli in these pages—or, I should imagine, in the entire Codex. But if one knows the origins of Nahuatl words, pipiltzintzintli means *noble child prince*." He looked up at me and smiled. "And Topiltzin—"

"Means *Our Prince*," I cut in. "And...and he is a little boy in the story. A noble child prince."

The old man's grin widened. "Who grows up to be a wise sage, nourishing himself by bathing once a day in sunlight and drinking water from a holy spring."

"As a plant does!" Leaping to my feet, I began pacing back and forth on the grass. Everything was slotting into place: Gillies's passion for botany, his interest in the healing properties of plants. I recalled how, on that bumpy, squeaky ride to Kennedy's house, I had found Gillies examining a flower in the grass—how we talked about the deadly nightshade, belladonna. *"Beauty, and the beast,"* Gillies had said. *"Yet a plant is neither good nor evil. It is simply as it is intended to be."* And then of course there was our conversation that same night, while we stood on the porch watching the moths plunge helplessly into the exposed flame. *"We are taught that only death reveals the mysteries of the afterlife,"* he had said. *"But what if there is another way to find out? A back door into the divine. What then?"*

"A back door into the divine," I said, turning to Lyle. "A way between worlds. A sacred plant that bestows its user with knowledge of the afterlife, its identity hidden, concealed within the—" I snapped my fingers in the air, having suddenly caught on to something else. "Gillies likened the Codex to a magnificent tapestry that had been created to hide a single yarn of great worth. A yarn being another word for a *story*."

Lyle sat nodding vehemently. "The story of Topiltzin would not have looked at all out of place in the Codex," he said.

"And with it being common folklore, the Church was unlikely to pay much attention to any anomalies in Fray de Sahagún's version."

"And his name for Topiltzin," I said. "The Divine Sage. Surely it must be a type of sage."

Lyle smiled at me. "That would be my guess. Sage has purple flowers, just like Topiltzin's cloak."

"But why this particular plant?" I asked him. "You said there were several magical plants, yet Gillies implied that the codex was written to protect and hide just one."

"Because the story of its origin challenges the most powerful story in the history of Christianity," Lyle replied. "As I mentioned before, the Toltecs believed the plant bore the legendary flower that was stolen from Paradise." He glanced up at the saplings growing upon the walls. "The legend has always struck me as bearing an uncanny resemblance to the story of Adam and Eve in the Garden of Eden, except that here it is the goddess of beauty and fertility, Xochiquetzal"—Lyle pronounced the name *sho-chi-ket-sal* —"who lived in Paradise with her husband Tlaloc, the God of Rain, until one day she was tempted by the rakish looks and irresistible charm of the dark creator god, Tezcatlipoca. The two became lovers, and Tezcatlipoca convinced Xochiquetzal to steal a flower from Paradise and bring it down to Earth so that mortal men and women might have access to divine knowledge. This was forbidden, and when Xochiquetzal's theft was discovered she was banished from the heavenly realm—whereupon Tezcatlipoca kidnapped her and took her down into the Underworld. Although, in other versions she goes of her own accord and becomes his consort."

"The forbidden fruit...stolen from Paradise." I ran my hand

through my hair, trying to grasp all that Lyle was saying. "And you think the Church would know of this myth?"

"I don't see why not," he said. "There were many missionaries in Mexico at the time of the invasion."

"Could it even be the same story as that of Adam and Eve in the Old Testament—told through the mouths of another race of men?" I looked the reverend squarely in the eye. "In which case the reappearance of this sacred plant could shake the very foundations of Christianity."

"Which is why your friend is in grave danger." Lyle clambered to his feet. "And why he needs your help."

I watched him wander out into the ruins, clutching the four remaining pages in his hand. Upon reaching the far end, he stood looking up at the belfry. The morning sun had risen into the stone arch and hovered there like a shimmering golden bell, casting a beam of sunlight upon the old man. Lyle, in his colourful poncho and straw hat, lifted his hands in a gesture that was both dramatic and authoritative, as if he were welcoming the sun into this forgotten house of god. I thought again of how similar the reverend's life was to that of Bernardino de Sahagún centuries before him. Lyle, too, must have developed a deep love and respect for the people of this land. Bernardino de Sahagún was the custodian of their greatest secret, and now Lyle, three centuries later, held the key to its unveiling.

I walked across the grass to join him.

TWENTY-THREE

Acapulco, Mexico, 26th March 1822

LYLE HELD out one of the pages as I approached. It was the page bearing the illustration of Quetzalcoatl in his green headdress, with a serpent wrapped around his leg and a quetzal flying above him.

"We must work on the assumption that Mr Gillies wishes to draw your attention to these words," he said, pointing to a line of Nahuatl that had been underscored. "The phrase here has been omitted from the Spanish translation. It reads: *Let Quetzalcoatl's light be your guide through the darkness.*"

I considered the phrase, and then the title beneath the illustration, *Dios de la Estrella de la Mañana.*

"Lord of the Morning Star," I said. "The morning star is Venus—could this be Quetzalcoatl's light?" But then I shook my head. "I fail to see how a planet could guide anyone. Planets are not like stars; they do not have a fixed location in the heavens."

Lyle flipped the page over to the illustration of

Tezcatlipoca. He drew my attention to the Nahuatl words that were underscored.

"Once again absent from the Spanish translation," he said. "It reads: *In Tezcatlipoca's kingdom, the stars forever shine in the eternal night.*"

"His kingdom being the Underworld."

The reverend nodded. "The text tells of how Tezcatlipoca, together with his divine counterpart, Quetzalcoatl, created the present world under the Fifth Sun. Tezcatlipoca ruled the night, and was feared for his powers of destruction and his knowledge of sorcery. The Aztecs saw him as a force of change and the ruler of mankind's destiny. He would roam the Earth in the form of a jaguar. They also knew him as Ehécatl, the Night Wind—in this elemental form, he would enter their homes and manifest as a figment of their dreams, laying down challenges in which they must face their darkest fears. Those who prevailed gained the Lord of the Night Sky's blessing and protection."

Lyle handed me the page bearing the illustrations of the basket weavers and of a woman cradling a child. He placed his finger on the underscored line of Nahuatl. "This line is a little different. The first part appears in the Spanish translation—*el niño es mantenido a salvo por su madre*: 'the child is kept safe by his mother.' But in the Nahuatl, there is a prefix *teo* on the word 'mother,' *nantli*, which makes it: 'the child is kept safe by his *divine* mother.'"

"The divine mother being...the goddess who stole the flower?" I suggested.

"Xochiquetzal? It might well be." Lyle shrugged. "The second part is omitted from the Spanish. These words translate to: *She will show the way.*"

I ruminated on the phrase, *the child is kept safe by his*

divine mother, she will show the way, while Lyle turned over the page. The other side held the illustration of the stonemasons at work. "Stonemasons were regarded as the master craftsmen," he said. "They created the idols that were worshipped as a channel to the gods." As there were no pencil markings on this side of the page, Lyle moved swiftly on—this time to the page with the illustration of the gigantic tree, along whose branches walked naked men and women. The title beneath the tree read *El Árbol del Mundo*: The World Tree.

"In Aztec legend, the world tree connects the many realms of existence," Lyle explained. "These figures are the souls of the dead on their path to enlightenment." The reverend pointed to the Nahuatl words that were underscored. *"The tree that sustains all life has roots leading into the Underworld."*

The roots sprawled out beneath the surface of the ground, surrounding a starlit subterranean cavern in which Tezcatlipoca sat on a throne, holding his obsidian mirror. Lyle drew my attention to the deity's outstretched arm. Tezcatlipoca appeared to be pointing towards one end of the cavern. I followed the line of his finger into the tangle of roots that lay beyond the cavern. There was a symbol there, a spiral within a square.

I looked at Lyle.

"The Aztecs regarded the spiral as a symbol of progression and change," he said, handing me the page. "Letting go and surrendering ourselves so that we may become enlightened. The square represents the material world that exists about us, the elemental forces of nature—earth, air, fire, and water. The inscribed spiral, as you see here, is a mystical symbol that represents the path leading from the material world into the divine." Lyle's eyes widened, his eyebrows rising high upon his forehead. "Each of the four pages contains the same inscribed spiral concealed somewhere within the pictorials. It may well have been what Mr Gillies was looking for when he removed these from the Codex."

I rifled through the pages. The old man was right: the design was on Quetzalcoatl's shield, and embroidered on the child's sash, and there—as Lyle handed me the last of the pages —in the illustration of the sacrificial ritual, embossed upon the alter on which the victim lay.

"*Tonatiuhtiz*," Lyle said, reading the title beneath the illustration. "*He will become as the sun*."

"This, this is the place I must find!" I said, tripping over my words with excitement. "The Divine Sage is here"—I pointed to the familiar figure in his purple cloak and headdress—"and Gillies said in his letter that he needed to be somewhere by the solstice. It has to be here, Father, this place where the ceremony was held."

I told Lyle what Gillies had said about the ceremony; how a Chosen One embarked on a dangerous quest. "If he survived the quest, the ceremony took place at noon on the solstice," I said. "Whereupon the Chosen One was sacrificed through a bite from the golden serpent." I tapped my finger on the snake that Topiltzin held aloft. "The golden serpent might be...it might be a vessel in which the sacred plant was administered, or even some sort of ceremonial piece."

"Or they might be one and the same," Lyle said, his eyes returning to the page. "Fray de Sahagún's Spanish account tells us that during *Tonatiuhtiz* the Chosen One is killed by a bite from a deadly snake." He then placed his finger beneath the words underscored on the Nahuatl side. "But here it reads: *He who consumes the golden serpent will know death and be liberated into light*."

"Consumes," I said. "The golden serpent is eaten?"

Lyle raised a snow-white eyebrow in my direction. "There are many words for death in Nahuatl, including death through sacrifice. Fray de Sahagún has quite deliberately written 'to *know* death,' and to know death might not mean dying in the physical sense, but to become enlightened, liberated into light. To become *as the sun*. Which ties in with the properties of the sacred plants—granting those who consumed them divine knowledge."

I was left somewhat confused by this. Had Lyle not just convinced me that the sacred plant was called pipiltzintzintli? All that about the Topiltzin, the child prince, being used to disguise the name of this plant.

"Are you suggesting there are two names for the same plant?"

"Often these sacred plants are prepared in a special way before they are consumed," he said. "Either because they are poisonous, or because the potent effects will not be released without other essential ingredients. The name of the preparation can be different to the name of the plant." He pointed to the illustration. "Notice how Topiltzin, the Divine Sage, is holding the golden serpent."

"Could it represent the fruit?" I suggested. "The flower might be purple, and the berries golden?"

Lyle beamed at me. "Yes. Yes, I like that."

But then the old man's face softened, and a look of concern filled his eyes. "Have you considered..." He hesitated, and seemed to deliberate for a moment as to whether he should continue. "The letter written by Mr Gillies... His conviction that you are the essential element in his quest."

"What of it?" I said, taking out the letter again.

"He mentions premonitions."

"I do not believe in such things," I said, somewhat dismissively, as I reread Gillies's letter to Sir Walter.

"And the alignment of coincidence," Lyle went on. "Is that not what we are witnessing here, this day? I have not made the journey to the port for nearly three months, yet my visit could not have been more timely for you. It is as if our paths were destined to cross."

I looked up from the letter. "I am not quite sure what you are implying, Father."

"Things are not always what they seem," Lyle said, his eyes meeting mine with a steely gaze. "We see the world as cause and effect, but where destiny is concerned, the rule is reversed. The effect is written first, and the cause emerges as a trail of choices and coincidences that lead the way." The old man turned his gaze once more to the sun hanging in the belfry. "If Mr Gillies has the seer's gift, he may have foreseen what he calls his *untimely demise*. And he may also know something about your destiny, Captain, which you have yet to discover for yourself."

TWENTY-FOUR

Tepic, Mexico, 6th June 1822

THE CHILD IS KEPT SAFE BY HIS DIVINE MOTHER, SHE WILL SHOW THE WAY

THE TREE THAT SUSTAINS ALL LIFE HAS ROOTS LEADING INTO THE UNDERWORLD

IN TEZCATLIPOCA'S KINGDOM, THE STARS FOREVER SHINE IN THE ETERNAL NIGHT.

LET QUETZALCOATL'S LIGHT BE YOUR GUIDE THROUGH THE DARKNESS

HE WHO CONSUMES THE GOLDEN SERPENT WILL KNOW DEATH AND BE LIBERATED INTO LIGHT.

IN GOOD WEATHER, the journey up the Mexican coast from Acapulco to San Blas would take no more than three weeks; but by the time we had set sail, it was late April, and the stormy season had settled in. Though the sun would rise each morning into a promising blue sky, by midday the skies were inevitably filled with thick, grey cumulus clouds, and the winds would become scattered and difficult to harness. On some days, the weather broke in the afternoon and the rain fell in heavy sheets that soaked us to the skin and left us thoroughly miserable. On other days, when the clouds remained, we would instead face a stifling humidity that persisted well into the night and afforded us little sleep.

This sullen and frustrating weather persisted for six long weeks as we clawed our way up the last five hundred miles of coastline. With every day that passed, I became increasingly worried that my chances of finding Gillies in Tepic were slipping away. Wherever he was headed, he intended to be there by the summer solstice. The news from Captain Morris that Gillies was last seen talking to the captain of a whaling ship, together with an indication in the stolen pages that Topiltzin fled east across the water, left me quite certain that Gillies was headed out to sea: to an island, I suspected. I had of course thoroughly scrutinised the charts on board the *Conway*, but they contained little detail of the surrounding ocean save for a few islands just off the Mexican coast from San Blas. There could be dozens more that had been omitted, not to mention all the uncharted islands that lay as yet undiscovered by cartographers. And on top of all that, how could I possibly get out to this island by the solstice without abandoning my duties? There was a million pounds worth of gold and silver waiting for me in Tepic!

It was not until the morning of the sixth of June that the *Conway* sailed into the tranquil bay of San Blas—and with little over a fortnight until the solstice, I could afford to lose no more time in finding Gillies. Having secured the ship, I dispatched orders for a boat to take me ashore and informed the officers that I would be away for several days.

The residents of San Blas had never seen an English merchant ship of the *Conway*'s stature arrive in their port, and the wharfs were filled with people eager to sell their wares and exchange news with us. Among the clamouring crowd, a British official was waiting for me with further instructions from the Admiralty. A guide had already been organised to take me to Tepic, which was a day and a half's ride inland. There was, however, some delay as my horse was being shod by the farrier, and I seized the opportunity to talk with the sailors on the wharf. "Has anyone seen or heard of a man named John Gillies?" I asked. "Sickly looking gentleman, with bushy whiskers and tight curly hair. Walked with a cane." "Might have been looking for a ship to take him out to sea."

My enquiries were met with apologetic smiles, shrugged shoulders, and shakes of the head. Nobody recalled having seen such a man.

The town of San Blas sat perched on a nearby rock face, which rose a hundred feet or more out of the nearby swampy plain. It was little more than a collection of narrow streets and houses, with a small church and a central plaza. No bustling marketplace or street sellers, no merchants running out into the street to greet me—as was usually the case. The townsfolk were polite enough when I spoke to them, though it was clear they cared little about the ships that came and went from the harbour. These people were the day labourers and fishermen: the merchants all lived in the city. I began again with my enquiries—but no, nobody had seen or heard of a man matching Gillies's description.

I thus decided to continue on to Tepic that same day. The

ride took me first across the misty mangrove swamps before climbing steadily on a track through dense jungle. Slender trees raced up from the tangle of lush, wet undergrowth, their branches hanging with pendulous creepers that moved gracefully in the breeze. Now and then, I passed through a village of cane huts and the muddy children would run giggling alongside my horse.

A halfway house was located in a larger settlement on the other side of the forest. I had intended to stop here only to take supper, but fell in with an English party on their way to the port who advised me against continuing after nightfall, as the path traversed a high ridge. Although my guide seemed rather ambivalent towards their concerns, I decided to take their advice and stay in one of the rooms, rising at daybreak to continue on my way. The morning ride was a steep ascent up the mountainside, and I reached the ridge just as the sun rose over a distant mountain, spilling its golden light into the valley below. The ride along this spectacular edge was exhilarating; the world about me seemed boundless, and I was filled with a sense of tremendous privilege.

By the time I began the descent down the mountain track, it was late afternoon. The rooftops and smoking chimney pots of Tepic were clearly visible on the valley floor, wrapped in the coils of a meandering river. The clouds were gathering steadily overhead, darkening by degrees as I crossed the cultivated plain upon which the city had been built, and as I rode into town the heavens opened in a torrential downpour. In spite of the deluge, I splashed through the tree-lined streets, enjoying the experience. The city was quite beautiful in the rain, all emptied of life. The parks and garden were bursting with flowers, and majestic churches and government buildings lined the river.

News of the *Conway*'s arrival had already arrived in Tepic, and I spent the afternoon drying off in the residence of a local dignitary while the merchants and government officials came and went, leaving their documents in an ever-growing pile. The Mexican gold we were to transport back to England would be used to purchase goods for the purpose of trade. I was informed it would take three days for all the necessary arrangements to be made and paperwork to be signed.

Which meant I had seventy-two hours to track down John Gillies.

In the days that followed, I was unable to escape from official business during daylight hours, but made my excuses when it came to the evening entertainment. Wandering through the busy night markets and dropping by the taverns, I asked around for information on Gillies. Finally, late into the second night, I discovered the inn where he had been staying. The landlord was a burly, unwashed sort, and no sooner had I spoken the name John Gillies than his face darkened.

"He still owes me a week's rent," the man said, scowling. "Disappeared in the dead of night a month ago, leaving half his belongings—worthless as they are."

Having pacified the man by paying the money that was due, with a little extra for the inconvenience, I enquired as to what Gillies had left behind.

"A pile of old clothes and some pictures," he said with a dismissive shrug.

When I asked if I could take a look at the pictures, the innkeeper agreed and went to fetch them. I recognised all three as he handed them to me, one by one.

There was the fanciful sketch of the *Conway*, navigating Cape Horn under the watchful eye of Quetzalcoatl, the Plumed Serpent.

Then there was the portrait of Legge. I had forgotten how lifelike it was—how his eyes seemed to shine that alluring and translucent blue despite it being a charcoal drawing.

And then there was the dark sketch of the man in chains, the man Gillies told me he had met in a dream.

Sensing that he might be in possession of something valuable, the innkeeper snatched the sketches from my hand. "These are now my property," he said. "But they are for sale, and I shall sell them to you at a good price."

The price he offered was ludicrous, and my poor attempts at bargaining fell on deaf ears. In the end, I bought only the portrait of Legge. Had he known it, I would have paid any amount of money for this, every note in my pocketbook. Placing the sketch carefully in my saddlebag, I decided that I would hang it on my cabin wall, where it would serve as a reminder of the day we arrived in the port: that glorious morning of the swimming race, when I watched him leap from the channel board and splash across the bay, running naked onto the beach with his arms in the air.

During the night, the rain fell heavily. In the confines of my small room, which leaked water from the ceiling, I studied the pages of the Codex by candlelight. I knew the five underscored lines of Nahuatl by heart, but as much as I recited them aloud and studied the illustrations alongside each one, I felt no closer to finding the golden serpent. I found myself thinking about the Spanish sea captain that Gillies spoke of, the one he said had gone in search of Topiltzin's tomb around Bernardino de Sahagún's time and failed to find it. According to Gillies, the mariner had become acquainted with Fray de Sahagún in Tepic. Was that why Gillies wanted to come here? Was there something in Tepic that he needed to find out? Something I needed to find out too?

When morning came, I rode to the military fort on the outskirts of the city. My intention was to look at the naval records dating back to the late sixteenth century, when Bernardino de Sahagún had been alive. Having negotiated access to the library, I returned later that evening once my duties were finished for the day. A soldier greeted me at the entrance and escorted me down a rabbit warren of corridors. Upon entering the library, he lit the oil lamps and then left me in peace to peruse the bookshelves, which filled the walls from floor to ceiling.

There was no ordering system to speak of, the books having been placed on the shelves in a somewhat haphazard fashion— and apart from that, I was not entirely sure what I was looking for. In the hours that followed, I climbed up and down the ladder, reading the titles embossed on the spines, pulling a book out now and then to blow the dust from its cover and skim through the pages. As the grandfather clock in the corner of the room began chiming eleven, I came across a book on islands in the East Pacific, which was published in 1623. Casting my eye down the index at the back of the book, I was thrilled to see the name *Captain Martín Yañez de Armida*, which I instantly recognised as the name of the mariner Gillies spoke of.

Turning hurriedly to the page in question, I read the short paragraph on Yañez. It said that in 1608 the captain embarked on a voyage to an uninhabited volcanic island called Santo Tomas. Yañez was in possession of ancient maps and believed the island was originally called the Island of the Divine Shepherdess, as named by the early natives of the country who had travelled some three hundred or more miles out to sea on a raft. On his return, Yañez renamed the island Isla Socorro, after the Divine Shepherdess of the Catholic Church.

And there was a footnote:

* La Virgen del Perpetuo Socorro, the Virgin of Perpetual Help, is a title given to the Virgin Mary as depicted in the Hodegetria, the popular icon in which the Holy Mother gestures to her son as the Way.

My heart leapt. Returning to the bookshelves, I searched madly for a book on Christian art and, finding one, ran my finger down the index until I came to the word *Hodegetria*, then turned quickly to the relevant page.

My eyes fell upon an image that was all too familiar. It was a depiction of the Madonna and Child that I had seen many times in paintings, murals, and stained glass windows: the Holy Virgin cradling the infant Christ in one arm while gesturing to him with her other hand, her head tilted lovingly in his direction.

I had seen this somewhere else.

Unfolding the pages from the codex, I sought out the illustration of the mother and child. Yes, I was right—the same tilt of the head, the same gesture towards the infant, and the Nahuatl text underscored next to the image.

The child is kept safe by his divine mother, she will show the way.

Isla Socorro, the island of the Virgin Mary—she who shows the way. I had found the island!

Now I just had to find out where Isla Socorro was. The library contained several detailed charts of Mexico, and I rolled one out across the table. Holding the candle over the chart, I surveyed the waters of the North Pacific Ocean.

And there it was, four hundred miles southwest of the mainland. The tiny island I was looking for.

TWENTY-FIVE

San Blas, Mexico, 15th June 1822

WE WERE READY TO DEPART. The *Conway* sat low in the water, her belly filled with gold and silver to the value of a million pounds. With such an amount of treasure on board, I stationed two men on guard at the hatchway to the hold. The hatch itself was securely locked, and I remained in possession of the only key.

Having completed the final checks, I returned to the main deck to see the last of the provisions hauled up over the bulwarks: crates of squealing pigs and clucking chickens, barrels of ale, salted meats, sacks of flour. The sky was leaden and a strong northwester blew in from the sea, flapping the sails wildly as they were hoisted aloft. It was certainly not the best of days for sailing; the wind would carry us south, but we would be pushed constantly back towards the coast. In order to catch the trade winds to Cape Horn, we needed to cut our way some distance out west.

At least, that was what I told the crew.

Isla Socorro was too remote and insignificant to appear on the charts I kept on board the *Conway*, but I knew exactly where it lay and plotted a course that would take us there. By my estimation, we would reach the island in three days—or quicker, if the weather turned in our favour. I informed the *Conway*'s officers, in a casual way, that I was eager to conduct an additional experiment on the invariable pendulum. I said that I had located an island that might be suitable—omitting to say its name—if the winds took us in that direction. We would not stay there for long, I told them, perhaps a couple of days at most. Enough time to conduct a short exploration and take a few recordings.

Enough time, I secretly hoped, to find the golden serpent.

Unfortunately, rather than an improvement in the weather, we were to witness the strong winds worsening as the day continued. By late afternoon, a dense bank of clouds marked the horizon. The storm came that evening with great force, and for the entire night, the sea had us at its mercy. With the bowsprit swinging like the needle on a compass, and the waves crashing over the bulwarks from every direction, it became impossible to maintain a steady course. I remained at the helm throughout the night, refusing to give in, gripping the wheel and bellowing out commands through sheets of rain. I was not about to let this tempest shatter my hopes of finding the island, not after I had come this far. The island was out there in the raging sea, and I *would* find it.

The malevolent weather finally yielded at daybreak, but still the sky remained obscured by a blanket of thick, grey cloud. There was no telling how far we had been swept from our bearings or in which direction—and if that was not dismal enough, I was suffering from a dreadful headache.

I struggled through the day, short-tempered and irritable. When the storm came back for a second night, my temper blackened further still. Striding back and forth on the deck, I belted out orders in the torrential rain, yelling at the men if they slipped and fell, if they were too slow to catch a loose line, if they misheard my commands, if a sail was torn. Every crack of thunder worsened my headache. The bright flashes of lightning tore through my eyeballs and left me groping for the handles on the wheel, half-blinded. As the hours passed during that wild and tempestuous night, my bitter mood turned all the more morose. By now, we could be a hundred or more miles off course. Damn the cursed weather!

Ordering the crew to keep the *Conway* against the wind, I returned to my cabin and slammed the door. The sea still heaved outside my window and the cabin lights swung overhead. Sitting down to a plate of the cook's stew, and holding onto my whiskey glass to stop it from sliding across the table, I listened to the tireless creaking and yawning of the ship.

My head was pounding. I could not recall ever having such a headache. I drained my whiskey, hoping it might numb the throbbing pain. As I was refilling my glass, there was a knock at the door.

"George—good," I said, opening the door to see Birnie standing there. I had quite forgotten having sent for him.

The doctor came inside and glanced around at the mess.

"It is this blinding headache," I said, returning to my whiskey and knocking it back in one go. "I need something to ease the pain."

Birnie frowned. "How long have you had it?"

"Two days solid."

"You look washed out." Resting his thumb above my eye, he pulled up my eyelid. "Look up. All right. Now look down." He raised my chin with his hand. "Open wide. Tongue out." He then felt my pulse, nodded to himself, placed his hand on my forehead. "Have you been feeling feverish?"

"A little, yes."

"Anything else?"

"Restless, I suppose. I am finding it difficult to concentrate."

His eyes fell on my empty glass. "You should stay off that stuff. Drink water, and plenty of it."

"It is probably just lack of sleep," I said dismissively.

"Even so, the alcohol will—"

"Less of your nagging, George," I snapped. "Do you have something for this headache or not? Bring me some laudanum."

Birnie looked offended. "I'm not *nagging*," he said, glancing at the cabin door. "I'll go and get my blood-letting implements. We should try to relieve the pressure behind your eyes first."

"All right. Yes. Whatever you say." I rubbed my temples, then released a sigh. "And I apologise for being so ill-tempered. It is just this relentless weather—and this damned headache."

"Get some rest," the doctor said. "I'll be back soon."

I ushered him out and closed the door, then went to fetch the whiskey bottle.

There was a loud crack of thunder. The ship rolled suddenly, causing me to pour the whiskey over the back of my hand. My dinner plate slid from the table and smashed on the floor.

"To hell with this tempest!" I yelled, and in a fit of rage hurled the whiskey bottle at the wall. It shattered, sending shards of glass everywhere. The ship lurched again, and I lost my balance, landing on my hands and knees. I felt a stabbing pain in my hand—a piece of glass was lodged in my palm. Gritting my teeth, I pulled it out, and watched a rivulet of blood trickle from my hand.

"Damn you!" I shouted. "Damn you to hell!"

The ship rocked violently and one of the cabin windows flew open to the night. The wind howled into the room and the rain poured in and drenched the seating. Clambering to my feet, I made my way to the window and stared into the darkness. The swell surged and fell in giant crests of white foam. Forks of lightning tore across the sky.

"You have won!" I yelled into the storm. "I am beaten, do you hear? Keep your damned island, keep your damned golden snake! I want no more of this curse!" All at once I felt a maddening need to be free of the stolen pages, as if they were the very cause of the violent weather, and my violent headache. Were they not responsible for the entire unravelling of my life? Everything was fine before I had set eyes on the damned things! I should never have taken a step into Gillies's lodgings that day. I should have let the man die on the frozen deck that night—then all this would not be happening. Charles would still be alive. We would not be lost at sea in this damned storm, and I would not be endangering my ship for a promise I had not a hope in hell of keeping. The pages were a curse and I wanted them gone, destroyed forever. I would toss them out of the window and watch the heaving sea swallow them up!

Staggering back across the cabin against the corkscrewing of the ship, I pulled open the drawer of my bureau. As I reached for the pages, however, I caught sight of the charcoal sketch of Legge lying beside them. I took it out instead.

The sight of the lieutenant's gentle eyes and handsome face made my heart sink.

"I have failed you, Charles," I said, my voice breaking.

"The golden serpent is lost to us. I tried, but it is no use. I am sorry. I am so sorry."

Legge gazed up from the page, his eyes reassuring me, his lips holding the traces of a smile. *There is still time*, he seemed to be saying. *All is not yet lost. Weather the storm. There is still time.*

Slipping the picture back into the drawer, I walked over to the mirror. Ever since the lieutenant's death, I had forgone my old routine of observing my reflection as a way to compose and distance myself. Looking now, I saw that I was older. I looked weary. My eyes carried dark bruises beneath them, and the wrinkles in their corners had deepened considerably. I caught sight of a few grey hairs poking from my beard, and when I tugged at one, it refused to yield.

An almighty crack of thunder then broke through the night, and with the flash of lightning that followed I felt a searing pain shoot through my temples. I clenched my teeth and stifled a groan, pressing my hands onto my eyes. Oily pools of colour swirled before me, and when I removed my hands, the colours remained, obscuring my vision.

Holding onto the back of a chair, I blinked heavily and waited for my sight to clear. When it did, my blood ran cold at what I saw. It was my reflection in the mirror: my hair had thinned considerably and was as white as snow. And my face... It looked haggard and drawn, as if I had aged thirty years or more! Struck with terror, I stared at this aged version of myself while he stared back at me through confused and watery eyes. Behind my reflection, the furnishings of the cabin had vanished. The room he stood in was stark and white.

I shut my eyes tightly, counting each breath, waiting for the delirium to pass. Because that was all it was, I told myself, just a moment of delirium—and when I looked back into the mirror,

I saw with tremendous relief that I was myself again. The chairs and dining table of the cabin were reflected behind me, the ceiling lamp swinging overhead, the cabin window opening and closing as the ship rocked.

And yet I did not feel right.

My arms and legs carried a dull ache. Glancing down at my hands, I saw that they bore thick blue veins and the creases of age. My mouth felt dry and chalky. What was happening to me? And the room... Turning around sharply I realised that I now stood in the white room, barefoot, and dressed in a night-gown. There was a narrow bed in one corner, and a writing desk. The window looked out onto a tidy lawn with gravel paths and a stone statue.

I was inside the mirror!

Confused and panic-stricken, I ran to the door and tugged at the handle—it was locked. Banging on the door with my fist, I cried out for help. When nobody came, I kicked the handle violently until at last it flew open. I entered the dark passage-way, stumbling into a space surrounded by ladders and open to the elements. I was back on board the ship, on the gun deck beneath the main hatch, the rain falling in torrents from above. Through the hatch, I could see the mast swinging back and forth, and caught sight of a shadowy creature running across the yardarm. I watched it slide down the sail, ripping the canvas with its talons.

Reeling backwards in shock, I slipped and fell on the deck.

Grotesque figures emerged from the dark corners of the gun deck. They moved towards me, staring vacantly with their lifeless eyes, their faces distorted by wicked smiles.

"Get away!" I yelled with all my might. "Get away from me!"

The pressure inside my head was unbearable. I gripped my

hair, as if doing so might stop the crushing pain. The ghoulish figures surrounded me. I began flailing helplessly as dozens of hands gripped my limbs, their voices muted and incoherent. I struggled and kicked, but they held me fast. There was nothing I could do, not a chance of escape—and yet I kicked and fought for my life as the world about me faded away.

TWENTY-SIX

HMS *Conway*, North Pacific Ocean, 18th June 1822

A BRIGHT FLAME tore through the darkness. Shielding my eyes, I caught a brief glimpse of my surroundings before the light went out: barrels of powder, a workbench, carpentry tools fixed to the wall. I could hear the rhythmical clanking of the bilge pumps, the acrid stench of tar burnt my nostrils. Where was I? In the hold somewhere? In one of the storerooms?

Someone was with me in the darkness. He cleared his throat.

"Who's there?" I called out. My mouth was parched, my voice dry and lacking strength. "Why am I down here?"

There was silence for a while, then the sound of a match being struck. The dazzling flame returned, and this time it rose up and lit the tip of a cigarette. I made out a stubbled chin and thin lips.

"Kindly tell me what the devil…" As I moved my legs to stand up, I felt something sharp bite into my ankles and heard the rattle of chains against the deck. I continued in my attempt to scramble to my feet, but the man stepped towards me and his boot collided with my chest, taking the wind out of my lungs and knocking me to the floor.

"Stay down," he said in a foreign accent.

I was clamped in leg irons! My mind reeled as I took stock of my situation. Why was I was being held prisoner on board my ship? Still nauseous and confused, I struggled to remember what I could: there was the storm, and I retreated to my cabin with a blinding headache. Birnie came. And then what? Had I fallen asleep? Lost consciousness? I remembered seeing my aged reflection in the mirror, and then that white room.

And now here I was, chained up in the hold. Had pirates or privateers captured us during the night? I fought to stay calm. I had to think clearly.

"Who are you?" I called out. "What is it you want?"

A bright orange spot glowed in the darkness as the man drew on his cigarette.

"You are in something of a predicament, are you not, Captain?"

"Stop lurking in the shadows," I demanded. "Reveal yourself, you coward."

With the burning end of his cigarette, the man lit the wick of a lantern sitting on the workbench. The pale yellow light flooded the storeroom, and I saw then what a miserable state I was in—stripped to my underclothes and breeches, my shirt filthy, my ankles raw and bruised from the rusty leg irons.

A tall, lean-faced man with a crooked nose returned my gaze. I recognised him. He was one of the new sailors we had taken on board in Lima—the new cook.

MUTINY! The word echoed in my mind as I sat sucking in the rancid air in shock. *There has been a mutiny!* It must be the gold, a million pounds worth down here in the hold—the mutineers were going to steal it.

"There is not a chance you will get away with this," I said, keeping my voice as steady and composed as I could, despite the turmoil that was rising inside me. "The Admiralty will not rest until they catch every last one of you, and recover every ounce of gold taken from this ship."

To which the man laughed haughtily. "The *Admiralty* is to hear about a captain who was chained up like a beast for the safety of his crew. A foolish captain who took part in black magic and lost his mind. Several of your crew will bear witness to how they found you drooling and speaking in tongues in the hut of a native witch. And they will all remember this very night, when you went mad during the storm."

"You will hang for this," I hissed.

"You are not listening," the man replied, quite calmly. "There is no mutiny. The *Conway*'s captain has lost his mind." He sucked on his cigarette. "But we are fortunate. The first lieutenant has taken command."

Wollaton. Was he the leader of this?

"Mr Wollaton has neither the skill nor the brains to command this ship," I said sharply. "Let alone escape the fleet of ships that will come after you. You have made a terrible mistake listening to the plotting and conniving of that incompetent fool. Mark my words, you will be caught and hanged."

"Still you do not listen," my jailer cut in, casually admiring his fingernails. "And perhaps you underestimate your lieutenant. As post-captain, he will receive ten thousand pounds for transporting the gold back to England. The Admiralty will have not a thing but praise for his efforts. In all likelihood, he will receive a promotion." An ugly smirk grew across his lips. "Perhaps they will make him commander of this very ship."

"A ship's captain cannot be declared unfit to sail without the written consent of the ship's surgeon," I snapped, challenging him with a stare. "Where is Mr Birnie?"

The man picked up the lantern, holding the light high above his head as if to further intimidate me by revealing the hopeless predicament I was in. "We are less than a day's sail from Isola Socorro," he said. "A fortuitous opportunity presents itself, do you not think?"

He knew about the island. Did the mutineers intend to bury a portion of the gold there and transport the rest back to England? In my weak state of mind, I remained bewildered and confused. And who were *they*? How many of the crew were involved in this mutinous act?

"You have kept me alive," I said, desperately trying to regain control of my wits. "There must be a reason."

"You may still be of use," he replied. "Although I am not so sure. You do not strike me as a man who likes to cooperate, nor one that I can trust." He lowered the lantern. "And besides that, I have what I want now. It is merely my natural inquisitiveness that draws me to Isola Socorro—which you so conveniently marked on your charts. We can afford a few days looking for the treasure, but if I return without it then no matter. I still get my pay. I am not a greedy man."

Isola Socorro. My mind was racing. *Isola*, not the Spanish *Isla*...

The man was Italian! The intruder who ransacked my cabin and then escaped through the window, leaving his accomplice stone dead on the floor. One of the "hounds" who had come after Gillies. Now he was on board my ship masquerading as the cook, joining forces with Wollaton to incite mutiny—and no doubt the pages were already in his possession.

He raised his cigarette for another puff. "So...are you a man who likes to cooperate, or no?"

"You will get not a thing from me," I seethed, gritting my teeth.

The Italian regarded me calmly through his narrow, deceitful eyes. "We shall see."

Turning on his heel, he made for the door.

Enshrouded once again in darkness, the reality of my desperate situation set in. My ship was embroiled in a mutiny, and I had been played for a fool. How could I hope to convince the crew that I was not insane, when I was chained up like this in the hold? The Italian would continue to poison their minds with his venomous tongue—and no doubt Wollaton too. My blood boiled to think of the dour Yorkshireman standing at the helm, all sly and supercilious.

Where was Birnie in all this? Surely he would never fall for such a lie without insisting on seeing me? Had they disposed of him? The thought depressed me terribly. They needed the doctor to sign the declaration committing me unfit to command, but what then? I prayed that he was still alive up there.

In a fit of desperation, I began shouting for help. I shouted and shouted until my voice became hoarse, proclaiming myself of sound mind, proclaiming the crew had been tricked, proclaiming the cook was an imposter—but no answer to my cries ever came.

Throughout the long hours that followed, I staved off the feelings of panic and despair looming in the darkness by concentrating on the movement of the ship. *I am still the captain*, I told myself again and again. *The crew will come to their senses and see they have been lied to. They will start asking questions soon enough. Aye, someone will come.*

I just had to stay alert. Remain calm. Someone would come and rescue me.

Tuning my senses to the creaking and straining of the hull, I focused on gauging our trajectory across the ocean. We were maintaining a steady course now. Over the hours that passed, I kept track of the time by listening out for the dull clang of the ship's bell ringing the change of watch. Shortly after this, I would hear footsteps crossing the deck above me, followed by a second set of footsteps retracing the same path: the men guarding the hatch were changing over.

An entire day passed, and not a soul came down to the hold. The feelings of anxiousness and despair, which had now firmly taken root, were interspersed with fits of anger, where-upon I would yell curses into the darkness. As for the ship, I had at some point in the night or day—I knew not which it was —stopped following our course, although it was apparent that for quite some time the *Conway* had been losing speed. The wind was losing strength. Perhaps on account of this, the heat in the storeroom was rising steadily. I sat drenched in sweat and with a raging thirst. How much longer would I last without water? Perhaps a day at most?

As the hours drifted on, I began lapsing in and out of sleep, waking with a jolt to find myself trapped in the same, stifling darkness. I fought to keep myself awake by reciting verses I knew—Shakespeare, Lord Byron, and poems by my friend Walter Scott—but soon the words began to swim inside my head. Nauseous with dehydration, I lay on my back, tormented by the drip-dripping of water as condensation fell from the wooden beams in the darkness above me. As the *Conway* continued to slow by steady degrees, the temperature in the storeroom became ever more oppressive, until even the rats that scurried invisibly about me seemed to give in to lethargy.

I fell asleep, and found myself standing in my mother's bedchamber, in the house where I was born. The bed curtains were drawn, tied to their corners with lengths of platted rope. Sunlight poured in through two large windows, which looked out over the kitchen garden.

An attractive brass telescope with a polished fruitwood barrel sat on the windowsill. I picked it up and peered through the glass eye. On the other side of the garden lay a grassy paddock where two boys played by a horse pond, their shirts hung upon a nearby post. They were dragging a makeshift raft from the boat shed on the eastern side of the pond. Clambering over the gunwale, the two lay side by side on their raft, their hands clasped together as it drifted across the water.

Before the dream could unfold any further, I awoke. Staring into the darkness, I realised that I had long forgotten that day. The other boy was Robert, the son of a carpenter. He was a year younger than I was, an energetic, romping boy with thick black hair and deep green eyes—and taller than I by several inches. I remembered that day so clearly now. He and I, on that little raft, laughing and giggling in the sunshine. It was the first unalloyed happiness I had ever known.

But we had been watched by my father, from the very window where I stood now. And later that evening, I had peered through the crack in the library door to see my father pacing the room while my mother sat in a chair, sobbing. I never saw Robert again. I never went back to the horse pond and played on that raft. And when the summer was over, I packed my sea chest and said goodbye to my past.

I had shut that day away. Closed and locked the door, never daring to return. Yet now the door was flung open, and I remembered the happy child that I was: lying upon that raft with my heart so buoyant.

I lay there with tears filling my eyes.

Then, as my attention slowly returned to my surroundings, it struck me that something was odd about the silence in the storeroom. The bilge pumps had stopped clanking, but it was not only that—I was unable to hear the ocean. Not a creak from the ship. We were not moving.

I realised the cruel fate that must have befallen us. We had sailed into the doldrums, the menacing calms that plague the equatorial waters and could hold a ship for days, if not weeks. Up on the sweltering deck there would be not a breath of wind. The *Conway* would be sitting upon a sea that was as smooth as glass; her sails hanging limp against the masts, the portholes flung open to the heat. And with not a thing to do, the men would be slumped against the bulwarks mopping their brows, or dragging their feet listlessly about the deck, gazing out over the railings at a watery world as still and silent as a painting.

The *Conway* was stuck fast.

And here I sat in chains. A prisoner on my own ship.

Then all at once it came back to me: the sketch Gillies had drawn, the desperate man, sitting in the darkness with his head bowed low.

It was I.

I began to laugh through my aching teeth. "Can you see me now, John Gillies?" I called out, imagining him lying on the frozen deck with Birnie, Legge, and I crouched over him, the ghostly aurora dancing in the night sky over our heads. "Am I to die here in this sweltering cell? Is this what you saw? Is that what you saw, John Gillies?"

The last rasps of laughter left my lungs and I lay back upon the boards, utterly spent. Closing my eyes, I let in the delirium I had fought so many hours to resist.

In the dream that enveloped me, I was a boy once again,

standing on the wharfs at Liverpool docks with the enormous wooden hull of a ship looming behind me. Seagulls were crying and circling overhead. The wharfs were crowded with sailors slapping one another on the back, some lumbering their sea chests, others helping to load the ship. There was a fair wind, and I held onto my cap as I clutched a leather bag of my belongings, with my own small sea chest at my feet.

My father stood in front of me. He was an awkward, rangy man, and wore a black coat and black hat. He looked nervous, glancing up at the ship as it rocked restlessly on the tide, tugging against the ropes that bound it to the quay. I watched him take a deep breath, exhaling the air slowly through his pursed lips.

"You will be well looked after," he said, reaching into his coat pocket and bringing out a package tied with string. "I have spoken at length with Captain Hughes. He seems a well-meaning fellow." He took another deep breath. "It is for the best, son. Someday you will understand."

Hearing my name being called, I turned to see a cheery-faced man with blonde hair striding towards us.

"Mr Basil Hall?" the man said again. When I nodded diligently, he continued, "Well then, we had best get you signed into the muster book before we set sail without you." He winked at my father.

"This is the first lieutenant, Mr Brownlee," Father said, smiling at the man. "He has promised to keep an eye on you, son. Listen to what he says."

The blue-eyed lieutenant ruffled my hair with his hand. "First voyage is always a little daunting, but you'll get used to it soon enough. There is freedom out there on the waves. And so much adventure as any boy dares dream of."

My father thrust the package into my hands. "It is a journal for you to write in," he told me. "It is not a gift; it is a responsibility. Observe without bias and write accurately without embellishments. Your duty is not to please, it is to educate. So, no silly flourishes, do you hear?"

The lieutenant and another sailor picked up my sea chest and carried it across to a pile of chests being hoisted on board.

"Goodbye, son," my father said, holding out his hand.

I wanted to give him a hug, but he did not hold himself in such a way as to be amenable to my affections.

So I shook his hand.

And with that, he turned and walked away.

TWENTY-SEVEN

HMS *Conway*, North Pacific Ocean, 20th June 1822

I CAME to my senses spluttering and coughing, with water spilling out from the corners of my mouth and dripping down my chin. The storeroom was once again lit by soft yellow lamplight, and the Italian was crouched in front of me, gripping my jaw with his hand as he held a flask to my lips. Someone else was behind me, propping me up.

I drank greedily and instinctively until the Italian snatched the flask away.

The leg irons were off, lying open at their rusty clasps on the floor, but my hands remained firmly tied behind my back. Glancing past the Italian, I saw Wollaton leaning against the open doorway, and a shorter man concealed in shadow behind him. The lieutenant's face wore the same snide, self-satisfied smirk I had seen so many times on deck—only this time, it was more belittling than ever.

Four shameful, duplicitous men. Were they the ringleaders of this mutiny?

"You are to accompany us to the island," the Italian said bluntly. "Should you try to cause a disturbance, I will not hesitate to kill you."

Stepping away from me, he stood with his arms folded. He had more to say, I could tell, and I bit down hard to hold back the curses on my tongue.

"Then you will take us to the treasure," he added.

I released a grunt, mocking his haughty demands. "And I suppose you will set me free after that?"

The Italian shook his head. "Three of your more loyal crew are bound and gagged down here in the hold. Should you make a fuss, I will give orders to have their throats slit, and yours after. Mr Birnie, for one, will be—"

"Leave Birnie out of this!" I shouted, struggling against the man who held me.

"Calm yourself, Captain." The Italian exchanged glances with Wollaton. "Mr Birnie will come to no harm if you agree to accompany us peacefully. But you *must* agree."

"I wish to see him first," I demanded, scrambling onto my knees, then to my feet. "I will not agree to a thing until I see that Birnie is still alive."

It was then that Wollaton took a step into the room. He stood for a moment with his hands in his pockets, idly kicking his heels against the deck as if he were contemplating something.

"See, if it were up to me, I'd have done away wi' you hours ago," he said, a grin slipping across his mouth. "But *this*... This makes it all worthwhile."

Striding forwards, he clasped me by the shoulders and spun me around.

Birnie was standing behind me. It was he who had been propping me up. And while I stood bewildered,

Wollaton leant close to my ear. "Mr Birnie looks alive enough to me."

"See here, I am fine, George," I said, seizing what might be my only chance to convince the doctor of my sanity. "Whatever sickness took me during the storm, it has passed. These men... they are deceiving you, they..."

But I saw it then: the hostility in Birnie's cold gaze, and in his rigid, unyielding stance. He was one of them. Birnie was one of the mutineers. The notion was so jarring that at first I just stared at the doctor in shock.

"You killed Charles," he said.

"What?"

"He was recovering. He would have lived."

"George, I—"

"I saw that bottle on the windowsill." Birnie's eyes narrowed behind his spectacles. "I know what you did. And why. You thought he might talk—to me, to others. Confess his sins on his deathbed."

"George!" I pleaded. "Charles was dying, you know he was. And the bottle, I..."

"My friend was murdered," Birnie said flatly. "And I've every intention of seeing his death avenged."

Before I had time to speak further, my mouth was gagged with a dirty rag. Wollaton tossed a sack over my head, and it was tied tight at my neck. While I struggled to breathe against the heavy cloth, the men continued to talk in whispers.

"Do not attempt anything foolish," the Italian said, as someone untied the cords that bound my wrists. Then, with a shove, I was made to walk forwards, and heard the storeroom door shut behind me.

I was taken across the hold, past the cages of animals in their pens: a goat was bleating, and there were sporadic clucks from the chickens. I thought about all the gold stacked nearby in the wooden chests. Gold that would be delivered to England along with a pack of well-rehearsed lies that would tarnish my name. The thought made me sick.

More whispers, and then the sound of bolts being drawn back, and the squeak of hinges. We had reached the hatch.

"Give me a reason to slice you open, an' I'll do it wi'out a second thought," Wollaton said, as my hands were placed on the rungs of the ladder. I felt the sharp end of a blade press into my back. "Now climb."

I clambered up the ladder and was pulled roughly through the hatch by the hands of another man. Another traitor. How many of my crew wanted me gone?

Standing in silence, I listened to the others coming through the hatch before it was bolted and locked. They led me across the orlop deck, and up the ladder to the lower gun deck. We walked past the rows of hammocks, past the ship's mess—and all the while I listened hard beyond the sound of my own laboured breathing. Where were the crew? There was not a sound but the boards creaking beneath our feet. Was it night? It felt like night. The heat must have drawn the men up onto the main deck to sleep against the bulwarks.

Upon reaching what I realised must be the companionway stairs, my mind began to race. We were going up onto the main deck. What should I do when we got there? Yell out? I climbed the stairs with my heart pounding in my chest and my body tense and alert. My face was dripping with sweat inside the sack.

I was led across the deck, aware of the eerie silence. Where were the men? Why did nobody speak out? All I needed was a sign, just a single friendly voice, and I would shout for help and struggle to break free.

We ascended the steps to the quarterdeck. Footsteps and whispers continued around me. I heard the heavy creaking of rope—the sound of the jolly boat being lowered on its davits. A hand gripped my shoulder and I felt the knife blade return to the small of my back.

"Move it," Wollaton growled.

Having guided me across a plank into the jolly, they tied my hands again and I was made to sit down on one of the wooden thwarts. Others joined me, and the boat descended towards the water, hitting the surface with a splash. I felt the gentle motion of the sea beneath us, followed by a more severe rocking to and fro as the men repositioned themselves and unfastened the cables. I heard the sound of their oars knocking against the ship's hull, levering us away. We drifted for a few moments, then came the squeaking of the oarlocks and the rhythmical splashing of the blades cutting into the water.

"Farewell, old ship," I whispered from inside the suffocating cloth sack.

It must have been a good hour before the men stopped rowing. The boat rocked again as they swapped places, and then at last the sack was pulled from my head.

I was sitting at the rear of the boat. The Italian sat on the thwart in front of me, holding a lantern in his hand. Four men were at the oars: Wollaton, who was stuffing his pipe with tobacco; Birnie, who gave me the briefest glance, then looked down at his feet; a skinny deckhand, whose name I could not recall; and the pig-eyed Mr Trickett, our Master at Arms.

Mutineers, the lot of them.

Only then did I take notice of the impenetrable fog surrounding the boat, concealing all but a few feet of black water beyond the gunwale. Closing my eyes, I let out a silent curse. My kidnappers must have stolen me across the deck in this shroud of fog. I should have called out when I had the chance.

It was too late now.

Trickett tore up a loaf of bread and handed it around to all except me. The same went for the supply of water: they swigged from their waterskins without offering me a drop. At length, the Italian untied the gag about my mouth. He sat watching me carefully as he chewed and swallowed.

"Did you drug me?" I asked, glaring at him. I had been thinking about the headaches and the delirium I suffered on the night of the storm, and how my being declared insane was central to their plot to take the ship. "Something in my food? Or was it in my drink?" I shot Birnie a black look. "Was it you, George?"

"If it had been up to me, I'd have made sure we used enough poison to kill you," Birnie replied, returning my stare with one equally hateful.

"What is the matter with you, man?" I started. "Hearing you talk with such venom and such...such disloyalty. It is *your* mind that is poisoned now, not mine. Poisoned by lies and bitterness and—"

"Enough!" the Italian broke in. "Or I shall return your head into this sack."

Another hour or more passed, and all the while I sat gazing blankly into the fog. It was as if we were rowing through some other realm, a place of limbo estranged from time; as if there was nothing at all beyond the mist, no ship from which we came, no vast expanse of sea, no stars above us. Just an infinite fog. And we would row on and on, with my thirst never quenched, and my sores never healing, the men never tiring at the oars, the flickering light of the lantern never failing. On and on, for all eternity...

My vision blurred and I must have blacked out and fallen from the thwart, as in the next moment I was being roughly shaken awake by the Italian. After that, he let me drink from his waterskin and fed me two dry biscuits to eat. I did not believe for an instant that this was an act of kindness; rather, it was to keep me alive and in such a state as to be useful. After all, if he had wanted to kill me, he could have tossed me overboard. I savoured this knowledge like I savoured the taste of the biscuits and the last traces of water on my tongue. Turning my gaze back into the fog, I felt my spirits revive a little.

The night did at last retreat, and morning came as a pale, pastel blue haze. The fog still clung to the boat, but the colour had returned to the water, and now and then I saw fish swimming about beneath the surface. It was good to see other forms of life.

"Eeeeaase up." Trickett brought his oar out of the water and placed his finger to his lips. "You hear that?"

The others lifted their oars, and as the boat slid silently across the water, I heard the sound of gulls circling somewhere overhead.

All eyes turned beyond the boat. Towering cliffs were materialising from the fog, rising up from the ocean, sheer and impenetrable like the battlements of a great city. Dozens of waterspouts emerged from the rock, making the island look as if it had surfaced from the depths, still dripping with water, like a giant sea monster whose slumber we had disturbed.

TWENTY-EIGHT

Isla Socorro, Mexico, 21st June 1822

THE MUTINEERS SKIRTED the island looking for a break in the cliffs: with the water being so eerily calm, there was no danger of our being capsized or dashed against the rocks. At length, we arrived at a narrow peninsula that jutted out into the sea. Here, the cliffs had eroded to form a natural arch and several tall stacks, the rocky pillars standing like sentinels in the turquoise water. Beyond these, I could see a shingle beach.

The four men at the oars steered the boat in the direction of the shore. As we drifted into the shallows, I could see the pebbles on the seabed, and silver fish darting to and fro in the water.

The Italian shifted his position and then held up his pistol.

"Out." He pointed the barrel at my forehead.

I clambered over the gunwale and stood waist-deep in the water. The mutineers promptly followed. While they manoeuvred the boat to the shore, I waded alongside them, gazing beyond the beach at the grassy landscape that rose up into the fog.

The mutineers dragged the jolly up onto the shingle. Though my body was primed with a fierce urge to flee, I fought against the temptation. I was still weak, and the only exit from the beach was via a steep bank at one end. And with my hands tied behind my back, any attempt to escape would be quickly thwarted.

Standing close to the water's edge, I listened to the rattling of the waves as they folded on the shingle. I knew I must wait, bide my time. If I could convince my captors to begin an exploration into the island, a better opportunity might present itself: then, if I could run fast enough, and far enough, I might stand a chance of making it into the fog.

It was not much of a plan, what with there being five of them, four of whom carried pistols—but at least it gave me hope. Somewhere out there in the fog lay the only thing that mattered to me now: the golden serpent.

A renewed sense of determination burned in the pit of my stomach.

I had to escape these men.

Meanwhile, the mutineers were preoccupied with sharing rations of food and swigging from their waterskins. The sight was hard to bear, not so much because I was myself ravenous and desperate for water, but rather because I was forced to watch Birnie standing there amongst these traitors. It became harder still when I saw Wollaton slap his back in a sickening display of camaraderie.

Sitting down on the pebbles, I turned my attention back to the ocean. I could hear the screeching of a gull, and moments later I caught sight of an albatross flying gracefully towards me. It glided to the beach with its great wings outstretched, landing on a rock a few feet away, whereupon it began preening its feathers.

The sight of the bird reminded me of the sorry little creature Legge had rescued on board the *Conway* all those months ago. I wondered if it had survived. Could this even be the same individual, all grown up?

I found myself swept into a vivid memory of Legge playing his fiddle in my cabin, while the young bird sat on the back of a chair, squawking along comically. We had both fallen into fits of laughter. How I missed that sound, the lieutenant's cheery laugh—it always seemed to me so innocent, so untroubled. I thought of the warm summer evening after the picnic party, when Legge and I had stood upon the wall at the bottom of the garden, listening to the distant chimes of the sunset oration while the sun melted upon the horizon, spilling a river of gold across the darkening sea. I reimagined our walk through the moonlit hills to the abandoned farmhouse, feeling again the thrill of that enchanted evening, and how we had leant against the crumbling wall inside the garden, swigging from the wine bottle, while all about us the night cicadas chirped their song.

Drunk and happy as lords, we had stripped off our clothes and run about naked, whooping and laughing with not a care in the world. I caught him, and after we fell into the soft grass there came that unbridled moment in which I suddenly dared to kiss his mouth. I remembered the burning desire that coursed through my veins as our bodies intertwined, and how I climbed onto him, pinning his arms over his head. The way his pale white chest was flushed red with passion.

I would never forget the look in his eyes, nor his beautiful smile.

Next to me, the albatross had stopped preening itself. Cocking its head, it regarded me with its black pearl of an eye.

"I have been such a fool," I said. "Tell him I remember it all. Tell him that if ever I have been free in my life, truly free, it was on that night."

The bird opened its bright yellow beak and let out a shrill cry.

I turned to look up the beach. Trickett was loading his gun with powder.

"Go, before they shoot you." I kicked the shingle with my boot. Spreading its impressive wings, the albatross sprang into the air and flew away.

The Italian strode across the beach. He stood in front of me for a while with his hands on his hips. Then, crouching down, he fed me some water. I managed a few mouthfuls before he snatched the waterskin away.

"If you wish to stay alive, you must lead us to the treasure," he said.

I looked him square in the eye. "You intend to kill me. Why should I care about living for a few more hours?"

The Italian's brow creased into a frown while he thought. "If we find the gold, then you will be set free on this island," he said. "I shall inform the crew that we left you here because it was too dangerous to keep you on board with your madness."

"That seems something of a risk," I said. "What if I am rescued?"

He rose back to his feet, reattaching the skin to his belt. "Your men do not know the name of this island, nor where it is. And when the *Conway* returns to England with all its gold on board, I doubt the Admiralty will waste time searching the seas for a disgraced captain who lost his mind and is most likely to be dead."

"What cause do I have to trust your word?" I said. "You are a mercenary and a liar by trade."

The Italian laughed. "Perhaps you think me a mercenary, Captain, but I do not see it so. I see myself as a merchant, just like you. I obtain goods that others want, and I sell them at a price." He opened his coat so as to show me the stolen pages poking from his pocket. "Important men are willing to pay a lot of money for these."

"And even more for the treasure itself," I said, second-guessing his intention. "Though it is quite clear you were told very little about what this treasure is."

"Neither do I care," he replied, though I saw his shoulders tighten.

"I am right, am I not?" I said, goading him. "Whoever hired you instructed you to retrieve the pages, but refrained from telling you *why* they were so important. Not that I blame them —they must have known what a cold-blooded reptile you are."

"My employers are wealthy men," he said. "When it comes to getting what they want, money is no obstacle to them. They will pay me well for retrieving the pages, and a hundred times more if I bring home the treasure."

"Unless you keep it for yourself," I said. "Deliver the pages to Italy having already stolen the treasure. Mind you, I suspect your fellow mutineers will want a cut."

I noticed the Italian's lip twitch in irritation. "You are wrong," he said. "I intend to hand everything over to my employers..." He grabbed hold of my hair and yanked my head back. I felt a knife blade press against my throat. "And I do not like playing games."

"All right... All right," I gasped. It was time to convince the ringleader of the mutineers that I was worth keeping alive. "There is a piece of treasure... The golden serpent. It is buried in a tomb somewhere on this island."

He let go of my hair and took away his knife.

"It is rumoured to have magic powers," I said, glancing up to see his response. "According to legend, the golden serpent can open a door into the divine."

The Italian held my gaze for a time, his eyes hard and unreadable. "I have little interest in what lies beyond this world," he then said with a dismissive shrug. "One day I shall die and find out for myself. Until that day comes, Captain, I am quite happy to wait." He looked up towards the island. "The fog is lifting. It is time to go."

They left the deckhand to guard the boat, in case there were natives on the island who might steal their only means of returning to the *Conway*. He was told to fire his pistol at the first sign of trouble, at which point the expedition would be aborted immediately.

As we walked up the beach, I turned around for one last look at the ocean.

Wollaton climbed up the bank first, and I was instructed to go next. With my hands tied, I slipped and fell several times during the short scramble. When I finally reached the top, the remaining three men followed.

We thus began our ascent up the island, first through a tangle of scrub and then out into open ground, the dense white fog always remaining a few hundred feet beyond us, as if it were an ethereal curtain being slowly and deliberately drawn back by an unseen hand. Throughout the steady climb, I was made to stay between Wollaton and Trickett, the Italian marching out in front, and Birnie trailing behind at a distance. We walked for several hours like this until, upon reaching a rocky outcrop, the Italian called out that we should take a rest. The temperature was rising and we were all of us dripping with sweat, our brows raw with sunburn despite their being no sign of the sun through the fog. I sat down in the shade beneath the rocks, trying to ignore the sound of the other men gulping water from their skins.

The island fell away below me, an undulating carpet of green rolling down to the shingle beach and the eroded stacks of the peninsula. I could see a mile or so out to sea, its surface as smooth as a millpond. The *Conway* would be somewhere in the fog beyond, though it sat across the other side of the island. I wondered what might be happening on board the ship. If the fog continued to rise, what would happen once the island was in view? Would the sight of land bring my men to their senses?

The Italian walked over and stood next to me, sucking on his cigarette. He followed my gaze out to sea.

"Your crew believe you to be cursed," he said, as if having read my thoughts. "In their eyes, it is you who is to blame for the storm, and the death of the wind, and this fog that cloaks us." He blew a plume of smoke into the air above his head. "They knew we were taking you off the ship, and yet they each turned a blind eye."

His words stabbed me like the cruellest of knives.

"There is no longer anyone on board to poison their minds," I said, as calmly as I could. "How long will it be before they come to their senses and realise they have been tricked?"

"We will be back on board before nightfall, with or without this precious golden serpent," he said, looking noticeably riled. "The *Conway* will sail back to England with Lieutenant Wollaton at the helm."

It gave me some satisfaction to know that I had planted a seed of doubt in the Italian's mind, though I needed to be careful not to push him too far. Scrambling to my feet, I glanced up the mountainside. The summit was at last revealed, a flattened tabletop of rock with sheer cliffs on the western side, and what looked like a gentler climb on the eastern slopes. Beneath the cliffs lay a carpet of trees.

The sight struck me as familiar.

"Show me the pages," I demanded.

The Italian hesitated for a moment, eyeing me with caution. Then, tossing his cigarette over the plateau, he took out the stolen pages.

I told him to find the illustration of the mother and child.

"This one represents the island," I said, gesturing to the illustration with a nod of my head. "The divine mother and child, as depicted in the Hodegetria."

The Italian squinted at the page. "La Madonna Odigitria."

"Also known as La Virgen del Perpetuo *Socorro,*" I said. "Now turn the page over."

And just as I had thought, the illustration of the stonemasons bore a striking resemblance to the scene we looked upon now; the rocky outcrop, and beyond it scattered boulders rising like monoliths from the earth, and then the distant cliffs—identical to those in the illustration, even down to the cluster of trees beneath them.

The Italian saw it too, and smiling with delight he held the page up in front of his eyes, comparing the two scenes.

Held aloft like this, I noticed something else—not so much within the illustration as *through* it.

"She who shows the way," I gasped.

The Italian looked at me for an explanation.

"The illustration on the other side. You can see it when you hold the page up to the light. And the Virgin's hand, it is gesturing towards—"

"The cliffs." The Italian brought the page closer to his eyes. "No...not to the cliffs. To the forest beneath them!"

By the time we approached the outskirts of the forest, the

morning sun had burnt away the last of the fog. The shade beneath the trees looked cool and inviting, but I was made to wait while the Italian stopped and examined the stolen pages. Wollaton stood next to me, holding his waterskin at a height so that I was forced to watch the water falling into his mouth and running wastefully from his chin.

"Such a shame about Mr Legge," he said, wiping his mouth with the back of his hand. "Ending up wi' a knife in his liver like that."

"Your knife?"

I saw it then, the acknowledgement in Wollaton's eyes. I saw the way his lip twitched as he tried to conceal his mirth.

"You coward," I seethed. "To sneak up on one of your own and attack him from behind, then hide away like the cockroach you are!"

"One of me own?" he scoffed. "That Miss Molly were never anything of the sort. None of you are—not you, not Mr Legge, nor that prancing Mr Darby. Types like you, lording over the rest of us like you are better." He took a step closer, glowering at me, his sun-blistered face inches from my own. Pulling out his dagger, he pressed the blade into my stomach. "Aye, it were me that put a knife into your little friend."

I breathed hard against the anger that boiled beneath my skin. "Go on then, do it!" I challenged him. "I am not afraid to die, and every second I live is another second I have to find a way to kill you first."

Wollaton pushed the blade harder against my flesh. He glanced in the direction of the Italian, who was looking our way. "Truth be known, I don't want you dead," he said, slipping the knife back into its sheath. His countenance darkened, his eyes narrowing. "I want to break your legs an' your arms, an' drag you to a rock where you can watch us sail away wi' all your treasure. An' you'll know that I'll be standing at the 'elm, commanding the crew, an' I'll be sleeping in your cot, an' eating at your table, an' shitting in your latrine." A cruel smile spread across Wollaton's lips. "An' I'll take the greatest pleasure in knowing you will die there, against that rock, knowing that I beat you. Tekkin' your ship. Tekkin' your command. Tekkin' the ten thousand you're due for bringing the gold back to England." He shielded his mouth. "An' tekkin the life of that little whore of yours an' all."

I was standing face to face with the man who killed Legge. I looked into his vile, treacherous eyes, took in every pockmark on his leathery cheeks, the curl in his lip, the droplets of water clinging to his wiry beard, the rancid smell of his breath. I despised this man.

And yet he was right. He had taken everything from me— but I was not done yet.

Without a word, I turned away and walked towards the trees.

TWENTY-NINE

Isla Socorro, Mexico, 21st June 1822

THE FOREST SEEMED ANCIENT. The trees were carpeted in moss and strung with ivy, and the air was moist and earthy. The remnants of the fog still dripped from the fronds of gigantic ferns and glistened on the surface of the boulders that were scattered across our path. All about, I could hear the chattering and whooping of birds and the buzz of crickets.

We walked in single file, bathed in the soft green light that filtered through the canopy. There was an unsettled air amongst my captors. The Italian, Wollaton, and Trickett all walked with their guns at the ready, starting at every crack of a branch or rustle in the bushes nearby. There had been no talk of natives since we left the beach, but if they inhabited the island, this was the most likely place for an ambush.

While the mutineers kept a lookout for these would-be attackers, I surveyed the forest. I was looking for a tree that might represent the world tree illustrated in the Codex. After the page containing the illustrations of the Divine Mother and the stonemasons—which had brought us this far—it seemed logical that page with the world tree followed next. *The tree that sustains all life has roots leading into the Underworld.* This would then leave the page about Quetzalcoatl and Tezcatlipoca, which made reference to the Underworld, and then finally the page about the ceremony of *Tonatiuhtiz*: the page with the golden serpent.

But what sort of tree was I looking for? A tree that had existed in Bernardino de Sahagún's day, when the Codex was written, would be well over two hundred years old by now. If it dated back to the days of the Toltec Empire, then it was several hundred years older still. Could a tree live that long? It was possible; I remembered having once been told about a great oak in Somerset that dated back to the time of William the Conqueror.

Some way into the forest, I spied a majestic fig with an enormous sinewy trunk, and branches that sent masses of tendrils down to the ground. Straying from the path, I waded through the undergrowth to take a closer look. The sound of gunfire cracked through the air and I ducked instinctively, thinking the shot was aimed at me. I turned to see Trickett holding his pistol, the smoking barrel pointing towards the forest floor.

"You *idiot!*" Wollaton yelled, shoving the Master at Arms out of the way as he gazed down at the path. "Now the whole bloody island knows we're here!"

"It was a snake!" Trickett retaliated. "And if you've got such a problem with my shooting it, then go ahead and take the lead yourself."

Wollaton stamped his boot on whatever remained of the poor creature. "You could'a just shooed it away wi' a stick—or walked around the bloody thing!"

"Aye, well, like I said, you go first," Trickett said in a huff.

The two men continued to bicker until the Italian marched in to resolve the argument.

This was my opportunity to break and run. I felt a rush of nerves. If I could get far enough away before they noticed, I could dodge amongst the trees and hopefully avoid getting shot. It might be my last chance.

I looked about. Where was—

A hand seized me firmly by the shoulder.

"Don't," Birnie said. His tone was not so much reprimanding me as insisting I should take heed—and so too was the look in his eye.

"George, you cannot let these men succeed," I pleaded. "Whatever your grievances with me, you *must* lay them aside. There is far more at stake here than—"

"Save your breath," he cut in, his eyes darting in the direction of the Italian, who was striding towards us through the undergrowth. "I'm not on your side."

Returning to the path, we continued on through the forest until the trees broke apart and we found ourselves on an escarpment that ran along the coast. The sheer drop to the ocean was several hundred feet. Further along this precipitous edge, the grey cliffs rose all the way to the summit, where numerous waterspouts sprung from the rock, sending sparkling ropes of water down to the sea.

The mutineers stopped to drink from their waterskins again. I was so desperately thirsty that I had to look away. How much longer could I survive without water? It seemed to be everywhere, and yet I had not a drop to drink. In the grip of this torment, I found myself opening my dry lips and imagining I could drink the fresh water as it fell from the waterspouts.

Even when I looked back into the forest, I thought I could hear the distant sound of...

Suddenly, a thought struck me.

"This way!" I yelled and hurried back towards the trees.

The mutineers chased after me, shouting that I slow down. I followed the perimeter of the forest until the trees ended abruptly at the cliff face. Having skirted the smooth, grey rock, I then turned back onto a natural path through the ferns. The sound I had recognised was growing louder, unmistakable now as the low rumble of water. I dashed ahead with the other men at my heels.

Emerging into a clearing, I found myself standing before a semicircular wall of rock that stood higher than the treetops. A waterfall cut through its centre, glittering in a beam of sunlight as it cascaded over a series of ledges and plunged into the shallow pool below, casting a shimmering rainbow into the misty air.

The Italian caught my arm. "This place is mentioned?" He was clutching the stolen pages in his hand.

"*The tree that sustains all life,*" I said, nodding towards the waterfall. "The rain clouds are its canopy, the waterfall its trunk, and the water that seeps down into the earth its roots. Yes, it is mentioned!"

The Italian had a wild glint in his eye as he took in the falls.

"Now, untie my hands so I can drink," I demanded.

He eyed me suspiciously. "And have a better chance of escape?"

"Four men against one, and three of you armed with guns," I replied. "I should say the odds are stacked against me."

Tucking the pages back into his pocket, he threw me a reproachful look. "Your hands remain tied, but you can drink."

I knelt down on a flattened rock at the side of the pool and submerged my face in the cool water. The sensation of quenching my thirst was nothing short of euphoric: I felt as if the crystal-clear water was coursing down my throat and then running through my veins, revitalising my spirits. When I was done, I sat back and breathed in deeply, taking a moment to admire the beauty of this spot. Saplings grew upon the ledges of the falls, their lime-green leaves filtering the sunlight. Butterflies danced and chased one another above the pool. The striated rock around the edges of the waterfall was cut into a deep overhang, as if an area slightly more than a man's height had been scooped out with a giant spoon.

There was no denying the place had a sacred and hallowed quality about it—this lost waterfall, hidden away in a forest on a remote island cloaked in fog. How long had it been since the sound of human voices had disturbed this tranquillity? If there were no natives on the island, it could have been centuries. I wondered if the Spanish sailor, Captain Yañez, had ever found the falls when he came to the island two hundred years ago.

As I sat listening to the steady rhythm of the waterfall hitting the surface of the pool, I noticed something rather curious. The water in the pool was not very deep, and became gradually shallower as it stretched across to where I sat—but there was no sign of a stream leading from the pool. So then where did all the water go?

Looking about for an explanation, I saw a dark crevice in one corner of the wall of rock. I climbed to my feet and skirted the pool. Yes, there was the answer: the water appeared to be draining away through the crevice. No more than three feet high, it might only be visible when the waterfall was relatively tame—as otherwise it would be submerged.

Had the seasonal rains hidden the crevice from Captain Yañez?

The Italian was standing at the water's edge with his hands on his hips. "What is it?"

"The pool drains into the rock below," I called back. "There must be a space. Underground caves."

"And we go this way?" he said, still feasting his eyes on the opening.

"*The tree that sustains all life has roots leading into the Underworld*," I recited, splashing back through the shallow water at the margins of the pool. "This is the way. I will stake my life on it."

All eyes turned to Birnie, who carried the lantern strapped to his belt. Having placed it on the ground, he took out his tinderbox and then seemed to spend an eternity striking his flint before there was any sign of a flame. "It's this misty air," he said, carefully replacing the cover. "The wick was damp."

The doctor skirted the pool and then stepped into the shallow water next to the crevice. Crouching down, he thrust the lantern into the opening. "I cannot see much," he called out, "but there does appear to be a space on the other side." He lowered himself onto all fours and, holding the lantern inches above the surface of the water, stuck his head and shoulders into the crevice. "Most certainly a space."

Crawling forwards, he then disappeared from sight.

Trickett hurried after him and called through the opening. "You alive in there, doctor?"

"There's a tunnel," came Birnie's muffled reply.

The Master at Arms dropped onto his hands and knees and was next to disappear.

"Now you," the Italian said, turning to me.

"I need my hands." I spun around so he could untie the chords that bound my wrists.

"Tie 'em in front," Wollaton said, taking out his pistol and pointing it at my chest. "He can use his elbows."

It was by no means an easy manoeuvre, scrambling through the crevice on my elbows and knees. When I was through, I looked about the cramped and musty cave in which I now stood. Sunlight flooded through the opening, and the walls glistened with a film of moisture. Birnie was standing by a dark space at one end of the cave. It was the entrance to a passageway; and once the Italian and Wollaton were with us, the doctor led the way, a pearl of yellow light cast around his silhouette as he walked into the darkness.

We were descending into the mountainside, the low rumble of the waterfall fading away behind us until only the sound of our boots broke the silence. The passageway began to narrow considerably, and before long it was barely a man's width between the slippery walls. I thought we were reaching a dead end, but Bernie shuffled forwards with the lantern, pressing his back against the wall.

Each of us followed, squeezing through the gap in the rock. We emerged into a dome-shaped cave some twenty feet across. A stream ran along one wall. Aside from the gap through which we had come, there were three other passageways leading from the cave. Birnie walked around each of them, shining the lantern into their gloomy depths.

"Which one do we take?" he said. "The wrong choice and we could be lost down here forever."

I looked around at each of the passageways. Had I missed something in the Codex? My eyes turned to the stream. *The roots of the tree*, I thought. *Follow the roots of the tree.* The water disappeared under a low shelf at one end.

Low, but not too low to climb under.

"Bring the lantern," I called to Birnie, and stepped into the stream.

The doctor hurried over and joined me.

Sure enough, on the other side of the shelf lay a tunnel.

We followed it along its length, splashing through the shallow water until the tunnel came to an end. We were in another chamber, this time one with only a single exit. The air within the corridor beyond was stale and suffocating, but we had little choice. The passage led to a natural stairway, which spiralled down into the rock. As we descended, step by crumbling step, the air became less fetid and the sound of water returned; a deep, resonant rumble that became steadily louder.

The stairway ended and I stepped out into an open space. The light from Birnie's lantern did little to reveal how large it was, but from somewhere out there in the darkness came the thunder of a waterfall.

Birnie held the lantern high above his head. As he did so, the walls and ceiling of the cavern began to sparkle with hundreds of points of light.

"Well, would you just look at this," the doctor said with a gasp. "Pyrite. The mineral can absorb and reflect light."

I gazed up at the glittering display, realising that this was more than just a natural spectacle. Each piece of pyrite had been meticulously placed within the rock to form constellations of the northern and southern skies. I could see Cassiopeia, Orion, Draco, and Taurus. The mighty Scorpius, my favourite of all the constellations, climbed the far wall snapping its pinchers, with the red star Antares glowing in its heart.

There had been nights on board the *Conway* that had looked just like this. Nights without a moon, where I would stand upon the bow, struck dumb by the enduring beauty of the heavens; marvelling at how the constellations continued each night in their path across the sky, and in total separation from the affairs on Earth.

"In Tezcatlipoca's kingdom, the stars forever shine in the eternal night," I said, turning to Birnie. "They brought the stars down here. They created the Underworld."

I saw something then in the doctor's eyes: a look of solidarity. A look that said, *I am with you. Do not say a word.*

My heart leapt.

Right at that moment, Trickett snatched the lantern from Birnie's grasp. He strode ahead into the darkness, then stopped suddenly and began swinging the lantern to and fro as he gazed around.

"Come see this!" he shouted back. "It's—"

There came a crunching sound, that of crumbling rock. I watched as Trickett performed an absurd series of movements in an attempt to right himself, but it was too late. Flailing his arms pitifully, he tipped forwards and disappeared from sight.

As the light descended with him, I caught a glimpse of our surroundings. We stood upon a high ledge, which formed a walkway around the perimeter of an enormous cavern. Along the walkway, I could see entrances leading back into the rock. The waterfall was across the other side, plummeting from an opening in the ceiling, and crashing over the ledge before falling several hundred feet into a black lake, which filled the basin of the cavern. Then the light went out and the cavern plunged into darkness, leaving only the pyrite heavens sparkling above us.

"Trickett!" I heard Wollaton call out in the darkness. "Trickett! Answer, you damn fool!"

But no reply came. I wondered if the Master at Arms had died from the fall, or whether he might still be alive somewhere down there, but unconscious. Perhaps he was drowning in the lake?

Whatever his sorry fate, Trickett was gone.

For quite some time, we all stood in a stunned silence. Without the lantern, there was little chance of finding our way back. And what of the way forwards—walking blindly along the ledge unable to see any gaps or fallen rocks along its length?

One thing was for certain: if ever there was a time to make my escape, it was now. As I reached out into the darkness, looking for Birnie, my hand touched the barrel of a gun.

"My finger is on the trigger," the Italian growled. "Prove to me you know the way, or you are a dead man."

I said nothing.

The barrel was now pressed against my chest. "Do you know the way or not?"

"Give me a moment. I need to think." I gazed up at pyrite constellations. I had found the island—the Divine Mother. And she had shown the way to the forest—the illustration of the stonemasons. We had discovered the waterfall—the illustration of the world tree—and followed the water here, into Tezcatlipoca's kingdom with its pyrite stars.

Let Quetzalcoatl's light be your guide through the darkness.

"Dios de la Estrella de la Mañana," I said, recalling the title beneath the illustration of Quetzalcoatl. "Lord of the Morning Star."

Venus.

My eyes cast about wildly as I studied the familiar patterns of light. Patterns that I had seen so many times, on so many nights throughout my life. Patterns that I lived by and were tattooed upon my mind.

Being a planet, Venus did not belong to these patterns.

I searched the constellations for a star that was out of place.

And there it was—glinting in the darkness across the other side of the cavern.

"I have it!"

The Italian seized me by the shoulder. "Lead the way," he said, stepping behind me and poking his gun into my back. "My pistol is loaded. If you move suddenly, or I cannot hear your breathing…"

I ignored his threat. The glowing fragment of pyrite sat near a strip of darkness that cut down through the constellations: I knew this must be the waterfall. Choosing the direction that avoided the need to cross the falls, I took my first steps along the ledge, with my back tight against the wall. Without the use of my hands to steady me, I was ever conscious that I might lose my balance and be the next to fall over the sheer drop, which lay just inches beyond my feet.

And thus we began on our way, one cautious side-step at a time. Every so often, the cavern wall would disappear behind me as we passed one of the entrances onto the ledge. Sometimes the air seemed cooler in the passage beyond; sometimes there seemed to be a breeze. But all the while I kept my eye, and my mind, fixed on that single piece of pyrite further along the walkway.

We had made it a quarter of the way around the cavern when Birnie called out that the stars were fading. He was right—without the light from the lantern, the pyrite was losing its glow. I quickened my step, my foot groping ahead in the darkness for obstacles before I flattened my heel. As we neared the waterfall, the air became wet with spray and the ledge became treacherously slippery. A little further still and I felt water rushing over my boots.

The stars in the cavern had all but faded away, and the piece of pyrite my eyes were locked upon was now little more than a faint speck. *Ten steps further*, I told myself, and slid my foot along the ledge. *Nine. Eight. Seven.*

I knew the Italian was still next to me, because he kept prodding me with the barrel of his gun. As for the others, I could not tell. Against the roar of the waterfall, they could have fallen to their deaths without my knowing.

Six. Five. My heart sank as the last glimmer of the pyrite Venus died away—and all the other stars with it. The darkness surrounding us was complete.

There was no stopping now. *Four more steps.*

Three.

Two.

The waterfall thundered in my ears.

One more step.

I kicked the wall with my heel. It was still solid. I was certain this was the spot.

Another step still.

And another.

Had I made a terrible mistake?

One more step...

Kicking back my heel, my foot continued into an empty space. I turned to face the rock and felt ahead with my bound hands: they broke through a film of water into the hidden entrance. I threw myself through the opening, my heart racing in my chest and my mind dizzy with exhilaration. The other men followed. First the Italian, then Wollaton...

"Holy Mother of God," I heard Birnie curse, as he came through. "That was"—he caught his breath—"the most terrifying experience of my life!"

It was only then that I realised the rock surrounding us was faintly visible. Wollaton must have noticed this too, and he raced ahead down the dark passage, leaving us to chase after him. There was a sharp right turn, after which the light became brighter still, and I could see Birnie next to me, with Wollaton's silhouette striding out in front. On the next turn, the source of the light was finally revealed at the far end of the tunnel. Daylight! We broke into a run. Upon reaching the dazzling light, I saw it was a circular hole only a few feet wide.

"I shall go first," the Italian said, excitedly. "Then the captain. The doctor after, and then you, lieutenant."

It was a tubular tunnel through the rock. Once the Italian was through to the other side, his back blocking my view of what lay beyond, it was my turn to climb in. I began wriggling forwards as best as I could. Spinning around, the Italian peered through the hole at the other end and chided me to hurry up. I felt my boots being grasped and I was given a hard shove, after which the Italian reached in and seized me by the collar, pulling me through and sending me tumbling to the ground.

Scrambling to my feet, my eyes still adjusting to the stark daylight, I saw that I was in a magnificent cave. Sunlight poured in through a circular opening above, an oculus in the ceiling. The walls of the cave were overgrown with thick, green vines and feathery ferns; and where the vegetation was absent, the bare rock revealed innumerable cave paintings. Men with spears chasing antelope; women gathering stems of corn. I saw a vibrantly coloured quetzal with a crimson breast, a spotted jaguar, a snake with open jaws. There were sea creatures such as sharks and rays, and curious beasts with a human torso and the head of an animal.

A stream cut across the centre of the cave in a channel, the water exiting to the outside world via a crevice, through which I could see the unmistakable cobalt blue of the ocean. This must be one of the waterspouts I had seen. All along the length of the channel grew a tangle of leafy plants with long, tapering inflorescences bursting with purple-and-white flowers.

Pipiltzintzintli. I knew it instantly.

I had found it, the mystical plant of the Toltecs. The legendary flower stolen from Paradise by the goddess of beauty, Xochiquetzal. I had found pipiltzintzintli. I had found the divine sage! And yet hardly had I the time to register this than my eyes fell upon something else.

Indeed, not something, but some*one*.

On the other side of the channel lay a grimy figure, slumped against the wall with his arms limp by his sides and his head hanging down towards his chest. His trousers were torn at the knees, and his shirt was stained with blood. A tin cup lay in the dirt beside his hand, and next to it a cloth bag, and a lantern.

I walked towards him, but the Italian caught me and threw me against the cave wall. "Stay where you are," he warned me, grabbing my neck as if he meant to throttle me.

Birnie was now through the tunnel and stood rubbing his eyes.

Releasing me from his grip, the Italian waded through the channel and lifted the man's head. I stared in disbelief.

It was John Gillies.

"As I live and breathe," Birnie gasped, leaping over the channel. He crouched in front of Gillies and took hold of his wrist, feeling for a pulse, then tried again with his fingers against Gillies's neck. "He's still alive!" the doctor called out, and reached for the tin cup. "The man needs water."

Wollaton had by now climbed through the hole and marched over to where Gillies lay. "That man just will not bloody die," he said, taking out his pistol. "Well, I shall see to it meself this time, and he had better—"

"Give him water," the Italian ordered, cutting the lieutenant off. "I intend to take him alive."

Hurrying back to the channel, Birnie knelt down to fill the tin cup with water. As he rose back to his feet, he threw me a look that was charged with urgency, and then glanced in the direction of Wollaton and the Italian, who were still leaning over Gillies.

Away, he seemed to be mouthing.

Whatever he was planning, I knew I had to act fast.

"There, on the wall," I said, raising my wrists and pointing across the cave. "Do you see it—the snake?"

The Italian turned around. "What of it?"

"It is in the Codex."

The Italian and Wollaton exchanged a glance before both men walked over to the wall and began examining the cave paintings. Birnie, meanwhile, hurried back to Gillies, the water splashing over the rim of the tin cup.

"Tell me which page," the Italian called out, taking the stolen pages from his pocket.

"The illustration of the sacrificial ceremony," I said.

Birnie was now crouching in front of Gillies. He glanced anxiously over his shoulder to see if the others were looking—the two men were preoccupied, the Italian rifling through the pages in his hand, the lieutenant inspecting the cave wall. I watched the doctor move the cloth bag. It was then that I saw what he was trying to tell me.

There was a pistol.

The Italian turned to look at me, and then at Birnie. The doctor had shifted his position so that the two men were unable to see what he was doing. Having picked the gun up, he was checking to see if it was loaded.

"The golden serpent," I called out. "This is the last clue.

See how it is next to the colourful bird? That is a quetzal." I was stalling for time as best I could. "The two together signify Quetzalcoatl, the supreme deity." I stepped across the channel.

Birnie was now standing with the gun behind his back.

"Yes, I know who Quetzalcoatl is," the Italian said, gazing at the wall. "But the serpent here is green, not golden." He spun around and saw that I had moved. "And I thought I told you to—"

"Drop your weapons!" Birnie yelled out. He swung the pistol nervously towards the Italian, then towards Wollaton, then back to the Italian.

Wollaton already held his gun in his hand. The Italian was reaching for his.

"Drop your weapons, or I'll shoot!" Birnie shouted.

The Italian's face darkened. "And *who* will you shoot?" he demanded, tossing down the stolen pages. "You have one shot, and two men to choose from."

"Either way, it'll even the odds," Birnie said, swinging the pistol back to Wollaton.

"Assuming your aim is good," the Italian said. "Is the gun even loaded?"

"I doubt he's ever fired a pistol," Wollaton said with a smirk. "Let alone killed a man. It would be against his 'ippocritic oath. Is that not right, Mr Birnie?"

"I'm here to avenge the death of my friend," Birnie said, his voice cracking. The strain he was under had turned his face crimson and brought out a thick meandering vein on his temple. As I took a step closer to him, I saw his finger tighten on the trigger.

"Charles, this is for you," he said.

The charge hissed as it ignited, and the gun went off with a bang.

THIRTY

Isla Socorro, Mexico, Solstice 1822

CLUTCHING HIS CHEST, Wollaton stared at Birnie in sheer disbelief. The blood was already soaking through his shirt and dripping from his fingers. Staggering backwards, the lieutenant fell against the wall of the cave. He slid to the floor, leaving a thick crimson mark amongst the painted figures and beasts.

The Italian reached immediately for his gun, his eyes filled with rage as he took aim at the doctor.

I stepped in front of Birnie to shield him.

"So be it," the Italian seethed, and without hesitating a second longer he pulled the trigger.

My whole body tensed as I saw the hammer spring forwards on his pistol, sending forth a shower of sparks as the flint struck the steel.

But no hiss came from the priming charge—just a dull thud.

The powder was damp.

It was an undignified fight that followed. I leapt across the channel and ran headlong at the Italian. Throwing down his gun, he reached for the dagger that hung from his belt; but before he had time to withdraw the blade, I careered into him and sent him sprawling, tumbling to the ground myself. When I looked up, Birnie was upon him, all swings and blows. The Italian yelled curses and struck Birnie hard in the jaw. He reached for his dagger again, and Birnie fought to stop him.

I threw myself upon the Italian and bit him in the neck.

"Aieeeeee!" he cried out.

His fist collided with my cheek, and I was sent reeling. By the time I had scrambled back to my feet, Birnie was upon the man, and they were struggling in the dirt. As they flailed and fought, I caught sight of a loose rock next to my feet. Pulling against the cords that bound my hands, I managed to pick it up —then, with a mighty blow, I brought it down on the Italian's skull.

His head fell backwards instantly, his eyes wild and unhinged. I hit him again savagely, and this time he toppled to the floor. When I hit him a third time, his body shuddered violently for a few seconds, then stopped moving.

The doctor and I stood for a while staring at the lifeless body and heaving air into our lungs. Birnie was bent over with his hands upon his knees. He spat out a mouthful of blood. Afterwards, he walked up to the Italian's corpse and rolled it over, pulling the dagger from its sheath. His hands were still shaking as he fumbled to cut me loose.

"We did it," he said with an exhausted smile.

I shook my head in disbelief, still catching my breath. "You are a brave man, George Birnie. And a good shot, at that!" I glanced across at Gillies, still slumped against the cave wall on the opposite side of the channel. "I should say we have him to thank too."

Wollaton was dead, the bullet having hit him clean between the ribs. Taking hold of his boots, I dragged his sorry corpse to the channel and Birnie helped me to throw him in. The lieutenant's body moved slowly towards the opening. His legs slid from sight, but the gap was narrow and he became stuck at the waist.

Stepping into the water, I placed my boot on Wollaton's shoulders and gave his body a shove. He shifted a little. Another push, and he slipped silently through the gap. He was gone now, falling some unknown distance down the cliff face, his body finally breaking against the rocks, or plunging into the sea—it no longer mattered, only that he did not remain in this sacred place.

As for the Italian, we lifted his corpse into the channel and disposed of him in the same unceremonious way. Once his body was out of sight, Birnie and I flopped down against the wall of the cave.

"You are the best of men," I said at length, offering the doctor my hand. He clasped it tightly. There were no words to express how I felt for him at that moment. His unswerving loyalty. His friendship. I wrapped my arms around him in the tightest of embraces. Yes, Birnie was the best of men, the very best.

We talked then. Birnie began by telling me when it was that he realised something was amiss.

"At first, I thought you might have caught a brain fever," he said. "I declared you unfit to command as a necessity. When Wollaton took over, he insisted you be taken down to the hold so as not to frighten the crew." The doctor grimaced. "After your appearance on deck the night before, ranting and raving in the storm, there were all sorts of rumours about curses and the like. Oh, and you were right—they were poisoning you all along."

"With what?"

"Mercury," he said. "A bottle of the stuff had disappeared from my chest a few nights previously, though at the time I simply thought I'd misplaced it. I spied it quite by chance on the night after you were taken to the hold. I was seeing to a burn on the cook's hand, and there it was, sitting on a shelf. That was when I started to put the pieces together—your violent headaches, swings in mood, feelings of nausea. By then, the crew were already convinced you'd gone mad. I knew that if I began shouting that this was all part of a mutiny, nobody would listen—and more's the point, I was likely to end up with a knife in my back and tossed overboard."

He sighed. "So, I decided that the best thing I could do was to play along—which was when I came up with the idea to convince Wollaton and our imposter cook that I despised you and wanted you dead. I knew that if they had so much as an inkling that I might be deceiving them, they wouldn't hesitate to kill me. I had to be convincing...and to do that, I had to convince myself as well."

"Trust me, you were convincing," I said, shaking the doctor warmly by the shoulder.

Birnie kicked the dirt idly with his heel. "I overheard him, you know—Wollaton, when he told you that he killed Charles. I was out of sight behind a rock, tying my bootlace. I was so bent with rage that I might have killed him right then and there. But they'd made sure I wasn't carrying my gun—they didn't trust me *that* much." He threw me a smile. "At any rate, it wasn't easy saying those things to you, and I'm sorry. Charles loved you dearly. Every day he spoke about you, and I saw the way his eyes lit up at even the mention of your name. I always knew that he was holding on just to see you again, and in a way I blamed you for the pain he was enduring as he fought against death. I suppose that's why…on that evening, when we were out in the garden—"

"I am glad you said what you did," I said. "I was in a very dark place, George. I had been lost for some time."

Birnie nodded. "Do you know, I think Wollaton killed Lieutenant Darby too. There was just something odd about the way Darby disappeared in Callao like that."

"Yes, I suppose, being higher in rank, Darby stood in the way of Wollaton taking command."

Birnie shrugged. "I guess we might never know the truth."

We sat in a contemplative silence. I listened to the babbling water as it ran through the channel, my eyes set upon a thin beam of sunlight that shone through the oculus in the cave roof.

Reaching into his coat pocket, Birnie withdrew a folded sheet of paper. "I almost forgot," he said, handing it to me. "This was in your bureau."

It was the portrait of Legge. There was nothing in the world I would rather have been given at that moment. Gazing into the lieutenant's eyes, I recalled the day he arrived at my lodgings in the Almendral wearing that silly straw hat. That first day.

"I miss him," I said. "Every day."

Birnie nodded. "As do I."

I glanced across the cave at Gillies, slumped against the wall like a puppet cut from its strings. "The artist is over there."

"Yes, I thought as much," Birnie said. "John was very fond of Charles. I saw that right from the start."

Folding up the picture, I handed it back to him. "Keep it."

When Birnie politely refused, I insisted. "Please, George. I want you to have it."

Having sat for a while longer in the quiet tranquillity of the cave, I began telling Birnie everything I knew about Gillies and the quest that had brought us here. Gathering up the pages of the Florentine Codex, which lay scattered across the cave floor, I told the doctor how Gillies had broken into the basilica in Florence where the codex was locked away, how he had tried to persuade me to take the pages back to England, how I had refused, and how I had learnt that the object of his quest was something called the golden serpent. I told him how the pages had ended up with Legge, and how I had sworn to my lieutenant on his deathbed that I would find the golden serpent. The doctor listened intently, asking questions now and then.

Then I told him all about Father Lyle and the clues in the Nahuatl text, and how the reverend had revealed the true secret that lay behind the pages: that the treasure was not gold, but something far more valuable—a mystical plant, hidden from the Church since the fall of the Aztec civilisation. I explained how the story of Topiltzin in the Codex was but a metaphor to hide the identity of this plant, which the Aztecs knew as pipiltzintzintli—a plant that was thought to bear the sacred flower stolen from Paradise in Aztec legend.

"Fray de Sahagún called it the divine sage," I said, nodding towards the plants lined along the channel.

Birnie leant forwards and snapped one of the plants at the stem. "It certainly looks like a type of sage," he said, examining it. "The squareness of the stem, and the leaf shape. And this inflorescence of tubular flowers." He crushed a leaf in his hand, lifting his fingers to his nose to smell the aroma. "The name of the genus, *Salvia*, is derived from the Latin *salveo*, which means to save, or to recover."

Showing him the illustration of *Tonatiuhtiz*, I said that the ceremony appeared to involve both the divine sage and the golden serpent, and took place at midday on the summer solstice. *"He who consumes the golden serpent will know death and be liberated into light,"* I said, reciting the words underscored in the Nahuatl text. "I thought perhaps the golden serpent might be berries from the divine sage."

"Sage plants don't produce berries," Birnie said, inspecting the inflorescence. "The seeds form on this long thin spike."

"Then I confess I do not have a clue what the golden serpent is," I said with a sigh, and then gestured in Gillies's direction. "There lies the man with all the answers. Is there any chance he will live?"

"It's unlikely," Birnie said. "But he might save us again before we're done here. We have his lantern." He glanced up at the oculus in the cave roof, through which the first bright sliver of the sun had appeared. "It's a little strange don't you think, that we find ourselves here on the day of the solstice—and it can't be far from noon."

"I am not so sure it is a coincidence," I said. "Everything seems to be..."

Feeling a tickling sensation on my skin, I looked down at my arm to see a tiny black insect clambering amongst the hairs.

I nudged Birnie.

"It looks like a small species of bee," the doctor said, holding out his index finger so that the insect might climb onto it. Instead, it flew away across the cave.

A curious thought then occurred to me. Climbing to my feet, I went to inspect the flowers along the channel.

They were teeming with these insects.

Was it possible…?

Crouching down in front of one of the flowers, I watched an insect emerge from its depths, all laden with pollen. Having spent a moment fanning its wings on the lip of the flower, the insect rose into the air and flew away towards the thick mass of vines that covered the far wall of the cave. I sprang to my feet and chased after it, then began tearing down the vines with my hands.

Stripping away the vegetation, I feasted my eyes on a cave painting about eight feet tall. It was of a female deity sitting upon her throne, with a child suckling on her breast. She wore two plumes of green feathers in her hair, and her nose was pierced with a thin rod. The painting was decorated with hundreds of gemstones: enormous pieces of jade dangled from her ears and dazzling rubies adorned her throne.

It was Xochiquetzal. I knew it for certain. The goddess who stole pipiltzintzintli and was captured and taken down into the Underworld by Tezcatlipoca. Painted next to her, and as tall as she, was a rangy plant that could only be the divine sage. Coiled around its stem was a magnificent serpent, its scales a mosaic of gold leaves.

Pulling down the remaining vines, the serpent's head was revealed. Its ruby-encrusted tongue stretched out beneath an alcove in the wall. Inside the alcove sat a tubular earthenware pot. It looked ancient and fragile, and I noticed a small hole in its centre. As I peered closer, a stream of insects began emerging from the hole. They swarmed the surface of the pot, and many more flew into the air.

There was a sweet fragrance emanating from the alcove. Honey—it was unmistakably the smell of honey.

Birnie was standing next to me now.

"Look at your shirt," the doctor said.

I noticed then that my shoulders and arms were covered in the tiny black bees, which ran about greeting one another. They seemed to be arranging themselves into thin lines, whereupon they began fanning their wings frantically—as if their bold intention was to lift me up into the air.

And not a single insect had landed on Birnie.

Carefully removing the pot from the alcove, I blew away the dust covering its surface. It was decorated with a macabre-looking face, painted with flowers in colours that had long since faded. The hole, from which the bees continued to emerge, was situated within the mouth. One of the end sections of the pot looked as though it could be removed, and when I twisted it gently, it released a squeak. I twisted it a little more, and with a light tug the section came loose.

Thick, golden honey dripped from the open end.

"The golden serpent," I said, exhilarated by my discovery. "Honey made from the nectar of these sacred plants!"

I collected the honey in the palm of my hand. Using the tip of my finger, I gave it a taste. It was deliciously sweet, and quite unlike any honey I had tasted before: distinctly citrusy and also slightly medicinal in flavour.

"You just told me that whoever consumes the golden serpent will know death," Birnie said, shaking his head worriedly. "Captain, I really don't think you should be—"

"*Will know death and be liberated into light,*" I said. "Human sacrifice was forbidden for the Toltecs. This is about knowing death through enlightenment. The honey is not poisonous, trust me."

A gust of wind blew through the cave. I watched the inflorescences of purple-and-white flowers sway and nod in synchrony along the length of the channel.

Birnie and I exchanged a glance.

"The wind has returned," he said, his eyes suddenly brightening. "The *Conway*... She will set sail!"

I smiled at him reassuringly. "You must go, George. Take the lantern."

The doctor shook his head vehemently. "We leave together, or we do not leave at all."

"Then let me do this," I said. "I feel as if my entire life has led to this moment, as if it were my destiny—and it is almost noon. I cannot leave here until this is done."

We stood looking at each other in silence, and all the while a swarm of bees gathered above my head in a humming cloud. There was not a thing the doctor could do, or say, to change my mind. He must have known this as he turned his gaze to the pool of honey in my hand and, shaking his head, released a heavy sigh. "Let's get this over with, and then we can go home."

It did not take long for the potent effects of the honey to take hold. I felt this at first as a slight giddiness, which brought in its wake a curious lightness to my being. I was standing next to the channel, and as I continued to ponder my jovial mood, I thought I saw something move on the cave wall. It was the serpent—its golden scales were shimmering. As I watched in astonishment, its coils began to tighten and relax around the stem of the plant.

I felt the urge to say something to Birnie, but thought better against it. The doctor was preoccupied with Gillies, gently lifting the tin cup to his lips in an attempt to feed him water.

I blinked heavily. In doing so, I found myself suspended within a universe of thousands upon thousands of stars. The experience was rapturous and all-consuming. I felt as if time itself no longer existed, and that I was an eternal being. When my eyes reopened, I saw that Birnie had not moved an inch.

Returning my gaze to the wall, the serpent's tongue was now flicking in and out of its mouth, its head turning this way and that. As I stood there, struck with awe, it descended from the stem of the plant. Upon reaching the floor of the cave, the magnificent creature then shed its scales before my very eyes, leaving behind a pile of gold leaves as it transformed into a thing of light. I watched on, speechless, as this breathtaking apparition wove across the cave floor towards me. Having encircled my legs, it then made its way over to Birnie and Gillies.

The doctor stood back with a jolt.

"Captain!" he called out, turning to me with an elated look on his countenance. "His eyes just opened!"

As Birnie began patting Gillies on the cheek and shaking his arm, I watched the sliver of golden light move to the centre of the cavern, where a sunbeam shone with full force through the oculus in the ceiling. Squinting my eyes, I saw that the sun was now positioned over the hole.

It was noon.

It was time for *Tonatiuhtiz*.

The light-serpent slithered into the sunbeam, which then turned a luxuriant gold. Above my head, the bees were swirling in an ever-thickening swarm. I walked across the cave and stepped into the fountain of light. As I did so, the humming of the bees increased to a crescendo. I could hear nothing but a vibrant, resonant sound, which seemed to reverberate into the very depths of my soul.

Closing my eyes, I was once again drifting among a sea of stars, in an inner universe unrecognisable from the night sky I had gazed at all my life. I felt wholly at one with this place, as if

I were a star myself, floating in the wondrous heavens, and burning as brightly as any other.

Then came a twisting, pulling sensation, as if my mind was being stretched like fresh dough. I felt as if a hidden eye deep within my thoughts was struggling to open. I felt it quivering, tugging against its invisible eyelid.

And then, all at once, it opened.

THIRTY-ONE

Kennedy Residence, Valparaiso, 1st November 1821

I WAS STANDING in the wood-panelled corridor that led to the back of the house. It was evening, and the lamp on the wall had been lit. Everything was just as I remembered: the smell of wood polish, the oil painting of Valparaiso harbour, the hall table with the vase of wildflowers. Sweet briar, picked from the garden in the hills.

It was as if I had never left.

The door at the end of the corridor was ajar, and in the room beyond, I could see an empty bed. As I walked towards the doorway, I caught sight of him, my lieutenant, dressed in his uniform and dozing in the armchair by the window, his face lit by a golden beam of evening sunlight.

My heart was filled with such joy I thought it might burst.

I stepped into the room. Legge opened his eyes and gave me a drowsy smile.

"Captain," he said, and then his brow furrowed. "You look... Are you all right?"

I glanced at my reflection in the oval mirror above the fire-place. My shirt was torn and covered in dirt, and there were cuts and bruises on my face and arms.

"Oh Charles, I am better than all right," I said, as I hurried across to him. Kneeling beside him, I took hold of his hand. "I am returned!"

Legge remained somewhat confused. "You have only been gone a short while." He drew a heavy breath, his lungs rattling as he exhaled. "You went to fetch George..."

"This entire day has passed for me, and many more besides," I said, gazing into his translucent blue eyes. Eyes that I had swum in so many times and never dreamed I would do so again. "The golden serpent, Charles... I found it! It truly is the way between worlds. It has brought me back... to this day. To *you*."

"The golden serpent," he whispered, and I watched the realisation slowly dawn across his countenance. "The way between worlds..." He blinked heavily, as if his mind might be deceiving him. "I care not if this is my delirium, I welcome it."

"I am here," I said, and kissed his hand. "I promised you I would find it, Charles. You were always with me."

He smiled. "Did I not tell you we are entangled souls?"

A warm breeze blew into the room. As the curtains billowed, I caught sight of the book, *Kenilworth*, on the windowsill, with the stolen pages still tucked inside. The little green medicine bottle sat next to it.

Legge followed my gaze.

"It is time for me to leave this world," he said softly.

I stayed with him as he drank the contents of the bottle and drifted away upon a river of sleep. In those final moments, I lifted his fragile body into my arms and stood by the window, watching the leaves on the tamarind tree move together in the evening breeze. Legge's head was resting upon my shoulder, and I could feel his ribs beneath my hand barely rising and falling.

I thought again of that first glorious evening, when we climbed onto the wall at the end of the garden and watched the sun setting with such splendour. I thought of how, in the silence between the tolling of the bells, when the world below us was in prayer, we spoke of freedom.

"I can hear your heart," he whispered, when he was close to the end. I kissed the top of his head, holding him a little tighter, and knowing that his own heartbeat was gradually fading away.

When he exhaled the last breath from his lungs, it came almost as a sigh.

Looking out into the courtyard, I knew that somewhere beyond the rustle of the tamarinds, across the lawn and down through the fruit trees, two men would soon begin arguing. Everything was just as it was; everything would be just as it always would be. And I knew now that Charles Legge died in peace, and in my arms.

Having gently lowered his body into the chair, I returned the empty medicine bottle to the sill, and slipped the book beneath the chair legs. When this was done, when everything was in its place, I walked across the room and looked again into the mirror on the wall.

The man who returned my gaze had thinning white hair. He wore a hospital gown, and the room behind him was stark and white. But the sight of this man, my aged self, did not frighten me as it had once before. Looking into his tired and reddened eyes, I thought of all the years I had spent seeking reassurance from a proud captain who sprayed himself with cologne and picked the fluff from his epaulettes, when it was not he, but this man before me now who was my true ally. I had become lost unto myself, and he had gone in search of me.

I smiled at him, and he smiled back.

"I have missed you, dear friend," he whispered.

I reached out, and our fingertips met upon the glass. The surface of the mirror rippled as if I were touching the surface of a pond.

"And I you."

Tears clouded my vision, and in the next moment, I found myself sitting at a writing desk positioned by a window. A notebook lay open in front of me, its pages filled with ink.

Through the window I could see a neatly trimmed lawn with gravel paths and a small, stone statue in its centre. Swallows were diving for insects in the evening sunlight. Beyond the garden lay a stretch of untamed grass, and after that woodland. Beyond the woods, I knew there was a high perimeter wall.

Closing the notebook, I watched the sun descend into the trees, sending rays of golden light into the western sky.

And never has my soul felt so alive, and my heart so free.

ACKNOWLEDGMENTS

The Divine Sage is a work of fiction. The story is based on the voyage of Captain Basil Hall, as detailed in his published book, *Extracts from a Journal, Written on the Coasts of Chili, Peru, and Mexico, in the Years 1820, 1821, 1822* (first edition, 1824), together with further information about the voyage that I learnt from the surviving log of the HMS *Conway*, and letters written by Basil Hall and George Birnie regarding Charles Legge's death. Though many of the characters that appear in *The Divine Sage* are real, their portrayal within the novel, together with the plot itself, is the product of my imagination.

In writing *The Divine Sage*, I wanted to portray Basil as reimagining his voyage, and to achieve this I have sometimes blended his original words as they appear in *"Extracts"* with my own: this occurs in the descriptions of the ports (Valparaiso, Callao, and San Blas) as they looked in the 1820s, and the passage about the oncoming storm at Tehuantepec. The funeral scene at the Fort of San Antonio also deserves a special acknowledgement, as much of what appears in the speeches of Basil and Birnie is taken directly from the letters written by these two men following Legge's death. The same goes for Birnie's description of Legge's final days. When I read these letters, I was moved beyond words. Legge died from an abscess on his liver and Birnie operated on him in an attempt to save his life (Basil avoids any mention of Legge's tragic death in *Extracts*). Finally, there is one other description in the story that I need to acknowledge: the sunset oration, where the mules stop in the streets and the people stand in prayer. These are the words of Charles Legge. I am indebted to the Staffordshire Records Office for allowing me to view the surviving log of the *Conway* (which was written by Legge) and the accompanying letters written by Basil and Birnie. Without this precious resource, my story would not exist.

I have many people to thank for their encouragement, love, and support as I have walked the long and lonely road of novel writing. Thanks to Audrey Logsdon, my editor, for reading through several drafts of the manuscript and providing me with everything I needed to craft, reshape, and tweak the story until it became what it is today. Thanks also to Kahina Necaise, who copy edited a later version of the manuscript, and to Bron, Brendan, Jacinta, Steve, Andy, Maya and Chris, for their constructive suggestions, and for always being so enthusiastic about the story, and keeping me motivated to see it published. Thanks to Mum, for all her love and encouragement, and to my Australian family who fill my life with such fun and friendship every day.

Most of all, thank you to my husband, Darren Hocking, for believing in me and supporting me throughout this incredible journey. Darren, you are the love of my life. This book is for you.

Printed in Great Britain
by Amazon